THE NAKED EYE

written by
Paul Kane

Previous Publication History
White Shadows (*White Shadows*, Things in the Well, 2019)
The Cursed (Original to this collection)
Maddy the Monster (*More Monsters*, Black Shuck Books, 2018)
The Queue (Original to this collection)
Crumbs (Original to this collection)
Pure Evil (*Art of Horror site*, 2001)
Mortis-Man: Origins (Original to this collection)
Another Life (*The Life Cycle*, Black Shuck Books, 2017)

Encyclopocalypse Publications
www.encyclopocalypse.com

Contents

No Horror Without Hope

An Introduction by Cavan Scott

There is no horror without hope.

Hope keeps us turning the pages, keeps our heroes fighting to survive. Any minute they'll escape the jaws of death, they'll run into the sunlight, the monsters no longer snapping at their feet. They'll live.

And yet, as the final page turns we see that hope, that promise, dashed. If we hadn't felt just a glimmer of hope, we'd never succumb to the crushing heartbreak of defeat.

Cheery, eh? But isn't that why we return to short stories of terror time and time again? The short story is horror in its purist form, dropping you into a heightened situation where our heroes – and sometimes our villains – are having their worst day possible and, at the hand of a master, you're right there with them every step of the way.

Granted there are other delights to relish. The

gruesome thrill of exquisitely crafted gore. Your skin crawling as the tension mounts to unbearable levels. The perverse pleasure of discovering a new type of monster when you thought every trope had been done quite literally to death. But without the most human of emotions, without hope, these diversions are empty, all splatter and no substance. These are not the moments that haunt you when you close the book, that keep you up at night or looking over your shoulder in the day.

Paul Kane gets this. He understands it in his bones.

This collection has tension. It has monsters and, yes, it has its fair share of gore, but it has characters you believe in, that you root for, that you pray will make it in the end, because the alternative is too terrible to imagine. You're in there with them, hoping that the monster in the snow will let you escape, that true love will prove to be more potent than a bitter curse. This humanity anchors even the most heightened reality whether it's a retelling of an age-old fairy story or a modern morality tale when mad scientists try to bottle evil. And, boy, do you feel it where all hope is lost; where, like the couple who are queuing for a life-changing reservation, you slowly realise where events are leading.

Even when the action shifts into Paul's homage to the beloved comic books of his youth, the characters remain true. You believe every action they take, even those that lead to disaster, and wonder if you would have... if you *could* have... reacted differently.

It's fair to say that Paul is prolific. A glance at his back catalogue is evidence enough, and many of these stories link to other corners of his work. That only makes them more fascinating. For a true devotee, they are welcome additions to Paul's ever-growing library, but if you've never read any of his stories before, they are a tantalising hint of what is to come when you inevitably end up seeking out the stories and collections he mentions in his afterword. Whether Paul is turning his hand to adult or YA fiction, there's no mistaking the passion for the genre and the desire to get under his reader's skin.

But don't take my word for it, dive in and discover for yourself the humanity at the heart of Paul's particular brand of horror...

Cavan Scott
Bristol. February 2021.

White Shadows

It was like they'd been wiped from the face of the Earth.

Wiped out – not in the sense of being tired, but like you did with a pencil drawing that just wasn't working, rubbing out the bits that had gone wrong. Or using Tippex; yes, that was more appropriate. More like what had happened, the brush smoothing out something that had been there before. One minute here, the next—

Amy gaped at the spot where it had occurred; waiting, holding her breath. But the person didn't come back again, the one they had taken, snatched away. Didn't emerge, come out the other side waving that they were all right. And then there was the redness – just the briefest of glimpses, but it had been there, she was sure of it even at this distance. A smattering before there was nothing left at all, and *they* moved on in search of their next victim.

Her, probably.

How had she ended up here? Because she'd been off chasing after monsters again, hadn't she. The ones she'd been chasing all these years, ever since—

Never thought she'd actually come face to face with them though, not really. Although maybe it had been inevitable, perhaps she'd made herself a target? Unfinished business. Maybe she'd *willed* them into being? Or summoned them? After all, she waited most of the year for days like this one. Waited *every* year. Got excited when she heard the weather forecasts telling her what was coming, and then the radio telling them roads were closing, schools were already closed. Got excited, but not in the way other thirteen-year-olds (unlucky for some) might, because they would be missing lessons, and could play all day long. No, she was excited for different reasons entirely.

She'd once made the mistake of mentioning the 'hunting' to her Aunty Beth and Uncle Steve not long after she'd arrived here on the farm (crops predominantly, no animals), and they'd taken it to mean she was after The Abominable Snowman or something. A child's flights of fancy. And although the creatures she went out searching for whenever there was snow falling were definitely abominable, there was no fancy to this at all. No *fantasy* as far as she was concerned. She didn't believe in Bigfoot, in spite of the footage that often cropped up on those 'Unexplained' documentaries Uncle Steve liked to watch (she didn't believe in the Loch Ness Monster either, or UFOs). But she believed in the things that lived in the snow. That used it, bent it to their will.

The things that had taken her parents away from her at such a young age.

The therapist her aunty and uncle had taken her to back then said that often children would cope with tragedies they didn't understand by giving what had caused it an identity. "Putting a face to it, humanising it," the therapist – a well-meaning woman who dressed in chequered skirts, wore big, round glasses like the ones Harry Potter sported and spoke in a Scottish accent – had said. In this instance, Death, she suspected – though she couldn't have been more wrong about it all. Amy hadn't 'humanised' the Grim Reaper – if that was at all possible, when you were talking about something that was basically a skeleton in a robe carrying the kind of scythe Uncle Steve used to cut down the long grass out the back of the farmhouse. She didn't believe in that figure any more than she did those other myths; this wasn't some comic book. Death was something that happened to you, when your body couldn't go on. Being *killed*, now that was something else entirely.

And the things she was imagining... no, thinking about – they weren't just in her imagination, she knew deep down they weren't – *had* no faces. They certainly weren't huge furry beasts that wandered around out in the wild, occasionally getting snapped by a tourist or several.

"It was just a terrible accident, sweetie. These things happen," her Aunty Beth – Mum's sister – had told her. Aunty Beth and Uncle Steve weren't able to have children of their own, in spite of the fact they would have loved them, so had been delighted to take Amy in. All right, perhaps not delighted, because Aunty Beth's sibling had been killed when all was said and done, but they'd made the girl feel welcome and were bringing her up as if she was their own. Uncle Steve especially thought of her as the daughter he'd never had: relishing spending time with her, making bonfires and putting on firework displays come November 5th, or ferrying her to the pictures in town in the Land Rover. That one was a special treat, the nearest town being something like twenty miles away from them. There was a village nearby, of course – and just about visible from their farm – where the school, a pub and the local shop was, but it was a tiny affair. All in all, Beth and Steve had been good to her, had caught her when she'd fallen, become her family after—

A terrible accident. A thing that had happened.

But it had been caused by something, hadn't it? Amy often dreamed about it all, told herself it was the link she shared with her parents; that they were trying to tell her something. Trying to warn her. In those dreams she saw the winds that must have rocked the plane her mum and dad were on, the snow drifts that battered it, causing it to crash-land at the base of that mountainside – the middle of nowhere. Snow drifts that had got worse and worse afterwards, as those who'd survived stumbled from the wreckage and went off to try and find help. People like Amy's mum and dad.

A mayday call had been put out as soon as the plane started to get into trouble, but those who mounted a rescue mission had only been able to find a couple of people who were left – and they were delirious, mumbling about being separated from the rest of the group by the strange, isolated storms. Mumbling something about 'white shadows' as well, though the authorities had taken that to mean the figures of those they'd lost sight of in the snow. They hadn't been making much sense in all honesty: starving, frozen and traumatised. Amy had read all this much later, online – but that was after she'd 'seen' what they called the shadows herself (hadn't she? it *had* been afterwards she was sure of it!), in her dreams. The things that had taken at least some of the survivors, leaving no evidence to be found even when the weather calmed down.

Leaving no trace of her parents, not even their bodies. Lost, in more ways than one. Wiped off the face of the Earth. Thank heavens they'd had the sense not to take Amy with them on that particular trip up north, had been Uncle Steve's default position. Much further north than they were right now on the farm, off on holiday to a place they'd never been to before; they were trying to work their way around the world, had promised each other they'd do that when they had the money, back when they'd first met at university. One year Africa, the next the Caribbean or Canada. They'd taken Amy on a few excursions with them, but she'd been too young to remember much. For this one, this last one, they'd left her behind. As it turned out, to mourn for them.

To forever search for the things that had taken them, or so she believed in her heart of hearts.

In the summer she'd pretend to go off exploring, but really she was readying herself; preparing for days like this one. For the autumn to come, then passing into winter, so she might stand a chance of spotting them – perhaps even fighting them, defeating them. Destroying them, like some kind of hero. Amy would celebrate when the snow came – especially if there was even the slightest chance it would come down thick and heavy. Not because it got her away from school, though she did hate that (for reasons other than the rest of her class… she'd never really fitted in here, never had any real friends; was always the 'weird one') but because it would be time to hunt once more.

On that particular morning, she'd ventured out wrapped up in a big coat, scarf, bobble hat over her short, mousy hair, and ear-muffs; wearing boots that had a good tread and two pairs of socks. She'd told Aunty Beth she was heading out to make snowmen with the other kids her age, get into snowball fights and perhaps do a bit of sledging, but she had nothing of the sort in mind. The woman had made sure Amy had a flask of hot soup with her, just in case – which she put in her rucksack – and warned her not to go too far.

Uncle Steve had been filling up the portable heaters with fuel, getting candles and torches sorted out, in case there was a power cut, which – let's face it – was a distinct possibility out here. Sometimes they'd even empty their chest freezer when that happened and stick everything outside, so that the food didn't go off. He'd waved at her when she walked across the driveway, reminded her that there was always a chance the weather could turn, get worse later on (*hopefully*, she thought) and had called out: "You be careful out there Aimes! Be safe!"

She waved back, but made no such promises. How did she know what she'd encounter out there, what would be waiting for her, whether she would be safe or not? And wasn't there part of her that hoped she wouldn't be, after all this waiting, all this time with nothing happening? Amy had already decided long ago that if they never came to her, then she'd go out there seeking *them* once she was old enough to do so. But she figured that, y'know, where there was snow they might show up, that the storm had to start somewhere before heading even further north; but she had absolutely no idea how it worked. There had been no reports done on this kind of phenomenon. No documentaries on the things in the snow, those 'white shadows'. Had no idea that today would be the day. *The day…*

Especially as it had only started out with a fairly light covering, a few inches or so. Looked to her like that worse weather Uncle Steve had mentioned might never reach them. Some of those families out there on the fields that she passed, having fun with their kids, the way in to work blocked off as well as school, were probably hoping it never did – because moments like this were precious. It just made Amy grind her teeth, because she'd been denied that herself. Denied by the things that had taken her parents.

She'd scouted around, then finally camped out in a particular position to keep watch, sitting on a collection of rocks, breath steaming as it emerged from her mouth. Amy had taken out her soup and drunk some of it when she got too cold, sighing the longer she waited. She probably would have welcomed Death appearing, just to give her something to tackle – so that all of her training could be put to some use. Though she found herself chuckling at the thought of being able to 'kill' death. The ridiculousness of it. Then she reminded herself that if anyone knew what she was doing, they'd think it was just as crazy. Hunting things that she'd dreamed about, that she thought might be responsible for killing her parents years ago so very far away from here.

At one point she'd even hung her head, saying to herself: "Amy, what *are* you doing? Really, what the hell are you actually doing?" But that feeling inside her, the one that had been there for so long, that she truly believed in, was still there – it would keep her strong. Even when—

But then it had happened. A veritable blizzard, a storm whipping up out of nowhere. She'd witnessed it, like something organic growing – but growing fast. A few flurries to begin with, then heavier snow, coming down like a white curtain: but not everywhere, across the board. In sections, behaving so strangely. Amy had never seen anything like it, although something told her Mum and Dad had. That maybe it had been the last thing they'd seen.

Now it was happening, though – now this thing she'd willed, been preparing for, was playing out right in front of her eyes – she was as frozen as those legs of lamb that would inevitably end up in their garden once the power was gone.

Doesn't mean anything anyway, she told herself. Just because there was snow – there had been snow before today, in previous years – didn't mean *they* would come. That this would be them arriving, the things from her dreams. From those warnings.

Except… except it did mean that, after all. Because as she watched – watched, but did nothing, even after all that prep – it took someone. Amy saw it wash over a figure, some bloke walking his dog – who'd let it off the lead to get some exercise. Saw it erase him, that snowdrift. Heard the furious barking of the Alsatian, then its whining as it saw something that frightened it – an Alsatian, by the way! – and went running off in the opposite direction, away from its owner. Man's best friend, but it didn't cover anything like this.

The white had wiped the guy away – rubbers, Tippex – off the face of the Earth. And then there was the redness, the specks of it she felt sure she'd seen inside. Like it was eating the man or something, churning him up. No way was he going to emerge from the other side; he was already done for. There was no steam in front of her now, her breath held as she watched all this. Saw the drifts cast about, looking, searching for more people.

For her?

No… another family this time, maybe even one of those she'd passed on the way. Mum, dad, three kids of staggered ages ranging from really little to not far off her age (though Amy didn't recognise the kid). Moving, heading in their direction like a shark through the ocean. If the shark *was* the ocean.

That was the thing which got her moving. Steam coming now, breath coming, Amy got to her feet, clambering off those rocks, and began to run. She waved her hands, shouting, trying to get their attention because – somehow, goodness knows how – they hadn't even seen the snow, definitely hadn't seen the man vanish. They were too busy having a good time, the dad swinging his youngest child onto his shoulders.

"Hey! Hey you!" Amy was throwing herself forwards now, launching herself towards that family in an effort to try and help them. To save them! "Look out! Can't you see what's… *Look!*" Even if they didn't have a clue about what was really happening – and how could they, why would they? – the fact a white-out was heading their way should be enough. But they were still oblivious, to her and the danger it seemed.

Then it hit them like a tsunami: white on white. Amy was closer than she had been to the man who disappeared, and thought she heard screaming. Though it was difficult to tell through the ear-muffs, which she wrenched now from her head, pulling the bobble hat off in the process. But she lost her balance and stumbled, crashing head-first into the ground: raking up the ordinary snow and hardened mud that was there.

Crash-landing, like the plane at the foot of that mountainside. Middle of nowhere, like this place!

Dazed, she looked up, just in time to see more of those red specks. There were no screams now, however, only an eerie silence that had descended over the patch of land ahead of her where just a few moments ago there had been screams of a different kind: of delight and laughter.

Amy was scrambling to get up again, this time off the ground, and it was only now that the drift was turning on her, turning in her direction. She froze again, all of her training, all her preparation wiped from her mind as effectively as that family had been from existence. There was no sign of them anyway, no evidence that they'd even been here – and as the white stacked up to strike her, Amy saw the shadows those survivors had been talking about; shapes constantly shifting, easily mistaken for something natural, though there was nothing natural about any of this. The real snowmen, except these weren't men at all. They were the monsters she'd been looking out for, waiting for. The monsters that used the snow, that hid inside it. Them or something like them – their kin, *their* family.

Think! she screamed inside her own skull. *Think about what you were going to do.* And it was then that she remembered what she was still holding. Why she'd really brought it. Let her Aunty Beth think it was so she wouldn't go hungry, but there was another reason entirely; just one of the ways she'd thought of to battle the things.

Quickly, Amy yanked off the plastic mug on top and unscrewed the lid of the flask again. As the snow hit her, surrounding her, and she saw more and more of those shadows inside – the white shadows blinding her to everything else – she let loose with the hot soup. Spinning around, flinging it in all directions, she heard the sound of their pain – not unlike the whining of the Alsatian who'd scampered off when it saw what was inside the storm.

Yes! thought Amy. *I've wounded them…* Drawn blood from *them*, even if it was only figuratively speaking. Hurt the things enough to force them to back off at the very least, to leave her alone for the time being.

Because her vision was clearing, and she could see again now. The snow that had been bearing down on her, the white shadows, had retreated, had turned once more. But Amy's victory was short-lived, her triumph premature. Not only had she failed to react in time to save that man, the family – in fact the only person she'd actually saved was herself, some hero! – she'd driven the shadows in the other direction.

In the direction of the nearby village.

And suddenly the drift was gone, as if that hadn't really been there either, leaving Amy to stand by and watch – horrified – as the strange wind powered it down the hill towards the small collection of streets and houses.

Towards yet more potential victims.

* * * * *

By the time Amy got there, it was chaos.

Most people had remained inside their homes, thankfully, not wishing to venture out into the cold – but there were some who were inevitably heading to or from the shop, stocking up in case things got worse (oh, they were worse all right). There were more kids scattered about, playing in the streets, in gardens, and some of the adults were making their way to the local ale house to 'warm their cockles' as Uncle Steve called it when he had a glass of brandy on cold evenings.

So there was still plenty of choice, and nobody was expecting the band of whiteness to hit them, especially that hard. As she'd neared the village – trying to get a signal on her mobile, get through to Uncle Steve or maybe the authorities – it had looked to Amy like a bed-sheet being shaken. Like when Aunty Beth made the beds: flipping the duvet so that it rose up first, before covering the mattress.

The snow covered a couple first, walking hand in hand – probably just out for a stroll to enjoy the scenery, not caring about anything but being in love. It had been the woman who'd seen it first, trying to point with a mitten on and failing, but getting her partner's attention nonetheless... just in time for the whiteness to envelope them both. Amy squinted, but could definitely make out those red droplets again as the things inside the snow devoured them. There was no time for screams it seemed, or if there were any she didn't hear them.

A few children who'd been kicking snow at each other had seen what had happened though, and *they* began screaming – perhaps they'd even spotted the shadows inside the storm? That led to more adults being drawn to the scene, more fodder for the white which was sweeping over the village.

An old woman was gingerly making her way up the road, walking stick in hand. She looked over her shoulder at the noise, only to be confronted by a sheet of blankness heading for her. Then she tried to get away, even swung her stick backwards at something only she could see up close and personal. But as she twisted, began to fall, she was suddenly 'absorbed' by the white.

People were coming out of their houses to see what was happening, some emerging from the pub with drinks in hand. Panicked cries and waving couldn't stop it. The only thing that could stop it was Amy: finally reaching the village after putting on a spurt. Pushing aside thoughts that this was her fault, that she should have been able to do something before *they* even reached here, she shrugged the rucksack off her shoulder and opened it up, pulled something out. Reaching inside her pocket, she then found what she'd need to arm her weapon and crouched so she could take aim.

What she didn't want to do was inadvertently hurt anyone, but these people were going to get hurt anyway if she didn't take action. Were going to get killed, in fact…

Being killed, *now that was something else entirely.*

The figure of the Grim Reaper wasn't here, but there was plenty of death to go around. *Time to end all that,* thought Amy as she flipped open the borrowed lighter – the one Uncle Steve didn't use anymore because he'd quit smoking a couple of years ago – and lit the fuse. Because of the angle she'd rammed it into the grass verge at, the rocket didn't shoot up into the air like it was intended to do, but actually zoomed in on the wall of white bearing down on a clump of teenagers: exploding when it reached its target. That whining sound again, followed by the snow dissipating. Amy grinned, rooted around again in the bag for more fireworks that she'd squirreled away over time, when Uncle Steve's back was turned.

She fired off two more into the whiteness, which also exploded, and for a fraction of a second Amy thought she could actually see the dark outlines of those monsters inside it – writhing and contorting, clearly injured by her actions. She was just about to fire another when she felt herself being hauled backwards, dragged up by the arm.

To begin with she thought the white shadows had doubled back and come at her from the rear, were attacking her there because nobody was around to watch *her* back. Instead, she was pulled around and found herself face to face with a ruddy-cheeked man wearing a flat cap. "What're you doin', girl?" he demanded. "Are ye touched or summat?"

Amy didn't have time to explain, wasn't sure he'd understand even if she tried, but she still attempted it: "Things… in the snow. Taking people!"

His brow furrowed. "Things in the…" Then he gazed over her shoulder and saw for himself. Amy twisted back around as his grip loosened, in time to see an auburn-haired woman wearing a puffer jacket get sucked into the white, the now-familiar redness accompanying her 'abduction'. "What the…" said the man.

Amy pulled away from him, bent and reached into her bag once more. The whiteness was too close to fire at now, but she had another plan. She had been preparing for this for a long time, after all.

Pulling out two sticks, she lit both and handed one to the man – who just gaped at that now instead. *"Use it!"* she barked, then showed him how, thrusting the sparkler at the advancing shapes, which cowered away from the heat and light. Amy jabbed hers forward; if she could have borrowed that therapist's glasses right about now, she might have resembled a female version of a certain famous wizard. Moves she'd practised again and again, defensive and offensive, even in the summer months or in her own

24

bedroom. Preparing for this day. For *the* day, whenever it should come around.

The man who'd grabbed her attempted to do the same with his sparkler, thrusting it out – but then dropped it and had to bend to try and pick it up. As he did so, the white shadows seized their chance and simply wrapped themselves around him, as if folding a warm blanket around the guy. Amy gritted her teeth and drove at the ones in front of her harder and harder, fencing with them almost.

Someone from the pub had got the right idea, and hurled a bottle of spirits with a lit rag in the top just in front of where the white-out was gathering. *Yes*, thought Amy – *that's it! Bonfire!* A couple more 'bombs' cracked and shattered then, the flames lapping higher and creating a barrier between the shadow-things and the people they were after.

Amy found herself smiling once more; it wasn't just her against these things now, she had allies. She might even have an army if enough people figured it out in time. Amy hoped to God they did, because those things would take the entire village given the opportunity.

Her smile faded when she saw more snow rain down on the fires, putting them out as effectively as if a giant boot had just stomped on them – leaving the way clear for attack once again. Amy looked around for her bag and spotted one of the straps a few metres away. With a final slash of her sparkler, she ducked and rolled over to get to it – she needed to be firing off more rockets, more missiles at those creatures. But just as she made it to the bag, something snatched it away – whiteness sliding over it and dragging it out of reach.

Amy let out a cry. What now? Sparkler in one hand, lighter in the other, she did her best to protect herself, to ward off danger, but that wouldn't help the rest of the people out there. The bottles of spirits had given her an idea, however...

There was an empty car nearby, Amy turned and made for it – tossing her sparkler and praying that it was open. People tended to do that around here, the risk of anyone stealing vehicles minimal because it was such a small place. She tried the door and her heart sank briefly when she couldn't open it; then suddenly it popped, had just been jammed because of the cold. Amy swung the door open, searching around under the dashboard for the petrol cap release. She'd seen the Land Rover filled up enough times to know the procedure, and now Amy raced around the side and unscrewed the lid, just like she'd done with the soup earlier.

Ripping open the sleeve of her coat she jammed this in the hole where the petrol went. Then she lit the material and went back to the driver's side, reaching in and releasing the hand-brake now, steering the car towards the whiteness. Luckily they were on a slight incline and she only needed to push it a little bit, aiming it and letting it go. The people she could see scattered when they realised what was happening, getting out of the way of it – and the explosion, when it came, blew apart the whiteness there: shadows, snow, everything.

Amy nodded, dropping to the ground and sitting there panting for breath. Job done.

Or so she thought.

The white began to swirl again, piecing itself back together, building the wall back up once more. Facing her, moving towards her. She clambered back up again, running from the white shadows who were now out for revenge – and all she had left was the lighter, the tiny flame from that burning her fingers as she waved it back at the drifts.

She was concentrating so much on this, that the shape coming towards her almost hit her. Amy closed her eyes and braced herself, thinking that the shadows must have circled her to cut off her exit, but when she heard the squeal of rubber she opened them again. Realised by the size of the thing what it must surely be.

The Land Rover pulled up short, missing her by inches, but she'd never been so glad to see anything – or anyone – in her life. "Uncle Steve!" she yelled when she saw him through the windscreen, the wipers flicking away random bits of snow. Either he'd got the dropped calls from her or he'd spotted what was happening down in the village – the drifts that were heading their way – and decided to come out and look for her. Either way, he would have figured out her location roughly via her phone; it was always the way he could find her if she got lost.

Her uncle opened the door and grabbed the roof, pulling himself up and out of the metal cage – standing on the edge of the door-frame so that he was higher than the roof itself. "Aimes! Aimes is that you?"

She nodded, then added for good measure: "Yes!"

"What's going on here? What was that explosion?"

Amy skirted around the front of the Land Rover and opened the passenger side door, virtually flinging herself inside. "No time to explain. We need to go."

"Go? Go where?" Steve looked totally confused when he climbed back in and shut the door.

"Anywhere!" she shouted. "Just away from here. They're—"

But it was too late, the whiteness had reached the front of the Land Rover and the whole thing rocked up and down. "Holy..." Uncle Steve didn't finish his sentence, another shake of his car threatening to turn it over onto its side. He popped the brake, rammed the gear-stick into reverse and stamped down on the accelerator. "What's happening?" he demanded as he did so, backing up and around so he could point the vehicle forwards again. "What *was* that? The snow?"

"Not exactly," Amy told him. She twisted around in the seat, looking to see if the white shadows were following at all. They weren't; in fact they'd changed direction again. But the relief she felt at that was temporary, especially when she realised where they *were* heading. Not back towards the village, but over and across.

Over, across, and in the direction of their farm.

"Oh no," she whispered.

"What?" asked Steve.

"We need to get home," said Amy, turning back to face him. He studied the seriousness of her expression and didn't ask any more questions, didn't dawdle. He just put the Land Rover in gear and drove off the way that he'd come.

At certain points it seemed like they were racing against the snow, but when all was said and done the lumbering Land Rover – designed for power rather than speed – couldn't hope to compete with the way the wind was blowing that weather front. Or rather the way those things were using the wind to propel themselves along.

Nevertheless, with Uncle Steve coaxing more and

more out of his vehicle the further along the track they went, they were only a little way behind the wall of white heading for their farm. "When we get there, we're going to need those portable heaters," she explained to the man behind the wheel.

He'd frowned again, but nodded. Something had struck the front of the Land Rover – he understood that – and now it was heading for home. If Amy said to get the heaters, then he was going to get them! However, when they arrived back Amy was dismayed to see Aunty Beth coming out of the farmhouse to greet them, waving as she did so.

"Get back inside!" Amy was shouting, but of course she wouldn't be able to hear her over the noise of both the drifts and the engine.

Steve braked, almost skidding into a fence – but bringing the Land Rover to a halt. He was out and rushing towards his wife in seconds, Amy shouting after him about the heaters – to remember the heaters! He wasn't listening, though. Perhaps he thought he could get Beth and bring her back to the car? Or maybe get her into the house… though now she'd seen what *they'd* done back at the village, Amy wasn't entirely convinced they wouldn't just smash the whole building to pieces.

She watched, open-mouthed, as her uncle fought to reach her aunty – the band of whiteness on top of them now. And again, Amy was frozen solid, facing the prospect of losing another set of parents. Then something took hold of her, thoughts of her mum and dad giving her strength. As if the bond, the link that had been warning her was now telling her what to do. Amy got out and ran herself, looking over and across at what was happening. The white shadows weren't even bothering to disguise themselves now, because they knew these people had seen them. That made them even more of a target. And was it her imagination, or were they even bigger? Like the rage they were channelling was empowering them?

Then suddenly it had happened, Beth was torn away from them both – even as Uncle Steve was holding out his hand, fingertips practically touching hers.

There one second, wiped out the next.

Erased… wiped off the face of the Earth.

"*No!*" screamed Steve, looking about him, searching for any trace of his wife – expecting her to just come out the other side, a little the worse for wear but okay. Alive. That wasn't going to happen. Amy knew that wasn't going to happen. She sniffed back the tears; there was no time for mourning. That would come later, she knew that as well; as she'd done for her parents for so long.

Now was the time for action, the time to finish this once and for all.

They were coming, turning on Steve before he could do anything about it – before he could even properly process what had happened to Beth; the specks of red when she'd been taken and what it meant. Before he could come to terms with it happening to him as well.

Then suddenly someone was putting themselves between him and the white shadows. Amy, holding a heater in each hand. Not just warding the creatures off now, but fighting with them – punching them. And it was working, it was hurting them again. Uncle Steve could see it was and when she handed one to him, he helped his niece, pushing forwards with it like he was an old-fashioned knight with a shield.

The whining turned into a wailing, Amy and her Uncle Steve like Moses creating a pathway through the Red Sea. Ramming the heaters into the snow left and right, then fighting back-to-back like she'd seen in some of those action movies her uncle liked to watch.

Amy squinted, saw that the shadows were shrinking. "We're winning!" she called out behind her, but Steve simply grunted. He was getting some revenge of his own.

It wasn't long after that the storm abated, the whiteness disappearing and with it the shadows within. Amy's shoulders slumped, exhausted. She dropped her heater and almost collapsed – would have done if it wasn't for Steve catching her. Like he and Aunty Beth had caught her after her parents were taken.

He hugged her to him and they both broke down in tears. "We… we won," she said softly against his chest, but he couldn't really hear her – and she doubted he'd agree even if he could. They'd won, but at what cost? Look at what – who – they'd lost.

Lost, in more ways than one.

* * * * *

But Aunty Beth hadn't been the only one to become lost that day.

The man who'd been walking his dog; the family out on the fields. All the other villagers – gone. Taken by what the authorities later called a freak of nature, a snowstorm that came out of nowhere. An accident.

A terrible accident. A thing that had happened.

No one could explain where those people had

disappeared to, though. Why no bodies were ever found. And the more time that passed, it was almost as if the survivors of this isolated tragedy forgot what exactly had happened as well, and accepted the official line... the official lie. Perhaps it was easier than trying to get their heads around the truth. In some ways it was like their memories had been wiped, just like their loved ones had been...

Wiped off the face of the Earth.

Only Amy remembered, only Amy and her Uncle Steve – who she'd explained everything to. Even he'd had trouble with some of it, but he couldn't argue with the evidence of his own eyes. The only evidence that remained to back them up.

"Nobody would believe you," he said to her one night a few weeks after the memorial service, a glass of brandy in his hand. "No-one would believe *us*."

"It doesn't matter," she said to him. "We got them. We beat them. We destroyed them!" But even as she said the words, her voice wavered. Had they? Had they really? Could things like that ever really be destroyed? Her mind flashed back to the shadows piecing themselves together after the explosion and she had to wonder...

If there was another link now, between her – her family – and them. Perhaps there always had been, at least since the plane crash. Unfinished business. And she knew that neither her nor her uncle would rest easy whenever winter came again, though at least there was someone to watch her back now. Knew that they'd prepare, because who else was there? They'd *always* be prepared now. For a time when maybe, just maybe...

Those white shadows sought them out again.

The Cursed

He wished, every minute of every hour of every day.

Wished that he hadn't said those words. But that wish would never come true, not now. Wishes weren't as powerful as their opposite number, Stuart had come to realise. Were fuelled by hope rather than hatred, and nothing ever tops that last one – especially in this world. Hopes are dashed all the time; it was how he'd got into this mess in the first place. Living in hope. Besides, a simple wish couldn't undo what he'd done. Those words, a handful of words, but said with such feeling, with such…

Wished that he'd never said them. But he had. There was nothing he could do about it; not now, not ever. Said when he was drunk, and just a little bit high – but said with such conviction that the 'powers that be', the 'forces of whatever' had listened and taken pity on him. That was a joke in itself, because if anyone deserved pity now it was—

Then again, did people deserve pity if they'd got *themselves* into a mess? Willed it into being? However unintentionally, however misguided they'd been when it happened? But these kinds of things didn't come with a rule book, in spite of what you saw on the TV and in movies. The only rule was it had been done, and couldn't be undone. Not that he was aware of, that he'd been told. It didn't stop him wishing, couldn't stop him... hoping.

It had been, of course, about a girl. Always was, wasn't it? The classic tragedies. Romeo and Juliet and all that, star-crossed lovers, fated. Or about love, more accurately. Boy and girl, boy and boy, girl and girl, or whoever could feel that powerful emotional tug. The emotion that had fuelled the fire of so many great mistakes. That had caused people to lie, to cheat, to kill. And Stuart had considered that option, don't think that he hadn't. It just wasn't *him*: murder. Hadn't been back then, wasn't now. Would never be, especially as Stuart was so close to the end himself. He often wondered if all this might continue, once he was dead. Once the cancer that was currently working its way through his body was done with its task. When he succumbed to this delightful little disease, the scourge of our times. Would it just continue, in another place? The torment? Living... dying... dead. In hope? Eternally, forever?

Wishing that he'd never said those words, but they'd just come out. He'd thought them, and maybe that would have been enough anyway, but actually saying them: that gave them real traction, he now knew. If only he'd been more specific, that was where he'd gone wrong really, when you got right down to it. That was all it would have taken, he felt sure; a couple of words more. Some specificity, as that character had said in the film about dreams. A hook to hang it on, rather than a generalisation that could have meant anything. Could have killed her, or him, both or *all* of them for that matter.

But that hadn't happened either. Fate, or whatever the hell it was, had seen fit to keep them alive for this long, to play out this bloody pantomime until its conclusion. And beyond, if it carried on after death, as he feared it might.

Regardless of the state he'd been in, Stuart could recall that moment in time, that frozen moment he'd tweak just a little if he was in one of those VR machines or what have you, something from another one of those sodding SF movies he loved so much. Weren't they always popping pills to cure this, that and the other in those films? Kidney problems, sure – here you go, no more dialysis. Brain damage, yeah, here you go, take this with a glass of water and the neural pathways will repair themselves. Something eating away at your body, that's fine. That's just... It was usually at this point he'd start to cry uncontrollably; a condition he'd become used to over the years.

Back to that night, though, and to put it into some context, he'd had to endure all kinds of torture that week – back when Stuart hadn't really known the meaning of the word. Not real torture, not real pain. Psychological. Ironic really, as that was what he'd been studying at uni around that time. Around the time he'd first met *her*.

His inspiration, his everything.

His downfall.

She'd been hanging out in halls with friends of friends, like people did when they first got to that place. Homesick, not really knowing what was what. Arse looking a lot like an elbow. Loving the freedom and personal space but at the same time missing someone to do their laundry or make their meals for them. Huddling together in that shared experience, getting to know folk from all over the place, this country and abroad. Clubbing, getting wasted. Sleeping with complete strangers and making pals who'd be there for life, or you *hoped* would be. That word again.

Stuart had spotted her in the common room, chatting to one of the girls on his course called Heidi. Those two were from the same area apparently, or just down the road from each other, down south. A million miles away from this place in the industrial north. Where Stuart was from. Anyway, he'd paused in the doorway, dawdling there when he saw her. Didn't even know her name, just spotted her and froze. Another, altogether better moment in time.

She was wearing a tartan dress with thick black tights and trainers, her brown hair whoofed up on the top of her head. Those big, round glasses she used to wear back then only accentuated her equally big hazel eyes. Unlike most of the girls around her, she hadn't caked on the make-up. Her eyebrows were faintly drawn on, and didn't look like someone had been at them with a marker pen, her lipstick subtle instead of bright, glowing red. Stuart couldn't be entirely sure, but he always thought his heart had skipped a beat in that moment. Had assumed crap like that was just for stupid love songs and Valentine's Day cards – a holiday which he'd always hated before, but would revel in if whoever was running the show would just give him that girl over there perched on the arm of the battered sofa.

When Heidi – bubbly, hair dyed blue (this week), Heidi – called him over to introduce them, it seemed like his prayers might just be answered.

"Stu! Hey there, Stu!" Heidi had already been at the vodka that was being passed around. "This is Athena, can you believe that?"

Athena, like the Greek goddess, and he'd certainly

worshipped her liked one even then. Always thought, however, that she should have been named after Aphrodite. Not because she didn't have the intelligence or reasoning of Athena, but simply because he was captivated by her beauty. She'd pulled a face at her introduction anyway, said she wished (but you can't go back) she'd never told Heidi that. Another casualty of the vodka.

"My parents are kinda ageing hippies, out of their time. Athena's way too wanky." She preferred her second name, Maisie, or just plain May. Which was also beautiful, Stuart reckoned. May, when Spring had already sprung and you were on the verge of summer months. And when May looked at you a certain way, it was like the sun was shining on you in summer. You could feel the heat, the warmth. The love.

May had shaken his hand then, saying she was pleased to meet him – the feeling was definitely mutual – and that had been that. They'd spent the entire evening chatting, sharing likes and dislikes, comparing bands they followed, shows they watched, favourite movies. He'd been surprised when she'd come out and asked, "You like *Blade Runner*? And, bear in mind, I will judge you on this."

Like it? Was she kidding? "When a person is tired of *Blade Runner*, they are tired of life," he quoted, though Stuart couldn't remember who'd said it originally.

May nodded and laughed. She had such a beautiful laugh, like birdsong in the morning. Oh, he *had* got it bad. The more they talked the more he realised that if he didn't spend the rest of his life with this girl, this woman, then there would be no point to it at all. She could make or break him, that much was clear. It was just one of those things: Stuart had never been so certain about anything, ever. He was destined to be with her, in that George and Lorraine McFly 'density' way – another shared favourite – and if it didn't happen the universe might simply explode, or he'd just fade away into nothing. No such luck, sadly.

They'd had so much in common, so many shared experiences even though they'd gone to different schools. And from that evening on, the pair of them had been pretty much inseparable – regardless of the fact she was studying Health and Social Care (and an argument could be made that they were both sort of heading in the same directions with their career choices).

When groups of their friends had gone out, they'd inevitably ended up together in some corner drinking and trying to hear themselves think. Very often they'd bail on whatever club was having a happy hour (more like several hours) and find a quiet pub they could natter away in. Finishing each other's sentences, always knowing what the other one was going to say or ask. Yet it never seemed to progress from there.

"If you're not careful mate," his next-door neighbour in halls, Vikram, said to him, "you'll end up getting friend-zoned."

"I'm just… I just want to take my time, be respectful. May's worth it. I can wait."

"Just don't wait too long, is all I'm saying, before making your move."

Stuart couldn't say he hadn't been warned. All through first year and even into the second, after they'd been apart for the whole summer – which had been dreadful, messaging, phone calls and even visits not really cutting it as far as he was concerned – it had been the same story. "You know I think the world of you, Stuart," she'd tell him, "I'm just not ready for anything like that yet." She'd been hurt by guys in the past; he got it. He'd been hurt by girls. One especially he'd thought was pretty bloody special back in the dim and distant past of sixteen, and who'd totally trampled on his feelings. It had made him more than a bit gun-shy too, as he'd explained to her.

But then there'd been that feeling as well, the closeness that they shared. It was more than just friendship, surely? Was he imagining that? He thought the world of her too, was he projecting what he wanted to happen onto the situation? That ship sailed when she kissed him. Properly, full on, searching for the other person's tonsils with your tongue, kissing.

Okay, she'd had a few too many that night, was feeling particularly melancholy about how things had worked out with her love-life so far. "I mean," she'd pontificated, sitting on another couch in the flat Stu shared with a couple of other students, "why can't I find a guy like *you*, Stu?" May had tittered then at the rhyme, batting his chest with her hand.

A guy *like* me, he'd thought. Why *not* me? And he'd wished that night for something to happen, only for that to come true. Only for May to suddenly look at him intently over the rims of those spherical glasses, a look that practically caused him to melt. Then she was kissing him, and he was kissing her back. It was wonderful, he'd go as far as to say magical, and he was lost in the moment. Would have lived the entirety of his life in that moment, actually – which would have been better than living the one he had.

Except those kind of moments don't last forever. They end. And this one didn't end well. May was suddenly pulling away, saying how wrong it was. Mumbling shit like they were going to ruin their friendship and how much it meant to her, that she couldn't bear it if things went wrong.

"But… but it's not going to go wrong," he'd spluttered. Couldn't get her to see that at all. To see it was worth taking a risk, a chance on him and her. They weren't connecting now, were they? Knowing what the other was thinking? Weren't on the same wavelength at all. Then when she'd got up to leave and he'd grabbed her by the arm. It had been instinctive, a knee-jerk – elbow-jerk? – reaction, just to get her to stay so he could explain, tell her how much he loved her and wanted to be with her. The look she was giving him then, though. He'd blown it. Probably blown their friendship as well, even though he hadn't been the one to make the first move. Stuart had been waiting, so long – it really wasn't fair!

"I'll see you, Stuart." Not Stu, and she wanted to just get away from him. Out through the door and away, as far away as possible.

He hadn't helped himself by messaging repeatedly, trying to call her and leaving voicemails. Waiting to see May after she'd done with her classes, and she'd head off in another group. Waiting like some kind of stalker, some kind of creep. When he was so far away from that it—

"Mate, just leave it. Treat 'em mean and keep 'em keen." Vikram again, who had trouble pulling in a room full of single women. But Stuart figured he was right about leaving it alone. May needed some time and space to work things out, needed to know there was no need to feel embarrassed about what had happened. That they could wipe the slate clean, start again and maybe someday…

Unfortunately, what she did with that time was meet

Robert. Rob, as he liked to call himself. A Sports Science student with a six-pack and a smile so white you could set up camp in his mouth and study the polar bears. Fucking Rob! Which, of course, once he'd turned on the charm – which was the stuff of legend in their year – May started doing. He'd see them arm-in-arm on campus, and he'd see Rob just stop and pull her in for a snog – looked like he was trying to eat her face with those perfect teeth. Grabbing her arse at the same time (*he* had no problems differentiating it from an elbow), saying to everyone around that May was his. His property.

Ironically, she was okay with Stu after that – began talking to him at least, in short bursts anyway. Like he was safe now she had a fella. During an evening out, he'd made the mistake – when Rob was in the loo or wherever (maybe chatting up another girl somewhere) – of asking her what she saw in the guy.

"He's... Rob's just fun. I really like him," she'd said in all seriousness. They say love alters your brain chemistry, that you can't see anything clearly – and Stu couldn't really talk – that it's like a drug you crave at the beginning, wanting more and more. If so, May's brain was mush and she was so addicted she would have done anything just to have Rob look in her direction. Oh, he'd really done a number on her.

All charm, all smarm. People thought he was wonderful, even his exes didn't have a bad word to say about him. But Stuart could see it on him, the meanness there. The way he treated folk he thought were beneath him; a spoilt brat, only child. Golden boy. Who hadn't even moved that far from home; Stuart had moved further than him! That guy didn't have to worry about washing his own clothes, getting homecooked meals, because he'd pop back to the bosom of his middle-class family, for his mum to wait on him hand and foot and his builder father to bung him money, supplementing his loan. Everything handed to him on a plate.

May handed to him on a plate.

Why couldn't she see it? That she'd fallen into those same old traps, falling for the same kind of guy as before. That she'd get hurt again, same as ever. Stu had to listen to so many stories about that, could relate to some of them from his own perspective.

His suspicions about Rob had been confirmed when the bloke had caught him on his way out of the bar, shoving him against the wall. "Heard you and May used to be close." Used to be. Yeah. "Seems like you might be trying to worm your way back in. Well, one word for you: don't."

Stuart had said nothing, did nothing. What could he do, he was no match for Rob. Instead he'd nodded, run off when the thug let him go, his whole body shaking. Sat in his room trying to think of ways he could get the woman he loved so much, who he'd do anything for, away from that walking turd of a man. Came up with nothing. He couldn't fight Rob, and May wouldn't thank him for it anyway. She wouldn't even believe it if he told her the guy had warned him off.

All he could do was watch, and wait – the pain excruciating the more he saw them together. The nights were the worst, imagining them in bed together, doing all sorts. Rob doing all sorts to May (willingly, remember?). It was enough to drive a person mad, which looking back Stu guessed he was.

Crazy enough to drink himself into a stupor on that one fateful evening, to accept the dope Vikram offered him. Drunk and high, back in his room again, thinking about Rob pawing at May. What they'd definitely be doing on this of all days. On her birthday, and after he'd called in to her house party and seen them together. Stu had already sent a message wishing her a lovely day – risking one kiss: too many, not enough, overthinking it as usual – and that had been seen and ignored. Probably Rob poisoning her against him.

So there he was, after weeks, months of watching this shit. Out of his skull, wanting to do something – anything – that might… Veering between feeling sorry for himself, feeling sorry for May (who apparently gave not a shit), sadness at what might have been, and anger. Hatred. Directed at him, at her, remembering the night things had gone awry. How she'd 'led him on' as he'd said to her once afterwards, which definitely hadn't helped.

He remembered falling off the end of the bed, hurting himself. Tears pouring from his eyes, in just the right frame of mind to think those words (but don't say them!).

No, in the mood to fucking well say them out loud! Looking up and shaking a fist theatrically at nothing in particular. "I-I curse their relationship!" Didn't even need to say their names, because whoever, whatever, had heard him had known. Known his heart's desire.

Except it hadn't. What Stuart had meant was he wanted it to end. Wanted the pain, the torture of it all to stop. Wanted May *back*. Even as a friend, a best friend. Fuck, he missed her so, *so* much! Hadn't worked out quite that way, though, had it?

Had Stu been thinking then about the stories his

old gran had told him, the nonsense his mother had told her not to fill his head with. "Mum, please..." About the bloodline, the lineage reaching back to the middle ages and the trials. Where he'd come from and what he could do – if he put his mind to it. If he had his heart set on it.

He'd wanted to doom that relationship, and a curse was the way to do it, surely? Put a hex on it, a whammy, or whatever the fuck you wanted to call it!

But it hadn't done a thing, not that he'd been expecting it to. Over the course of the next few weeks, the next few months, he saw May and Rob together all the more. And her contact with Stuart was down to pretty much zero. He'd be lying if he said that hadn't affected his grades going into his third year, but in the end he got his head down and Stu just about managed to scrape a 2:2, rescuing it from the jaws of a 3.

At the graduation, his mum and dad there – the first time that man had worn a suit since he'd buried his own mother, Stu's nan – and proud of their son, the only one in their family to ever get a degree, never mind a middling one, Stu had seen May and Rob again. Him with his arm around her, his possession again. Their own parents hardly mixing, looking as uncomfortable as fuck.

She'd caught his eye at one point during the lengthy ceremony, turning round in her seat, and smiling weakly. Stu had smiled back, though it was the last thing in the world he'd felt like doing.

He hadn't bothered with the party afterwards, had headed back home instead; it was one of the last times they all spent together, because his dad passed about a year later from the same thing that was trying to see Stu off. But even as he'd eaten the celebratory roast dinner his mum cooked, watched an old SF movie with his father – who'd actually got him into all that kind of stuff, God bless 'im – Stu's thoughts hadn't wandered too far from May. From Rob and May. His thoughts wouldn't wander too far from them over the next few years, actually.

Life intrudes, however, and time works strangely. Goes by simultaneously in the blink of an eye and takes ages. It was a struggle to get work doing what he was qualified for, mainly because there were applicants more qualified than him. So he ended up working some shitty jobs in order to get a certificate in counselling, which was what Stu did till he hit his thirties. Listening to other people's problems to take his mind off his own.

And there were women, of course there were (he'd got lonely, as people do; we're not meant to be on our own). Lynda, the smoker, who cared more about her cat than Stu – it was mutual as it happened. She worked for the trainline, so the discounts came in handy, Stu supposed. When they'd broken up he felt like it had come as a relief to the both of them, the cat more upset than anyone. Then there was Georgina, George: he'd moved in with her for a little while. George was as close to the real deal as Stu got during that time, with her sweet, caring nature. In the end though he'd simply grown bored, the same old story.

"It's not you, it's me." It really was him. But she'd cried and cried, asked if there was anything she could do to make him stay. There wasn't. What a bastard. Should never have… led her on in the first place, when he knew – deep down he knew – that she would never be 'the one'. Only close, but sadly no cigar. Not even one of Lynda's dog-eared ciggies. Enough to fool himself for a while, but in the end he was just going through the motions.

Bev, Carol, Donna, Eve… Same old story. None of them knew – while they were with him – that they weren't the love of his life. Could never be that. Because they could never be:

May.

Stu heard, he couldn't remember where now as the shock of it caused him to go on a three-day bender, that she'd got engaged to *him*. May had got engaged to Rob. Bloody Robert. It had probably been through an old uni friend, cropping up and chatting about this and that. "Did you hear, so-and-so topped themselves? So-and-so got arrested? Can't say I'm surprised. And so-and-so got engaged, can you imagine?" He could, and the very thought of it made him want to gag. Bad enough they were still a couple, all these years later, that they had presumably gone off and got a place together, were living together. Because if they were engaged, they would be wouldn't they. Wasn't like the old days when you waited, like he'd waited. But to have pledged herself to him? To be together forever… Although how many marriages lasted in this day and age; what were the statistics again?

Didn't matter, they were still together, the pair of them. She *wasn't* with Stu. And that made him want to just get bladdered. He'd sworn off the drugs a long time ago, but that didn't mean he couldn't get so drunk in the pub he had no clue where he lived – in a flat, alone, at that time – and almost had to spend the night in a gutter. If it hadn't been for a friendly couple in a car, stopping to see if he was okay and pointing him in the right direction, he might have frozen to death that night. Lucky, eh?

Certainly not the example he should be setting to students if he got the job he was aiming for. Moving on from counselling – because there was only so much he could listen to without feeling suicidal himself, especially when people talked about losing their partners, whether it was a bereavement or to another person – he found himself eventually gravitating back towards the uni again. The same uni, as a matter of fact, which was where he saw her for the first time since attending the place. Not on campus but afterwards, because he was staying in the neighbourhood at a B&B for a couple of nights – just while he had the interview and met other department members on the psychology course.

He'd come away from the interrogation, by three senior members of staff – one of which he remembered from his time here – convinced he hadn't got the post. So Stu had wandered round town, finding a supermarket where he could get cheap booze to drown his sorrows in his room yet again. Turning a corner on one of the aisles, he'd seen her at the other end. Blinking once, twice, because he couldn't believe it – and also because she'd changed, had shorter hair than he'd known it before, smaller glasses, was wearing a plain dress – Stu had stood there gaping until he could figure out whether this was real or not. Some kind of mirage in the frozen section?

No. It was real. *She* was real. And anyway, she hadn't changed *that* much. He'd recognise his May anywhere. Except she wasn't his May, hadn't been for such a long time. Had never really been his, if Stu was being honest with himself. Which was why he should just turn around and walk away, walk off. Convince himself that he hadn't seen what he'd seen, like he'd persuaded himself that the job was forfeit.

Instead of which, she'd turned herself, basket

dangling from her arm with an assortment of items in it. She'd done the same thing, gaped down the length of the aisle. They must have looked almost comical, like something from an old Marx Brothers or Laurel and Hardy comedy. Cancelling each other out.

Then she'd mouthed something, head cocked, "Stu?" The lips forming his name, a confused look on her face.

What could he do but nod?

Then suddenly he was walking towards her, like a Jumbo jet on approach for a tricky landing. Taking just as much skill and concentration to get there safely. Stu held up his free hand, the one not holding his own basket. "Hey," he said, but his voice cracked and he was too far away for her to hear him anyway. He repeated the greeting when he was closer.

"Hiya. Oh wow, it's so…" She stepped forwards herself, as if she was going to give him a hug and he leaned in, but at the last moment they ended up doing the whole awkward handshake thing, mainly because the baskets would have clashed or maybe got stuck together. Lucky baskets. But then she gave him a peck on the cheek as well, hand on his shoulder to steady herself. He noticed, though, that her eyes were darting around, checking who was around her, as if someone might be spying and report back about it. There was nobody else in the aisle.

"How… I mean, it's so…" She didn't finish that the second time either.

"It… Yeah," said Stu, smiling. And it was.

"How are you?" May looked around again, but this time it was connected to her second question: "What are you doing here?"

"In the supermarket?" asked Stu. He wasn't trying

to be funny, he genuinely thought that was what she meant – because he was flustered – but was happy when he saw her laugh at the remark.

"No, silly. *Here*. Back here."

"Oh, yeah, right." He told her about the job at the university, making some kind of joke about it having a hold on him he couldn't escape. Nothing like the hold this woman had on him, though. Not even approaching… "So, yeah, there's that."

"Celebrating or commiserating?" May asked, nodding at the booze in the basket.

"I'm… not entirely sure," he replied. Didn't want to tell her that he thought he'd cocked it up by coming across as too needy, too desperate. Didn't want to do that again here, with her. Put that image of him in her mind again. Stu couldn't help glancing down at what she'd got in her basket: some veg, frozen chips.

"Nothing much changes, does it," she said then.

Oh, it does, he thought. *It really does.*

"What are you…" he asked, returning the favour.

"Just grabbing something for dinner tonight. I was looking for—"

"No, I meant…" Stu waved a hand and she laughed; they'd done the same thing. He hadn't meant here in the supermarket, but—

"Oh, right. We live not that far away. It's close enough for Rob's work at the gym, and so he can see his folks more often."

Stu frowned. *What about your folks?* he almost asked her. *When do you see them?* Not very frigging often, would be the reply. Assuming they were still around. Not his business, so instead he asked: "And what are you up to these days?"

May thought about it for a moment, then shrugged. "I was at the hospital for a little while, but the shifts… You know… The house keeps me fairly busy," she said eventually. "How about you, what else do you…"

"Oh, I'm…" He thought quickly and pulled this little gem out of the bag. "I do a bit of writing in my spare time. You remember, I used to talk about writing stories."

May beamed. "Those science fiction ones, yeah, I do! How's *that* going?"

"Had a few published actually." *Ha!* If you can call sticking them up on a site nobody reads published. They weren't very good anyway; it was probably for the best nobody had ever seen them.

"That's wonderful! You must be so pleased!" May smiled, and it was a smile of genuine delight for him, mixed – he thought – with a bit of pride.

Stu smiled back awkwardly. "Hey, listen. I'm around for a day or two, if you fancy, maybe…" What, a drink? Dinner?

May's smiled faded. "I'd love to but, actually, I was looking for the steak. It's steak night tonight, you see, and if Robert doesn't…" She stopped, laughed. "He likes a steak when there's a match on the telly. Oh, there they are!" Stepping to the side, she reached for the pack of steaks in the chiller section, and it was then that Stu saw it. The giant rock of a wedding ring on her finger; marking the territory again. Married; *of course* they were married by now. Couldn't stay engaged forever, right? Living together and married, and it's steak night, so—

"Okay, yeah. No worries at all. I might see you around then, if I… If things work out." They already hadn't, whether he got the job or not.

May smiled again, then looked about her a final time; he got the impression she was used to doing that while she was out and about. "That would be... Well, it was nice catching up, Stu."

"Yeah," he said, then watched as she put the steaks in the basket and wandered off, glancing back just the once and waving goodbye.

And he just stood there, when he should be going after her. Fate had seen fit to put them together again, it had to be for a reason! But what *could* he do? There was nothing *to* do. He couldn't make her see that all this was wrong, that she should be with him (fucking steak night, seriously?). That he'd take so much more care of her, that she'd have her freedom, could do whatever job she wanted to do, watch sci-fi movies instead of the bloody match if she'd just—

Too late, he rushed after her, rounded the corner that moments earlier he'd seen her turn, only to find she'd gone. Like some kind of magic trick, the disappearing lady. Or teleported? Stu checked every single aisle, raced to the check-outs, but there was no sign of May.

So that was that. He'd bought the booze, got wrecked, returned home and found out he'd got the job if he wanted it. Which would mean he might bump into her again, but wasn't that worse? Could he stand to keep seeing her knowing she was doing the shop for Robert's dinner that evening? Knowing she was returning home to him? Still with him, after all this time?

Stu thanked the uni for the offer, but declined it. Decided to go for another one in another city, somewhere he could try and get on with his life. Because he really needed to. Had to get over this damned obsession he had with a woman he'd met over a decade ago, had only kissed the once for Christ's sake!

He applied to a few unis actually, got into one of them, and moved. There had followed a few other flings, one with a fellow lecturer and another with a mature ex-student that had threatened to get quite messy, but life had gone on. Stu had job satisfaction, sort of, unless he was marking a particularly terrible assignment, and he actually did start to take his writing more seriously. His tales (all written under a pseudonym) were getting accepted into honest to goodness magazines this time, for honest to goodness cash. Not much, but enough to encourage him to carry on.

Then came the train. A journey back up to his mum's for Christmas. She'd married again, a decent enough guy called Colin who treated her well so Stu couldn't complain. Had even offered to watch a few films with Stu – "What do you say, we could watch that there *Star Wars* with Dr Spock!"; you can imagine how much that had made him cringe – but, as nice as the gesture was, it simply felt disloyal to his late father.

He'd only just made the six o'clock train, having left his shopping till the last minute as usual, so had clambered on board with his bags and was lucky enough to find a seat near the door of the carriage. Stu put his head back, closed his eyes, and let out a slow breath. When he looked again, he took in the rest of the people he was trapped with. A fat bloke in a suit who looked like he was a Christmas dinner away from a stroke; a mother struggling to keep two kids entertained, screaming at them when that didn't work; a guy wearing a vest in spite of the chilly weather, probably to display his collection of tattoos and piercings, and—

May.

Stu had to look twice again, gawking like the last time he'd seen her back in the supermarket. She'd grown her hair a little more since then, but only a little, wasn't wearing any glasses this time – laser eye treatment? more likely just contacts – and was wrapped up in a warm winter coat. May was staring down sadly at her drink (of tea, coffee, Stu couldn't tell, and probably didn't matter given the drinks on this service; it was brown, at any rate). The plastic cup was resting on a table which had four seats around it, all occupied. Stu looked, but couldn't see any sign of Robert.

It took a few stops before the woman who'd been sitting opposite May got up to leave the train. Without even thinking about what he was doing, Stu was up and making his way to that seat, lugging his bags. Was almost pipped to the post by a guy who was about to slide in.

"I'm sorry, I know…" Stu nodded to May, who looked up for the first time since he'd got on. Her mouth fell open in shock, then there was a twitch in the corner of her lips that could have been mistaken for a smile. May snapped out of her reverie, looked from Stu to the other bloke.

"Oh, yes. He's with me," she told him. If only that were true.

The other man backed off and Stu sat down, jamming his bags under his side of the table. "Thanks."

"Stuart," said May. "It's been a while."

"It has," he agreed. If she'd asked, he could have told her down to the minute exactly how long had passed since the supermarket. "How're things?"

"Good," said May, looking down again, avoiding his eyes. "They're... They're good. You?"

"Yeah. Same. Good."

He thought he heard the person on the left of him mumble something like "Get a room", but May didn't catch the remark so Stu left it. "You were after a job at the university back home last time I saw you, right?"

Stu let out a breath. "Didn't work out." Like so many things hadn't.

"That's a shame. I thought I hadn't seen you around."

Had she been looking for him? Stu wondered. "No, I got a gig somewhere else. I got on a few stops back. Just heading home for the holidays to see Mum and her fella."

"Fella?"

Stu's brow furrowed. "Oh, I thought I mentioned it when... Dad passed away."

May looked like she was going to burst into tears. "Oh. Oh, Stu. I'm so sorry. I didn't..." She reached out a hand for his free one – the one not clutching the bags under the table – and he let her take it. Let her give it a squeeze. "I've just been visiting my parents. I don't see them too often these days. They don't get on well with..."

Stu nodded, couldn't help giving that hand a squeeze back. "But they're okay, yeah? Still keeping well?"

It was May's turn to nod. "You know, my mum always liked you. Thought we might..." The nod turned into a shake. "Doesn't matter."

It did. It mattered *so* much, and it was the first he was hearing about this. But then he always did have a little chat with May's mum before she put her on the phone, if he was ringing her on the landline. Nice lady.

May shifted the position of her hand then, and he

felt the edge of her ring. Her wedding ring. She pulled the fingers free, reached for her drink but didn't have any. "And you, how are things with you? You happy?"

He thought about telling her about the published stories, but held back. Didn't feel the need to boast about stuff like that this time, although now it would simply be about telling her. There was so much he wanted to share with her, however, things that had happened not just since the last time he'd seen her, but before that. Huge chunks of his life she'd missed, and that made him feel like crying too. Instead, he just nodded as well and avoided her eyes now. "Yeah, happy." Far from chatting about the time that had passed, they sat pretty much in silence until it was almost time for May to get off.

"Look, May. If you ever want to—" Then he stopped, his heart sinking when he saw her rise. Having to dodge the edge of the table because of the swell of her stomach, pushing its way out of the coat. She followed his eyes, staring at the bump, and patted it.

"Not long now, a couple of months or so," she told him.

Stu felt like he'd been punched in his own stomach. It wasn't as if he hadn't known she was sleeping with Robert; had known it for such a long time. But inside there, in May's belly, was the physical evidence of that act and it made Stu sick. May wasn't trying to rub his face in that, although when the train lurched it almost happened for real. Then she smiled, and it was a genuine smile: she was going to have a baby. Didn't matter who the father was (it should have been him, not fucking Rob, that should have been his kid!). "I… congratulations, May."

"Ta. Oh, here we go! See you again sometime, eh

Stu?"

He held up a hand. "Yeah, see you soon." Wouldn't happen, Stu realised that. Might never see her again, and his last memory would be of her stepping onto the platform, then as the train pulled away from the station seeing a glimpse of Robert, grabbing her arm and linking them together. His property. Stu did cry then, not just for May, but her little one on the way. Imagine a father like that!

But it was still none of his business. Would never be any of his business.

Or so he thought.

The next time he heard from May it was several years – some grey hair and a stone or so – later, and it was her who got in touch with Stuart. He'd been surprised to see a message appear on his social media account, the same one he'd had all these years and kept in touch with people like Vikram through (twice divorced, he was looking for lucky lady number three). Hadn't been a secret or anything, May had even been a friend of his on there back in the day until her account had eventually disappeared. He could never bring himself to look at hers anyway, bad enough to see her and Rob together in person let alone galleries of photos featuring the happy couple.

"You happy?"

He'd nearly deleted the message because it had come through from an account he didn't recognise – not that he went on there much anyway – called 'Everyday Goddess'. Looking back, why he hadn't got the reference straight away Stu didn't know. It was how May – Athena – had been introduced to him. Then again, the internet was full of people calling themselves all sorts of bollocks

– and most of the women who contacted him were 'bots. There was also a photo of an owl, which he found out later on was one of the symbols of the goddess she shared her name with. It all added up to someone trying to keep this account a secret, and the message itself had sounded quite fraught.

"Stu, don't delete this!! It's me, May. I really need to talk to you." Turned out she was also using a computer at a library, because Rob checked her laptop and phone on a regular basis. She wanted to meet up, suggesting the next town along from where she lived (just far enough away, but not too far; somewhere she could make something up about visiting), the third weekend in June if he was free around then.

He was.

Truth be told he'd just split up with a lady called Janine, who he'd moved in with a couple of years earlier. She'd had kids from a previous marriage, and although that hadn't been a problem when they'd first started seeing each other – he'd been Mum's cool new friend Uncle Stu – living with her had been a different kettle of hormones altogether. The two boys, and especially the eldest who was heading into his teenage years, resented the time Stu spent with her and made his life hell, doing the whole 'who's in charge thing'. Their real dad, who hadn't given a shit about either of them up till this point, was soon back on the scene which had added another complication. The eldest lad started to emulate him, filling the house with toxic masculinity. They all seemed to think Janine was their personal servant, whether it came to picking things up or cooking or washing up, which apparently also extended to Stu. And in the end it had just seemed easier for everyone concerned if Stu packed his bags and left them to it. Last he'd heard Janine was back with the ex, more fool her.

He often wondered, when this latest attempt at a relationship had gone to shit, if that one hadn't been his subconscious response to the fact May and Rob were breeding. He'd show them, wasn't that right – and here was a ready-made family he could just slot into. When of course he was just gate-crashing someone else's party because he couldn't be arsed to plan one of his own.

All that was beside the point, though, because yes he was free and May didn't have to know anything about Janine and her clan and the total fuck-up he'd made of things there. (Slot in? Square peg in a round hole, more like!) But when he saw her, Stu realised he wasn't the only one who'd been in a mess lately. Ironically, as bad as it had felt at the time trying untangle everything with Janine, it was probably easier to get out of than May's situation would be.

"I think Rob might have been seeing other people," May confessed when they'd taken a seat in a nearby coffee shop, after she'd hugged the life out of him out on the street. "In fact I'm certain of it. When he's away like he is this weekend, on one of his trips for work."

Everyone knew what that meant, didn't they? Trips for work? Might as well be saying 'shagging anything that moved'. "I-I'm not sure what to say." Actually, he was – cheating fucking bastard, and cheating on May at that! – but Stu wasn't really surprised to hear about it. The only surprise was that May was just waking up to the fact all these many years later. Or was she?

"I mean, it's happened before. I found out about a couple of them, but, well, he promised me all that stuff was over. That after Penny came along, he'd put a stop to it." May looked much older than the last time he'd seen her, but then they were both getting older, weren't they? Closer to forty now than thirty, almost twenty years since they'd first met. Since he'd met and fallen in love with her.

Since he'd said those words. If only he hadn't—

Penny. A little girl, a daddy's girl. She might have been his, but it wasn't to be. "How old is…" He knew exactly how old she was, just hadn't realised she was a she. Penny. Pretty name, like her mother's.

"Almost seven, going on seventy."

"And where…" He looked around to illustrate, as if he thought she might have brought the little girl here and hidden her behind the counter to come out like one of those Long Lost Family shows.

"Oh, she's having a sleepover at one of her friend's. They're going on a treasure hunt, I believe."

"Right," said Stu. "And… Look, it's not that I'm not happy to see you, May…"

"You happy?"

"But what's all this got to do with you?" She let out a long sigh. "I… well, nothing. Not really. You don't owe me anything. I guess I just needed to talk to someone about it. A friend."

Owe her… He couldn't help himself, maybe it was the news about Penny, maybe it was the fact that if May had woken up to Rob sooner then… But she married *him*. She. Fucking. Married. Him! Stu found himself getting a bit annoyed. A friend? They hadn't been friends, not really, for such a long time. She must have seen the look on his face, knew what he was about to ask, because she answered his question in that weird way they had. That bizarre connection.

"I know, I know. I have no right to… But I don't really have any friends of my own, not where I am. I've sort of lost touch with them."

Shocker. You'd lost touch with me too, but you soon got back in touch when you needed me, Stu thought. *No. You don't have the right to do that, sit there and complain about your shithead of a husband who once pushed me up against a wall and threatened me. You don't get to—*

"Stu." Tears in her eyes again, as she reached out her hand just like she had on the train. "Stu, I don't know who else to turn to! My mum and dad don't want to know, they'd just say 'we told you so'. And, and…"

He was about to reply when he looked down at the hand that had hold of his. Looked down and spotted the bruises there on May's wrist. "God, did *he* do that to you?" Stu asked, a bit too loudly but was beyond giving a crap right that minute, and all of the anger just faded away. Anger directed at May, that was. Rob he wanted to flat-out murder, felt like it but would never do it because it just wasn't him. But still, Jesus Christ, her *wrist!* Blue and purple from where he must have had hold of her. It made him wonder what else the man had done.

"He was drunk, I shouldn't have said anything."

"May, there's no excuse for this. Not an excuse in the world for—"

She was crying freely, unable to hold back. "I just… I don't know what to do." May was looking at him like he had the answers, like he could save her from this. And he thought then to himself, perhaps this is it: perhaps this was the curse. The thing he'd been waiting for all this time. For it to kick in, for May to come to her senses? It had finally worked, in the most horrendous way possible yes, but worked nonetheless. There was still time. It would take some untangling, sure, more than his own situation had taken, but it could be done and it would be so, so worth it.

A little voice was crying out at the back of his skull that this was a mistake, that he'd just be inserting himself into another family that wasn't his own, even if Robert fucked off out of it, which he doubted the man would. Let Stu be a father to Penny? Bloody hell, he hadn't even met the girl and he was thinking about—

Not to mention the fact May had come here for a shoulder to cry on, that's all. Her life was complicated enough without him making it more so. Yet this was a start, wasn't it? A way of getting back to how they'd been. It was still there; she wouldn't have got in touch if it wasn't. They wouldn't be here unless—

She hadn't got anyone else. Nobody. Think about it, how you're being used. How much pain this woman's caused you over the years.

How much potentially she could still cause.

For some reason that didn't matter, all that mattered was listening to May, trying to help her. In the end, once they'd moved on to a quiet pub so she could have a stiff drink and they could carry on talking. Which they'd done, one drink turning into a few. Turning into many. Catching up on the time they'd missed, on what had happened in both their lives. Hers was so much worse than he'd ever imagined. May was expected to be a kind of Stepford Wife, perfect partner and mother, everything monitored and checked up on, which was why she couldn't risk a journey any further afield than this.

"Y-You just need to get out of there," Stu told her,

laying the groundwork, his words slurring. "Things will be a lot clearer when you do, I promise."

"But where would I...? I couldn't just—"

"You could stay with me," he said earnestly.

May looked down, then back up again. "I couldn't do that. Not after everything I—" She shook her head emphatically.

It was his turn to take her hand, squeeze it. He'd meant it only as a gesture of friendship, no funny business – same as the offer of somewhere to stay, though there was hardly enough room for him and his stuff let alone three people in the flat he was currently occupying (all that could be sorted out later, he told himself). As she'd done before, back at uni, it had been May who'd turned it into something else. Kissed him for the first time in such a long time. A lifetime. "I'm sorry," she said. "About before. I was just scared of losing you."

He wanted to say, to tell her that she'd lost him anyway though, hadn't she? That they'd lost all these years because of that one stupid mistake. But he kept his mouth shut, knew that anything he came out with might just ruin this moment, the same way as he didn't say to her "Are you sure?" when she suggested going back to the hotel he'd booked into that night, a much nicer one than the B&B he'd stayed in for the interview.

Didn't say a thing, just went back with her to that place, to his room: drifting, going with the flow. Drunk but not too drunk (he hoped). Was okay when she started to kiss him in the room, passionately, whispering to him: "I need this. Hold me Stuart, I just want to feel like I'm loved."

Stu opened his mouth to tell her that she was

definitely that. As much as it was possible to love anyone, he loved this woman. But again he held his tongue, even as she was turning the lights out (no, he wanted to see her, he'd waited so long; but then he thought about those bruises, where she might have more – never the face, they never go for the face, people like Rob). Then it didn't matter, because they found each other in the darkness.

Thinking back now, he only recalled flashes of that night, but remembered it being one of the best of his life. Nothing could take that away from him, could it? What was it Sarah Connor said about spending a lifetime with someone?

Although when he woke the next morning, he wondered whether it had even happened – especially when May wasn't there beside him (where she'd always belonged). Then he heard the sound of her in the shower, actually singing in the shower. Did that mean she was happy?

"You happy?"

He guessed so, Stu had never heard her sing when they were at uni together – not even when she'd got together with Rob, but then why would you? Stu didn't think he'd been any great shakes the previous night, but then had he ever really been? Had some moves, or so he'd been told, but—

When she'd appeared in the doorway, towel around her and hair dripping wet, he'd gaped again – just couldn't help himself. He'd climbed out of the bed and gone over to her, and she'd met him with a kiss. This was Heaven, surely? If Stu had been in Hell before, this was the opposite – like a wish was the opposite of a curse: one positive, one negative – but then he spotted another bruise on her shoulder and she caught him looking, pulled away.

Stu couldn't help himself, opened his mouth and it all came out: about what they needed to do now, how she should get away from Rob. Get Penny and—

It was too much. In the cold light of day, sober, it was just too much. May went very quiet, remained quiet all the while they had breakfast together. Another opposite of the day before when it had all poured out of her.

Then he'd seen her off at the taxi rank, she'd paid cash to get here and was going to do the same for the way back; no trace then. May had kissed him on the cheek, promised she'd be in touch about arrangements. To trust her.

So he had, but that voice was back again about her capacity to hurt him. *I hope you know what you're doing*, it said.

Hope.

That's what he'd done then, waited and hoped. Hoped and waited for May to get back to him through her Everyday Goddess account. Or just a goddess to him, nothing everyday about her. Nothing ordinary. A few days went by, and he thought fair enough – give her time to get herself sorted out. Time to talk to Rob, square things away, though Stu would have preferred to be around when she did that in case things got out of hand. Time to talk to Penny ("You're going to have a new daddy!" No. Too soon, *way* too soon).

But then a week went by, another weekend – the memory of the previous one turning bitter-sweet – a fortnight. And Stu started to send messages to her off his own bat, messages wondering how she was. Hoping (that word again) that she was okay. That she wasn't—

Dead. Let's be honest, he thought Rob might have killed her. Stu didn't come right out and say it, but the increasingly worried tone said it for him. Still no response.

Stu began to wonder if he'd made an arse of things again, come on too strong that morning when talking about the future and what *he* thought should happen. The last thing May needed was another controlling dipstick, out of the frying pan and into the—

Began to wonder again whether it had even happened at all, flashing right back to the morning when she hadn't been there. Had he imagined the whole thing? No, parts of it had definitely happened. But maybe the night, the sleeping together bit. Had he imagined that? Had he imagined May *wanting* him? Wished for it so hard that he'd made it happen in his own head, when all they'd really done was talk and fall asleep because of the booze?

Finally, just when he was about to go round there – although she'd been careful not to tell him where she, where they *all* lived, hadn't she – May had answered. She was sorry again, but there'd been an accident. Robert had been in an accident, a car crash, and she couldn't think about all this now, leaving or whatever. Because Robert needed her, she couldn't think about abandoning him when he needed her (Stuart needed her too, God did he need her and that twat had had years with May). Would take months for him to recover properly, if at all, so she couldn't... She just *couldn't*. It had been lovely seeing Stu again, but she was going to close down the account now – and if he thought anything of her he wouldn't try to get in touch again.

Stuart had stared at the screen even as he'd read the words, not really believing them while he was reading. Re-

reading them a few times, just to let it all sink in. It took him some time to draft a reply, because he wasn't quite sure what he was going to say that wouldn't be the literary equivalent of grabbing her arm (but not as hard, never as hard as Rob would do and only to stop her leaving when he couldn't really stop her from doing anything). Just as he'd fashioned his reply, was about to copy and paste it into the message thread, the whole thing vanished. Her account vanished, teleported away, not giving him any chance to respond to what she'd said.

He'd sat back again in the chair, frowning. Gazing, frustrated at the screen, his message and the redundant account. Back to square one, worse than square one! He'd have been better off if she'd never contacted him at all!

That one took a bit of getting over. Actually, he never really did. Wasn't sure he wanted to, or even if he could. Worse than the kiss, than May getting together with Robert in the first place. So much worse than any of the other bullshit, the chance meetings in the supermarket, on the train. Seeing the baby bump. His baby. What should have been Stu's daughter, Penny.

He contemplated hiring someone to track May down, track down their address and just head there to confront Rob – her? – about what had happened. For one thing, though, it wouldn't have done any good; once May had made her mind up about something that was that. For another it might just make things worse for her on a day-to-day (Everyday) basis when she had so much on her plate already, probably waiting on that moron hand and foot. Just like his parents, his mother, had once done. Stu knew nothing about Rob's injuries, but found himself questioning whether he might be putting them on, because he'd got wind of what was happening – how, was anyone's guess! Besides, it wouldn't come across well would it, tackling a cripple? Not his style.

He was left with no choice but to, well, leave it. Nothing he could do but hide away and lick his wounds. Again.

Told you so, that little voice whispered at the back of his mind.

Those next few weeks, few months, few *years* were probably the worst of his life. Stu tried getting back on the dating scene, but he was growing older and he seemed to have lost that ability to connect with the opposite sex. Most dates he went on were just more horror stories about past relationships, baggage. Either that or women came with kids in tow and he wasn't falling into that trap again.

He began drinking more, getting back into the recreational drugs, hanging out in some unsavoury places. It was at one of these called 'Mick's' that he met her. Not *the* her, because what would she be doing in a dive like that, but the closest thing Stu had come across in all this time before or since. Looks-wise anyway, not personality. That was okay, because he wasn't paying her to speak.

Trixie she called herself, though Lord alone knew what her real name was. At first it was just for company, so Stu could pretend. Very often he wanted her to just stay the night with him, stay beside him so he could wake up and see that face. The one which looked a bit like, but really, really wasn't, the love of his—

"*You happy?*"

It developed into something else then. They'd fuck, and it was here he'd see the difference, because this woman was so skilled in the erotic arts it was hard to conceive of her as May. Then that turned into a bit of an obsession, paying her for weekends on the trot, then wanting her not to see other clients.

It all ended with the police getting involved because he'd frightened the woman in question (who'd always thought he was a bit weird anyway) and Stu losing his post at the university, not that he was doing such a bang-up job of it anyway. Letting his students down when it was the last thing in the world he wanted to—

A bit of a wake-up call, that car crash (not an actual car crash, or May might have taken more notice of him, eh?). Kind of like waking up in a pool of your own vomit and realising you had to do something about your life, which he did on several occasions. Stu went to stay with his mum and Colin for a bit, where he dried out and swore off everything. They were good to him, much better than he deserved after shunning their help for so long; even shouting down the phone at his mother that he didn't need her (he *so* did).

When she'd asked him what he was going to do next, Stu had shrugged. "Haven't got the foggiest, Mum." It had been Colin, bizarrely, who'd given him the idea about trying to make a go of his writing.

"You've done well with those small stories of yours, why don't you try something longer now you have a bit of time on your hands?"

Why *didn't* he? There was nothing stopping him, like an actual job, which paid actual money. But Stuart gave it a go, it was something to do, and he actually found that he enjoyed doing it. In the meantime some of his shorts had come across the desk of an agent, one who'd just branched off to start her own firm and was scouring magazines for talent. Stu was about halfway through his magnum opus when she emailed him asking if he'd ever considered writing a novel. He told her what stage he was at, and she made him promise to let her have a look at it when he was finished – which spurred him on to actually finish.

Not only did he do that, but the agent loved it and sold it to a mid-list publisher for an okay amount of dosh. Enough to cover him while he was writing the next one, for him to get a place of his own again – within spitting distance of his mum and Colin – so he could carry on writing. The first book came out and was fairly well received. It was a bit of a Marty McFly's Dad moment when he unpacked his contributor copies and held it for the first time. Not *A Match Made in Space*, but definitely a love story – a doomed one involving time travel and a character's attempts to, as Sam would have said, 'Put right what once went wrong.'

It was the talk of the party when he got there; his gran's 100th birthday party, that was. Good genes, his gran, which she'd passed on to her daughter, she joked. Stu, however, had inherited more of his father's genetic flaws sadly.

"Going to be on those bestseller lists one day, aren't you son?" his mum was busy telling all the aunts and uncles, cousins and second cousins. Stu could feel his face burning red. Still, it was better than telling them about him being a pisshead and on drugs, chasing after a prostitute.

"We had hoped we'd see you settled with a nice lady by now, Stuart." That was the other one he got at the party, which just depressed him. He'd thought he might be settled with a nice lady too (not a lady of the night). One lady in particular.

Which had segued into a conversation about it with

his gran, about what he'd done. "I mean, I didn't really believe in... so I guess it makes sense. But *you* do. Believe I mean. You always used to say to me that..." He shook his head; this was horror not SF, and he'd never really liked the former (though his genre had the Force, didn't it? the Jedi and the Bene Gesserit?). Yet still he asked: "Why didn't it work?"

The wizened old woman had looked at him seriously, staring so hard he wondered if she could see him with all those cataracts. "What exactly did you say, young Stuart?"

So he told her, and she looked more serious than ever then. "But, don't you see? It did work. Your curse worked, Stuart. All too well."

What was she talking about, how could it have worked? May and Robert were still together as far as he knew. He told his gran as much.

"You cursed the relationship. If only you'd had a bit of patience, lad. Waited." But he *had* waited. Waited so long... "She might have just seen sense. Nature has to run its course. You clearly have a link, or you wouldn't keep finding each other. I'd go so far as to say you're right, you probably should have been together. She's your soulmate, but what you did messed all that up. Put a real spoke in the wheels."

Stu still didn't understand, not then. But the more he thought about it afterwards, the more he realised his gran was absolutely right. What he'd done had got in the middle of things he shouldn't, just like he'd done with Janine. Fucked everything up.

"They're tricky things, curses – which is why you should never use them lightly. They never work in the way you think, or hope, they might." She went on to say more, but Stu was still reeling from those first revelations.

But maybe there was something he could do about it. "How do I fix this?" he asked his gran, who simply shook her head. "There must be *something* I can do!"

His voice carried and soon relatives came over to see what the shouting was about. Before they arrived and he left, she whispered something to him. Something that saw him bawling his eyes out, even as he left the party and headed home, trying to resist calling into the off-license on the way. Trying to resist just taking a handful of pills and ending it all. Trying to resist making plans to find May and finally show up on her doorstep. Because none of it would do any good, only make things worse.

Stu's gran died a few months after that conversation, though everyone agreed she'd had a good innings. It was after Stuart's third book came out, and hit the bestseller lists immediately – his loyal fanbase spreading the word of mouth – after he heard there was film interest in his first two books, that Stuart was given the diagnosis. The first one. Life still had a few surprises left, it seemed.

His mum, his doctors, had been all about fighting it – and Stuart had done. Fought it with everything he had while undergoing the treatments. Concentrated everything on trying to get better, which he had done… for a few years anyway.

While he was in the hospital, though, he had a visitor. It was May, who came and sat by his bedside, tears in her eyes. "Oh Stuart," said the woman, taking his hand. There were lines on her face, the years had not been kind to her. But she was still as pretty as ever to him.

"What…?" He struggled to get the words out, but – as always – she knew exactly what he was asking.

"I had to come, when I heard."

Stuart thought about telling May, finally telling her about what he'd done. But he was too ashamed, not that she'd believe him anyway. Would probably think it was the drugs talking. So instead he just apologised.

"Sorry? What have you got to be sorry about? It's me who should be… I've been so…" She started crying freely then, not realising that none of it had been her fault. Not really.

Nature had to run its course.

"You happy?"

She told him about her life, that Penny was getting ready to head off to uni herself soon. That she was still looking after Robert, though most of the time he was confined to an electric chair (not the kind Stu would have preferred), which helped him get up and down so he could shuffle about on his Zimmer. When Stu looked in May's eyes he could see the strain on her, the strain she'd been under all this time because she was a good wife. A loyal partner, which was more than you could ever say for Robert. In his mind's eye, Stu imagined him shouting and growling at May, might still be giving her a back-hander or two if she got close enough; the sheer frustration for an active man would only have made things worse.

Before she left, May told Stuart to fight this and when he was okay, she'd come and see him again. He'd nodded, knowing that she probably wouldn't.

Indeed, Stuart wouldn't see her until he'd been clear of the cancer for a few years, not that it hadn't departed without leaving him with a few going away presents. The chronic fatigue, for one. Some were even side-effects of the pills he'd be on for life, however long that was.

Because when it returned it did so with a vengeance, the kind of cancer you didn't get over this time. At least he'd managed to see more of his books published, his creations turned not only into films but TV shows. The kind he'd watched himself as a kid. It was stupid, crazy money, and it helped pay for private treatment in the end. But it was all just about making him comfortable now. And you couldn't take it with you…

Couldn't take it with you, but he could leave it to someone. What he wasn't giving to his old mum, who'd had to bury her second husband only recently. Because, when he put the feelers out, sent for May this time because he knew he needed to at least put some of this right, she'd brought someone along with her.

A young man, in his mid-twenties. Stu had only needed to take a look at him to know, to realise. He was a real mix of May – who walked with a stick now herself, was back to wearing those glasses but with much thicker lenses – and himself. "Lance," she said to the boy after he'd escorted her into the room at the hospice which cost thousands a day, helping her by the arm when she almost stumbled, "this is an old friend of mine, Stuart. I've known him all my life."

"How're you doing?" the young guy asked.

"You happy?"

Stu waved a hand around at all the tubes running in and out of him, as he sat in his chair by the window, then laughed.

"Listen, would you give us a minute, love," May said to her son. He didn't look too sure, so she added: "It'll be all right."

When he'd gone, she pulled up a chair herself and

sat next to Stu. "D-Does he know?" asked Stu in a croaky voice.

May looked him right in the eye and shook her head. "I-I'm sorry, Stuart." They seemed to say that a lot to each other. Had said it so many times over the course of their lives. "That night when we… I convinced myself the baby was Robert's, from before his accident. But, well, look at him. I don't think Robert believes it himself, not really. He's got your eyes, Stu. I see you every time I look into them."

Stuart began to cry, held out his hand for May and she took it. "I have a son," he whispered. This world really hadn't finished with its surprises, had it?

May nodded.

"How… How's Penny?" he asked then. She was doing okay, had graduated as a doctor and gone off to work in some hospital down south. It was where her boyfriend worked, they'd met at university. Stuart couldn't help smiling at that. One kid who should have been his, another he'd never even known about. He'd missed out on both of them growing up, because of his own anger. His own jealousy. Now it was too late, all lost like those tears in the rain from their favourite shared movie.

Fuck.

Not even what he told May about his plans would make up for it.

"You can't, Stuart. It's too much." But it was only what they were owed and he insisted; his people would make all the arrangements. "He writes as well, you know," May told Stu. "He's quite good."

Stuart chuckled again, nodded. Then he started to cough and a nurse came in to usher May out, telling her Stuart was tired.

And when you're tired of Blade Runner…

Telling May she could come again another time if she wanted. But Stu knew that she wouldn't. That he probably wouldn't see her again in this lifetime, though there was always scope for this to continue after he was gone. After they both were.

Because hadn't his gran told him as much, that curses like that are unbreakable. "There's nothing you can do. They last an eternity," she'd whispered, just before he'd left the party.

He thought now, sitting and staring out of the window and feeling the life leaving him, realised that he should never have said those words. Or, at least, that he should have added those other couple which would have made it all right, less general: "I curse their relationship… to end."

Because in cursing the thing, he'd actually cursed it to last. Cursed them to live inside a damaged relationship that neither one of them could end, which was why May had remained, but also why Robert's affairs had never led anywhere. Why he'd always felt like she was his possession, something to never let go of.

"Nothing to be done. But in cursing them, you also cursed yourself," his gran had told him.

If he didn't spend the rest of his life with this girl, this woman, then there would be no point to it at all…

Could make or break him.

Curses rebound, never work out the way you want them to. Like in the old revenge thing, dig two graves. Or three in this case. He'd cursed them to keep going round in circles, maybe not just in this life, but in countless others to come. It might never end.

Yet still he had to hope, which was why he was wishing. In that last minute of his last hour of his last day. Wished for the last time he hadn't said those words, knowing it wouldn't come true.

Because wishes weren't as powerful as their opposite number, Stuart had come to realise. Were fuelled by hope rather than hatred, and nothing ever tops that one – especially in this world. Because hopes are dashed all the time…

And because he deserved the fate he'd brought upon himself.

Maddy the Monster

It was a time of monsters, or so she'd been told.

Had been for a while now, not that there was any way of marking the passage of time down there. Chained up, with four walls surrounding her and a dim light-bulb above which swung left and right in the draught that whistled through the locked and bolted door.

Not that it had been that much different before, where she was kept. But at least it had been bright; no windows, of course, that hadn't been allowed, just much better artificial lighting. She'd been provided with certain... creature comforts. A bed – not that she slept much – a chair, which was comfortable enough, and magazines which she'd read from cover to cover. The bits they hadn't blanked out, that was, for her own good. They were filled with beautiful women modelling glamorous dresses and wearing make-up to cover up their faces. Why, she had no idea, when they were probably much prettier without. Prettier than her at any rate. More... normal.

And she'd been given a name. Madeline, Maddy – that's what they'd called her, though she understood that wasn't her real name. It was just something they called her so it would seem less weird, like a pet or something. "Come along, Maddy. Don't struggle, be a good girl." Even though the tests hurt so much sometimes. It was for the benefit of others, she'd be saving lives – and who didn't want to think they were doing that? Being useful? "Some very sick kid's going to be feeling well again thanks to you," they'd say. So she'd played her part, all the while daydreaming about those women from the magazines walking through fields, bathing their faces in sunlight.

Free.

Still, it had been better than this, hadn't it? Back home – and Maddy couldn't help thinking about it as home, even now – she could move around, do as she pleased… up to a point. But it had been a prison, all the same. She'd been a prisoner, even though she didn't know any different. At least this place didn't pretend to be something it wasn't. You couldn't mistake it for anything other than a cell.

For a long time, she'd thought it was her fault. Figured they'd shot her with the tranq-dart and moved her because she'd started asking too many questions. Made too many demands. Got too curious about things as she grew older. Not about where she came from, why she was different – they'd told her that much. Told her she was special, with her scales and webbed feet, her tail and her claws – which needed to be cut if they got too long (couldn't risk any of the doctors or nurses getting injured as they went about their business). That they'd made her this way, specifically so she *could* help others. Cure all those terminally ill children. Surely, though, she'd said one day, that entitled her to some kind of reward – not just the chocolate bars they'd give her as a treat sometimes. Not just the jelly and ice-cream or movie nights with popcorn.

Something more.

Maybe even something out there, beyond the confines of her room. And they'd explain again and again how that wasn't really possible. That it had been tried before and the results had been... unfortunate. That's why it hadn't been done again. "Do you really want to be out there anyway, amongst people who don't understand what you are?" they'd said. "People who would run away from you, afraid? Or, even worse, hurt you?"

"But... but if I'm helping them?" Maddy had argued. "If I'm curing their children, then—"

That's when the hand would be raised and the discussion would be over. She'd remain in her room, where she was safe. Where no-one would harm her – apart from when the staff did their testing, naturally. Then it was necessary.

But she'd pushed, and she'd pushed – until they must have got sick of the questions, of the arguing. Because when she woke up again from her long sleep she was somewhere else. Maddy was here, manacled by the legs to the stone wall, barely able to see anything at all because the light was so bad – two bowls in front of her, one full of water and one of what looked like dried pellets. Food, if you could call it that. Certainly wasn't any chocolate or jelly and ice cream or popcorn.

Maddy had called out for help. Shouted so loudly her throat was raw by the time she was finished, so loudly her voice went completely and she had to drink all the water they'd left for her. Nobody came. Not for a long time. So she'd gotten angry, tugged at the chains, but been unable to break them. Had thrown the bowls across the room, the empty one and the full one – then regretted it when she began to get hungry. And she'd cried. Cried so much she thought she'd never stop. Whispered her apologies and begged to be taken back to her own room; she'd be good, she promised. She'd be a good girl, if they just gave her a chance.

When all the time it hadn't been her fault. She'd done nothing wrong. It had taken her a while to come to terms with that one, and had taken someone else to explain it to her. Barbara. One of the others they'd put in here with her, eventually. And that was one of the few good things about where she'd found herself; Maddy had discovered she wasn't alone, wasn't the only one of her kind in the world. Not by a long chalk.

She remembered now the day they'd brought the first, opening the door and almost blinding her when the light flooded in from the corridor beyond. Maddy blinked several times, her three eyes adjusting – and when they did she saw the guards (those men in military uniforms, armed to the teeth) carry in a boy who was covered in feathers and had what looked to be a beak. Unconscious, just like she had been to begin with, he was thrown unceremoniously into the far corner and landed on his front. Peering over, Maddy saw that he had ragged scars on his back, two running parallel, up and over his shoulder-blades; later she found out this was where he'd had wings and they'd been sawn off. Two of the men proceeded to shackle him as well, while another placed bowls down in front of the boy – one filled with water, the other with those dried pullets she'd eaten plenty of in the time she'd been shut away here.

When he finally came round again, he told her that he was E1k – which she refused to call him, naming him instead Eric – and that he'd been in a similar facility to hers. They hadn't even bothered to tell him the stories about the children before conducting their tests, though. Hadn't even given him a reason. Then one day they put something in his food and he ended up in there, with her.

"I-I have no idea what's going on," Eric confessed, tears flowing from his shiny-black eyes. "Are we going to die, Maddy?"

She didn't answer him. Couldn't, because she knew as much as he did. All they could do was wait, but at least now they could do that together. They weren't alone.

Maddy hadn't seen Eric in so long (felt like a long time anyway), and thought that perhaps he'd been on to something back then. That maybe he was indeed dead now. That they'd taken him away again and he hadn't survived whatever they'd put him through – more testing, just like they did with all of them. More samples, only they were less kind about it here than they had been back at her home. Back at the other prison, which hadn't looked like a prison but still was. Eric was probably used to that, hadn't been treated as well as her to begin with; no coaxing, just taking, like they did with his wings. Although these people might even have taken his life, which was worse. Maddy had no idea, no way of finding out.

Not even Julie knew, but then why would she? Julie was only the orderly when all was said and done, the dogsbody; the person in scrubs who came to take them away, to take them for the procedures. Wasn't her fault, and Maddy could tell that she hated what she was doing by the way she bit her lip all the time, hesitated before wheeling them into those rooms down the end of the corridor. Always asked if they were okay when she brought them back out again. She'd even patted Maddy on the claw once when she was bringing her back to the cell.

"It'll be okay, sweetheart," she'd told her, but then went back to biting her lip again. "In the end, it'll all be okay."

She looked a bit like the women in those magazines would look if they didn't paint their faces so much. Naturally pretty with her copper hair cut short and those blue eyes. Those *two* blue eyes...

Naturally pretty. Normal.

Every now and again she'd bring them their food and drink, but instead of water it would be lemonade and instead of those blasted pellets, she'd bring them what she could smuggle out from the canteen. Julie would put her finger to her lips and wink. If they found out, Maddy knew, she'd lose her job – a job she must so desperately need to be doing all this in the first place. Lose her job or... worse. Because those were some seriously nasty people who ran this place, no doubt about it.

Seriously nasty people who strapped them into all kinds of devices, forced them to endure pain like Maddy had never even imagined before. But in the end it would be all right, Julie had told her that.

She wasn't a very good liar, Julie.

But it wasn't until Barbara arrived that Maddy found out why they were doing what they were doing. None of the others had seen the outside world; not Ash, Tracy or Kevin. They'd all been 'transferred', just like her. Had only known life in one of those facilities. Barbara had actually seen it out there, knew what was going on – had seen snatches of it for herself.

Oh, she'd started out like them for sure. Had been

in a facility just like Maddy's, but for a good while longer, because she was much older than Maddy. In fact her skin was grey and wrinkly, though whether that was due to the fact that she had some rhino in her – as she often joked – Maddy wasn't sure. Wasn't even sure what a rhino *was*, to be honest.

"Been around the block a few times, that's for damned certain," she told them when she arrived – and had been chained up like the rest. They hadn't bothered drugging Barbara; probably thought she wouldn't be that much of a threat, as big and slow as she was. "And what's this?" Barbara had asked, picking up the bowl of pellets they gave her and chewing one before spitting it out again. "Tastes like crap!"

"It's all you'll be getting from now on," one of the guards told her. "So quit your whining."

"I'll whine all I want, thank you very much," Barbara told him, nodding as if to say 'and that's that', her chins wobbling with the effort. That had earned her a clout from the butt of a rifle; it connected with the side of her head and made a wet, thudding noise. "Ow!" she'd cried, but the guards had all just laughed.

When they'd locked the door again, footsteps echoing off down the hallway, leaving them in the almost dark with that bulb above them – and Barbara had stopped touching the top of her head and wincing – she'd told them her name and said: "Well then guys and gals, whadya see and whadya know?"

No-one had answered. Nobody really knew what to say to her. They saw very little and knew even less. So Maddy told her as much.

"I understand," said Barbara. "Okay then, let me

tell you what I seen. What I know about what's going on." She got herself into a comfortable position and that's when she'd said it for the first time: "This is a time of monsters, boys and girls."

"What's... what's a monster?" Ash had asked, his left tentacle snaking up and rubbing the back of his head.

Barbara had laughed then, even harder than the guards. "Aww, bless. Why, *you* are son." Then she'd looked around at them all in turn, stopping when she got to Maddy and winking at her just like Julie did. "But don't worry, that's not a bad thing – especially in such esteemed company as this. 'Course, some might disagree with that notion." She thumbed back at the door. "Some think being a monster makes you dangerous. Maybe they have a point."

"They're afraid," offered Maddy, remembering what the people back home had said to her. "They don't understand what we are."

Barbara clicked her fingers together. "Bingo! Give that girl a cigar."

Maddy frowned; she had no idea what a cigar was either.

"I mean, some do. Some understand, like the folk who made us – they know. But your average Joe on the street... No idea. They think we want to eat them or somethin'." She looked down at the pellets in the bowl once more. "Come to think of it, might be more appetising than what they're feeding you in here! But anyway, that's exactly right..." She waited for Maddy to give her name, which she did. "I like that, has a ring to it. Madeline... Maddy the Monster! And the rest of you?" Maddy, still smiling at the comment about her name, told her their names too and

Barbara had nodded in turn, as if trying to remember them for future reference. "Now, where was I?" she asked once Maddy had finished with the introductions.

"Afraid," Maddy reminded her.

Barbara clicked her fingers again. "That's exactly right. Human folk are afraid of us. Even the ones who do know where we came from, who made us. In fact they might be the most afraid of all! That's why we've been controlled, hidden away – and once we've outlived our purpose, what we were made *for*, we've been quietly disposed of again and again."

"But why? Why are they so scared?" asked Maddy.

"The simple answer is, we're different to them," Barbara told her seriously.

"They made us that way, though," Tracy argued, shaking her head in frustration – the dim light bouncing off her dark, shell-like skin.

"For a specific reason, sweetheart," Barbara told them. "Boy, you really don't know anything, do ya?"

"They made us to help cure the children," Maddy explained.

"Yeah, right, okay. I suppose so," Barbara replied. "I guess some children might have been helped along the way. Adults as well. But just as many have been hurt because they've used what they got from us in ways they shouldn't have done. To spread diseases, viruses – to wipe out enemies."

"They hurt, they *kill* their own kind as well?" Kevin seemed to be having trouble getting his head – which was atop an elongated neck – around this one.

"Oh yeah," Barbara said. "They fight amongst themselves all the time. Person against person, country against country. And don't even get me started on race and religion." She paused, looking at their puzzled expressions. "You guys don't know what those are either, I'm assuming. Sheltered childhood – literally. Okay, they're people with different-coloured skin, people who believe different things."

"They hurt their own kind for being different as well?" Maddy said.

"Yeah, sometimes they do."

"So what is… what is normal, then?"

"Look, it's complicated, Maddy. But they've been fighting less amongst themselves lately, let me tell you."

"Why?" she asked.

Barbara regarded her gravely. "Because sweetie, they have a common foe. Us! There's a war going on out there, kids – has been for some time."

"A war?" This was Kevin again.

"Yeah, you know – or maybe you don't. A really big fight. Started off small, but it's been getting bigger all the while. And it's all because of one man… monster, sorry. The person who's been setting us free, who I owe *my* freedom to actually; well, to his followers at any rate."

"Who?" asked Tracy, shifting position so that the bulb reflected even more off her dark, shiny exterior.

Barbara smiled now. "Michael, that's who!" Then she looked over at Maddy. "Michael the Monster."

Maddy didn't know why, but when she heard that name suddenly she felt hopeful, in spite of her surroundings.

"He's the one who first said it, who began spreading the word: that this is *our* time. That we would no longer be slaves. Oh, that means we do what the humans tell us to do – that we don't get a say."

"That we get to live in… steamed company," said Ash, with a grin.

Barbara laughed again. "Something like that, honey. That's the aim anyway, to get to live with each other – in freedom. That's what the resistance is all about.

"And what happens to the humans?" asked Kevin, neck arcing and drawing closer to Barbara.

"Depends on how hard *they* resist," she replied with a smirk, then shrugged. "Listen, I haven't seen much of the actual action. Bit too long in the tooth for that, see?" And as if to illustrate, she pulled up a corner of her top lip and showed them one of her tusks. "But I do know when they stormed the place where I was being kept – the only place I'd called home for so many years, that I'd given my all to, because, well, because like you those people had lied to me about what it was all for… When Michael's followers freed me, a handful of his people at most, there were not many like those bozos outside with the guns left standing by the end of it all."

"They were killed?" asked Tracy, slightly shocked.

Barbara shook her head. "I don't know. I do know that his people don't do that if they can help it. He says that's what sets them apart from the humans."

"You know him, then?" asked Maddy. She was intrigued now, wanted more details.

"I-I've heard stories about him," Barbara admitted. "When I was freed, they took me to a safe house. A place out in the country, a farmhouse where a few of our kind were living. You know, fields and such."

Fields, sky, the sun, thought Maddy.

"Somewhere the humans didn't know about, or so

we thought." She looked around her, at where she'd ended up. "Obviously they knew more than we realised. One dawn raid later, and here I am. Now those sorry sons of bitches *do* kill. I can testify to that." Barbara sniffed back a tear, looking away.

Maddy wanted more than anything in the world just to get up and give her a hug. Some of those people – monsters – had been Barbara's friends, that was obvious as well. "It's okay, it'll all be okay," she told her instead, mimicking Julie and having about as much faith in what she was saying.

Barbara dried her eyes with the back of her arm, turned towards Maddy again and attempted a smile. "Hey, I'm all right sweetie. Don't you worry about me. Stories, right? You wanted to know about Michael?"

Maddy nodded enthusiastically.

"Where to begin? From what I understand, he had a very similar start in life to the rest of us. Well, all of us as a matter of fact; monsters like we are don't exist in nature. Not really. I mean, there are certain animals folk call monsters – we're made up of some of them – but we're a different kettle of fish. Some of us are a whole load of kettles of fishes," said Barbara and chuckled again, her humour returning. "We were manufactured."

"Man-you-fac..." Ash began repeating and then just tailed off.

"Manufactured," Barbara said to try and help him. "You know, mass produced? No, that's not strictly true. They made a bunch of us, but no two are alike as far as I can work out. We're mish-mashes, but that's what makes us who we are."

"We're not normal," Maddy said, more to herself

than anyone.

"We're *better* than normal, sugar. We're the new normal! Or we will be by the time all of this is over. But where was I? Losing my train of thought again… Oh yeah, Michael. He started out like all of us: captive. Grew up in a facility like the ones I daresay you all came from? And I certainly did. But he asked too many questions."

Got too curious, thought Maddy – just like she had. "Was he moved to somewhere like this?"

Barbara shook her head. "No, no. These kinds of places didn't really exist back then. At least I don't think they did. They're something new. But I'll get to that in a second." She reached down and grabbed some of the pellets out of the bowl, palming a few into her mouth without thinking about it. Then she spat them out again with a "*Pahh!* Forgot myself for a moment. What I wouldn't give for some salted peanuts right about now."

And chocolate, jelly and ice cream, or popcorn, thought Maddy. This was like watching a film for her, the pictures forming in her mind as Barbara spoke, told her tale – or rather Michael's tale.

"Anyroad up, Michael didn't know any better, see? Like we didn't. Like you probably still don't, which is why I'm here to educate you." Barbara smiled. "Didn't know much about the outside world until he was given a taste of it. One of the humans where he was held, a doctor, persuaded the folk in charge to let him out. Just for a little while, but it was enough."

"He was *let out*?" Tracy gasped. "But wasn't he seen?"

"Ah, now that's the clever bit. He was taken out at a time of year when all the humans used to dress up as monsters anyway, so he could blend in. Not be noticed. Hiding in plain sight."

"The humans dress up as us?" Kevin asked.

"Well, not really as *us*. They dressed as made-up monsters."

"I thought we were made up... Manfatcured." Ash this time.

Barbara couldn't help laughing once again. "Not the same, kid. These were monsters from books, from films and such." Ash and Kevin were still frowning; they obviously hadn't had movie nights where they'd been kept. "Not real. Not like us. But yeah, the humans used to dress up like them, once a year for one day – one night actually. It was like a holiday, an... an excuse to party, play games, have a good time. Honestly, I think they're just jealous of us deep down. They want to be able to breathe underwater or turn into smoke, or fly. Just don't want to look like this." Barbara waved her hand up and down herself to show what she meant. "I hear that some have even been injected with our DNA to see if it will give them powers, but that was never going to work out. They just can't take it. At the end of the day, humans are fundamentally weak – that's why we're gonna win."

"Fun... and mental," Ash was muttering to himself.

"Yeah, exactly," Barbara replied. "But back to Michael... He was exposed to too much, and he wouldn't let it go. Instead of making him more compliant... Ash, that means he'd be less likely to kick up a fuss. Kick up a stink... Er, argue with them," said Barbara finally and the realisation dawned on Ash's face. 'Well, instead of that it did the opposite. And those people who were keeping him locked up decided to just get rid of him. Y'know..." The large monster pointed with her finger, the others curled around and her thumb was up in the air – then she brought the thumb down and made a '*bang!*' noise. "Michael caught wind of it, though, and escaped. I'm not sure if the doctor helped him or not, or maybe he just broke out. But anyway, he made it out into the great blue yonder."

It had been tried before and the results had been... unfortunate.

The pictures in Maddy's mind now were of those fields from the magazines, the blue sky with clouds, the sun shining down. That's what Michael must have felt for the first time when he escaped.

"Where did he go?" said Ash, asking the obvious question – another one of his tentacles flicking out.

"An old lady took him in," replied Barbara. "She was blind—"

"So she didn't know what he was," said Tracy.

"Oh, she knew all right – just didn't care. I think maybe she was lonely, same as Michael. And she was kind, like the doctor. He lived with her for a long time until..." Barbara's eyes brushed the floor. "Michael hadn't been idle though, while he'd lived there. He'd been preparing, researching. Looking for more of our kind, so that when the time came it wouldn't take long to free the first of us. Free us and start building his army. No more playing around, no more games."

Maddy pictured them now, breaking into somewhere like home. Incapacitating the people she thought she could trust, but who had shipped her off to end her days in this dark, dank place.

"Freed us and taught us, passing on information – making sure there were safe places for us to go, like the one I was in. That's where I learned more about the world, kids. And more about our leader. The person who started all this and is going to make a difference to it all."

"Michael the Monster," said Maddy, trying to imagine him now. She'd always really liked Eric, thought that maybe she even loved him at one point – though to think about that now he was gone and probably dead just made her sad. Perhaps it had only been because he was the first to keep her company? In any event, what she was feeling now was much more than what she'd ever felt for Eric. Love for a person, one of her kind who she'd never even met, but also something else. Admiration? Respect? Yes, all of that, but—

"Right," said Barbara. "I know exactly what you're thinking, as well. You want to follow him too, don't you? He sort of inspires that in all of us. Once he finds out what happened at that farm, he'll come for me. He'll come for all of us, I really do believe that."

"Things are going to be okay," said Maddy and for the first time she actually did believe those words.

"You betchya!" said Barbara.

"There's one thing I don't understand though," said Ash.

More than one thought Maddy, if she knew him at all.

"What's that, son?"

"Why we were brought here? Why keep us alive? Keep us locked away?" It was actually a pretty good question.

"Don't you see? That just proves how, after all this time, after all the fighting, the liberating, it proves that the tide is turning. They're getting desperate out there," said Barbara, beaming. "They need some of us left, to try and develop—" She remembered who she was talking to. "Try and come up with ways of fighting back! They're trying to make new weapons to use against us, but there's one thing they haven't quite figured out yet."

"What's that?" asked Maddy.

"Why, my dear, we *are* the weapons." She settled back then, the information passed on, just as Michael and his followers passed it on to her. Maddy could remember, see her now, leaning back. Recall her clearly in the days, the weeks that passed after that. Barbara never gave up hope, never gave up faith that he would come – wanted them to keep that faith too, even after she'd gone. Spoke like she knew she was dying (something that had happened back at the farm, maybe – a wound which hadn't been discovered because it was internal or something? Or had it just been her time? Whatever the case the experiments they'd conducted on her hadn't helped). She'd made them repeat it with her final breath, those words:

"S-S… say it kids. Come on, it's a time… a time…"

"It is a time of monsters," Maddy finished for her, as Barbara's head drooped to touch her chest and all of them began crying.

That had been so long ago, or perhaps only last week. They had no way of knowing. No way of knowing whether or not what Barbara had said was true, either. Whether there actually was a war going on out in the world, and if there was had she got it wrong about the way it was going? Were the humans actually winning – and if so, had they themselves contributed to that? Had the weapons created from them helped to turn that tide Barbara had spoken about back in the humans' favour? Had the story of Michael Barbara had been told, and passed on, even been real? It might have been a legend, a myth told to put their minds at rest – to give them a leader or a figurehead to look up to. Something to give them hope? After all, Barbara had never even met him, had she? Just the monsters who freed her, just the others where she'd lived who had obviously been killed in the attack. The humans had done that, found them and wiped all but her out.

There was no way of knowing, nothing to do but sit there in the dark and wait, and wait…

Until that one day, the day that wasn't the same as all the rest. Which didn't contain testing or them being fed – in fact the pellets and water didn't come at all that day, hadn't been brought in a good while. It left them hungry and wondering whether or not they'd been forgotten about. Or were they just not useful anymore and this was the humans' way of getting rid of them? Why kill them outright when they could simply leave them to starve? No. Julie wouldn't let that happen to them, surely. If she was still around. If she'd had a choice.

No sooner had she thought this than the door to their cell opened and the woman practically fell through, slamming it closed behind her.

"*Julie!*" shouted Maddy.

The woman looked back at her, then at the others sitting there in that dim light. It was difficult to see clearly, but there was fear in her eyes. Yes, definitely! Julie was afraid.

"Help… help me," she said, moving away from the door.

Maddy could hear them now, the loud bangs outside – in the hallway Julie had taken her down so many times. Like the sound Barbara had made when she pointed her finger and lowered her thumb. *"Bang!"*

Lots of bangs actually.

Julie repeated her plea: "Y-You have to help me. I didn't... There was nothing I could do to—"

Then banging of a different kind, something up against the door – hitting it, hard. Once more, followed by a third time.

And the door was smashed open, swung wide on its hinges so that it crashed up against the stone wall.

A body followed – one of the guards, flying through the air (no need to be jealous now) to land against the wall on the far side of the cell. Maddy heard bones cracking, and the man slid down the stone to land, unmoving, on the floor.

"Please!" screamed Julie.

Maddy could see more bodies littering the corridor, feet sticking out at odd angles, smoke obscuring the rest. Suddenly they were there, moving through the smoke.

Monsters. More monsters. More than she'd ever seen in her life.

"Steamed company!" shouted Ash.

A figure pushed through, obviously the one responsible for throwing the guard against the wall – who was now moaning, injured but not dead. This creature looked like his skin was made from the same stuff as the walls in there, hard and solid, his eyes little more than two craters in a craggy face. Flanking him was a woman who was the exact opposite, looked for all the world like she was made of that jelly Maddy had once eaten with ice cream; and see-through, so that all her internal organs were visible. Still more followed, making their way inside to free Ash, Tracy and Kevin... One of the monsters had what appeared to be a saw for a hand and was making light work of the chains that fastened them to the wall; another opened its mouth and spat some kind of burning solution onto the metal, which began melting it. The final one, who was as shiny as Tracy – but clear, as if he was made from some sort of glass – grabbed another chain and instantly it turned into the same substance. It took only a blow from the stone-monster to shatter it and release the prisoner.

Julie had her hands clasped now, kneeling and begging Maddy. "F-For the love of God, please help me!" she said, tears flowing down her cheeks. *God, religion. One of the things humans fought over*, thought Maddy. "Don't let them kill me!"

"They won't," said a voice she recognised. "Not if you don't give them reason."

Depends on how hard you resist.

Maddy looked up and saw Eric in the doorway; feathered yes, but also with a beautiful set of wings on his back. He flapped them once, twice and grinned at her.

"How—?"

"They didn't know I could do that. Grow them back again. *I* didn't even know myself. It was how I escaped."

Escaped? So it was Eric who had come back for them, Eric who'd led these monsters down here – had led the strike on this facility.

"Sorry it took so long, but it was really hard to find again. Hiding in plain sight like it is. I-I was in a bit of a bad way when I eventually landed. Disorientated, you know. One of the guards winged me – literally. Plus the drugs they'd given me…"

And with that Maddy was free as well, the chains

which had tethered her to the wall for so long now gone. She got up, almost fell over, but rushed across to Eric and fell into his arms.

"Hey, hey, it's all right," he said, patting her on the back as he hugged her. "It's all going to be okay now." And it would be, it really would! Maddy would get to see that bright light, get to see her sky, her fields and her sun. Was no longer a prisoner.

Julie was still crying, and when Maddy turned to look she saw another monster – this one with a snout and on all fours, a real-life dogsbody – sniffing at her. The woman was shaking, terrified.

"Don't hurt her," Maddy said to the canine creature. "She's… she's a friend. She's kind." The dog-thing looked over its shoulder, but wasn't looking at Maddy. It was looking past her to the doorway, where yet another of their kin had appeared.

"They do exist, believe it or not," it said. "I've known one or two of them myself in my time. The woman will be looked after, don't worry."

Maddy took him in, his many eyes and legs, the gills he was using to breathe – and she knew without anyone even having to tell her. Felt foolish for ever having doubted his existence. This myth. This legend.

Eric continued: "I was a mess, but then they found me. Fixed me up, good as new. His people."

"Michael," she breathed, and the name felt good coming from her lips.

"That's right," said Eric. "But how did you…?"

"Someone was brought here, wasn't she? From the farm, the safe house that—" Michael paused, shook his head. "Is she still…?"

It was Maddy's turn to shake hers now. "But she told us about you. About the resistance, the war. All of it!"

Michael nodded. "And… I'm sorry, I didn't catch your name."

"It's Madeline. Maddy," she told him, letting go of Eric. "Maddy the Monster."

He laughed. "That's right. A monster and proud of it! Good to hear. Now, it's probably time we were getting out of here, before reinforcements arrive to—"

"Time!" Maddy blurted out. Michael had been moving, turning away – and she wanted him to keep looking at her. Had to do something to make him look.

"Pardon me?" asked Michael. He was nothing if not a polite monster.

"A time," Maddy repeated. "It's something Barbara… She was the one from the farm…" Michael nodded. "It's something she said to me, something she'd heard that you said."

"A time," said Michael, smiling.

"It is a time of monsters," Maddy said proudly, recalling what her teacher, her educator, had said. Then she frowned when Michael shook his head once more.

He touched the end of her nose. "Not a time of monsters. Not anymore, Maddy. This is something else," he said, beaming – because she was as well. "Something *more*.

"This isn't our time any longer." Michael told her finally. "Instead this is an era. An age!

"Yes, it is the Age… The *Age* of the Monster!"

The Queue

It never seemed to end.

The waiting. The line, the queue. This bloody queue! Donnie checked his watch again, tapped it, then held it up to his ear. The damned thing must be broken again; shouldn't be, the amount it had cost him. Top of the line.

What he was used to now, what he'd become used to of late. Living the high life, instead of mixing with the low lifes. His old buddies from back home, back in the old neighbourhood. He barely saw them these days, was used to a better class of person.

What was that saying? You could take someone out of somewhere, but couldn't take the place out of a person. No matter how much you pretended.

No matter how much he'd made, using the money from that one last job to set himself up 'legitimately', not letting anything stand in his way. Well, *something* needed to be done, didn't it. If not now, then when? "But you're good at this stuff, lad!" He could see Fred's face even now when he'd told him he was quitting; that angry scar running along his chin. "Getting into places, an eye for the best quality gear." And it was true, he'd broken into so many houses and stolen so many things it was unreal. It was breaking out of them he had an issue with if he ever got caught and put in jail. He didn't want to keep living that life, the prospect of getting locked up with no freedom. Trapped. Looking over his shoulder all the time.

Ironically, that's exactly what Donnie did right at that moment, looking back and seeing the people there milling around in the queue. Faced front again, saw just as many ahead of them. What the hell was going on here? Why weren't they moving?

"Patience, love," said the woman beside him, placing a hand on his arm. It was what his old mum used to say, "Patience is a virtue." So religious, he'd had to hide what he did from her initially or she'd have been all fire and brimstone, but then of course the stroke got her. He'd never really known his father; maybe if he had—

It was what this lady had said to him before everything came right, so many times. Patience. Just a little longer. "Then we can be together properly."

Like this? thought Donnie. Yet another hotel, as nice as it was – five star, nothing but the best – another place away from prying eyes. In secret. No, they didn't have to do that anymore. It was all above board now. They didn't have to creep about.

"It's never been one of my strong suits," Donnie replied to the woman he loved more than life itself. More than anything in this whole, wide world. And he took her in now: short black hair like Uma from that movie, or the girls from that band who sang about staying with them on the moon; huge eyes like something from a Japanese cartoon, outlined in black; full, red lips he never tired of kissing. And that body... Good Heavens, what a body! Made for sin, it was.

Donnie's eyes travelled down now and his gaze lingered on her breasts – not too big, not too small, like that other breaking and entering expert had once said about the Bear's stuff: just right! – then those hips and legs. She was wearing a patterned summer dress today, but he'd never forget the first time he saw her at that party.

Hosted by a business acquaintance, someone he'd just done a very different kind of job for: a guy called George Young. Donnie was in security these days (what better person to advise on that?), had reinvented himself as a successful businessman in his own right, and he'd attended the birthday bash at the posh country mansion George owned. The décor was a little like the hotel they were standing in (standing, note, rather than moving, certainly not moving *forwards*) right now actually, with its gold-plating and pillars and sweeping stairway just off to the left of them through a foyer area that was obsessed with maroon. A stairway reaching tantalisingly upwards, to the pleasures of paradise that awaited...

No 'plus one' for Donnie on that occasion in the past, as he always preferred going to those kind of things unfettered. He'd never shaken that habit of scoping things out, observing, and on this particular occasion he'd scoped *her* out. Standing at the bar waiting for a drink to be poured, wearing a silver dress she looked like she'd also been poured into. Legs up to her armpits, encased in black tights or stockings, he couldn't tell which; hoped for the latter. Complete with that hair, it made her look like some kind of flapper from the roaring twenties.

He'd never been one of those guys who believed in

love at first sight, Valentine's cards with roses and hearts on them – but if that little bastard Cupid had been flying around at the party, Donnie could well imagine he might have fired a couple of arrows into him right there and then: into his body, his heart, even as the band played in the background 'All of Me'. He'd found himself drifting towards her, ignoring so many beautiful women who were present – red-heads, blondes – women he would usually have made a play for, enjoyed a one-night stand with and then never seen again.

This woman was different. Here was someone he could picture himself being with forever, and they'd never even spoken a word to each other. If it was true that everyone has a soulmate, someone they're tied to forever, who they're meant to be with, then this woman was his: pure and simple. Maybe not so pure, given the thoughts that were racing through Donnie's mind right at that moment.

She hadn't even looked up yet from the drink that had been served to her at this open bar, hadn't laid eyes on him so he had no idea whether this feeling was mutual. Let out a sigh of relief when she finally did spot him, looked him up and down – seeing a guy who kept himself in shape, filling out his black-tie outfit, his sandy hair trimmed short – and smiled. Wow, that smile – Donnie realised he'd crawl over hot coals, broken glass, would endure whatever tortures had ever been invented just for a glimpse of that. To bathe in its warmth.

"Hello there," he said, leaning against the bar, trying to remain composed and not do that sit-com turn where the little guy fell through a very different kind of open bar.

"Hi," she said back, and her voice was lyrical; a hint

of an accent perhaps, one she'd lost a good while ago. Been trained out of? But where…? Didn't matter, it just added to the uniqueness of her tone.

"I'm Treadwell. Donnie Treadwell." Said it like he was fucking James Bond or something; was dressed like him at any rate. Treadwell by name, Treadwell by nature – that was the usual one. Should have been 'Tread Carefully' he thought sometimes.

"Grace," she said then and sipped her drink, some kind of orange cocktail. Donnie suddenly realised how dry he was himself, turning and sticking a finger in the air to attract the barman's attention.

"What's that you're drinking?" he asked her, nodding at the glass with the piece of fruit sticking out of the top.

"A Slow Comfortable Screw Against the Wall," she told him, with a grin now.

Donnie couldn't help grinning as well. "Of course it is. Subtle."

All of me… Why not take…

"I just like them," replied the woman with the jet-black hair.

I'll bet you do, thought Donnie.

He wished he could do that right here and now in this hotel lobby, just rip Grace's clothes off and have her against one of those pillars or something. Donnie glanced around, wondering if any of the other people in this line would even notice. The people in his way.

"For God's sake!" one of them was moaning, a balding guy up ahead. "This is intolerable! What's happening, why aren't we moving, getting checked in?" He looked kind of familiar that bloke, and Donnie felt a twinge then, like he – they – should still be hiding away. Too used to all the secrecy… Then remembered where he was, with the jet-set, how there was every possibility he might have seen that bloke on TV or something. An actor, presenter?

"I think there must be some kind of convention on or something," a woman behind them replied to the question – not that it had been directed at her or anything. Donnie turned and saw a lady who'd had way too many facelifts for her own good, skin stretched taut over her bony features.

"What? Like a medical convention?" someone else asked.

"Who knows," the woman said, shrugging. Donnie winced, expecting the skin to split when she did that.

He looked at his watch again, remembered that it was broken. Sighed and started tapping his foot, almost knocked his suitcase over, that was leaning beside him.

"Relax," Grace told him. "I'm sure it'll all get sorted soon enough."

"Yeah," Donnie replied, not believing a word of it. He just wanted to get up to their room, unpack and… He was ogling her again. Grace. *Graceful*. That's what he'd thought back then when she'd introduced herself. That's how she moved, standing sideways on as he took his own drink from the bartender: a Martini. He'd refrained from adding 'shaken not stirred'.

"So, you're here for the birthday?" he'd asked, then thought to himself, *how fucking stupid!* Of course she was there for the birthday party, same as him. It was fucking invitation only.

It had made Grace laugh, though, like she assumed

he'd said it on purpose. If he'd thought the smile was heaven-sent, then the laugh was even better. It made him laugh too, made him happy. And he found that he wanted to make her laugh even more, wanted to make her happy too.

All of me... Why not take...

"Friend or relative of George's?" His client, the one who'd hired him to do the security work.

"Relative," came the reply. "I'm Grace Young."

Donnie nodded. This must be his daughter, then. He'd spoken about her once or twice in passing. He could do much worse than get involved with George Young's offspring, as loaded as that guy was. It wasn't that Donnie didn't have cash now, but he was nowhere near that level – Young was minted! Made it all through gambling. Not betting, that was a mug's game. But *taking* the bets, owning the betting shops. *Chains* of shops.

When the music switched to 'Happy Birthday', however, and a giant cake was wheeled out, a smooth master of ceremonies asking Big Boss George to join him on stage and the man of the hour, of the day – white hair and beard, big-bellied – had begun to make a speech, Donnie realised just how wrong he was.

"I'd like my beloved, my beautiful wife Grace, to join me up here to celebrate. Come on, Grace, where are you?"

Grace's smile changed then, to a plastered on one rather than genuine. Her eyes were apologetic as she placed her drink on the bar and moved away from Donnie, off to join her husband. Husband, *Christ!* He was knocking on for eighty if he was a day. George Young? That was a frigging joke! There were so many candles on that cake it was a fire hazard; Donnie could feel the heat from there.

And as George had pulled Grace to him – George and Gracie, for fuck's sake! – drawing her in for a sloppy wet kiss, it had almost made Donnie physically sick. Watching him paw and slobber over her, it was more than he could take.

Of course she was his wife, why wouldn't she be? Men like that could buy and sell beautiful women, though he'd found out later it hadn't been like that at all. Grace had fallen for the fellow – hard. She'd been an impressionable twenty-something, working in one of his shops when he paid it a visit. He'd taken a shine to her, invited her out – which she promised she'd had to think about before caving; the age difference and everything – then flown her to Venice for their first date.

"The most romantic place on earth," she'd told Donnie the next time she'd seen him. Told him over a drink in a hotel bar many miles away from where she lived with George, who'd been away on one of his business trips. She'd got Donnie's details from the guest list, had called him up out of the blue on his mobile saying that she'd looked for him when she was done on stage. Donnie had left early, couldn't stomach any more of that evening; as it was, he'd had a sleepless night thinking about the pair of them getting up to all sorts because it was George's birthday. Grace had looked sad when he'd told her that, explained they didn't really have that kind of relationship anymore. Not like in the early days.

"We'd been all over each other back then," Grace said, apologising when she saw the pain on Donnie's face again. She'd felt it the same as Donnie, when they looked at each other. When they were talking. Only a handful of moments, but… Well, that flying cherub had been firing his arrows pretty much all over the fucking place that night, hadn't he. Into the two of them for sure. Wasn't purely a physical thing, although it turned into that pretty swiftly – they'd checked into one of the rooms at that hotel after the drinks. And it had been electric, like nothing either of them had ever experienced before. Not just Donnie supplying what George wasn't capable of nowadays; he'd have been devastated if that that was case, but might still have considered the proposition just to be near her.

No, this was definitely the L word, even if neither of them spoke it until they'd met up several more times. Could break into anywhere, and he'd broken into her heart. Stolen it, the most precious thing he'd *ever* taken. "The thing is," Grace had said to him, laying in his arms in bed, both of them covered in sweat, panting, enjoying the afterglow of their third romp in as many hours, "I do still love George… I think." She'd felt him stiffen at that, and not in the good way. "I mean, I did. Until… He's been very good to me, Donnie. And my family. We had nothing."

"Like a sort of kindly uncle figure, that sort of thing."

"Now you're just making fun of me," she said, her turn to go rigid, and he'd apologised. Said he couldn't help feeling jealous.

"Have you ever thought about…" he started then, but didn't finish.

"Leaving him?"

"Well, yeah. I mean, I have money. Not as much as Uncle George obviously, but…" Donnie shrugged, as much as he was able to laying back on the pillow.

"It's not about… George is a good man, it would hurt him."

"Yeah, but, he's a big boy. He can take it, I'm sure."

Grace didn't reply, changed the subject by reaching her hand down and feeling for him again, stroking until he was hard. It was a good job Donnie had a fast recovery rate, and soon they were back to it.

Doing what he'd hoped they'd be doing right now, instead of standing and waiting for this bloody queue to start moving. Fucking hell!

"Patience, baby," Grace told him once more, which really wasn't helping. It was what she'd said back then as well. Patience, even when they'd been seeing each other for seven or eight months off and on. Having to creep about, being careful. George was old, but he wasn't stupid. Certainly wasn't that.

Then there had been that one time during a stolen afternoon, when she really hadn't been into it at all. Had swung her legs out and sat on the edge of the bed when they were done. "You okay?" Donnie had asked, sitting up, thinking it might be him. That she was *going off* him.

"Yeah, I…"

"Because if it's… If you're… I can just go, you know. If you'd rather?" And she'd burst into tears at that point. Cried so much he thought she'd never stop. Asked him to hold her tight, never let go, and he'd felt her shivering when he sat next to her, placing an arm around her. "What's happened? If he's done something to you, I'll—"

He could feel her shaking her head, even as it was buried in his shoulder. "No, no. Nothing like that, Donnie. It's just…" It all came out then, promoted by the notion Donnie might take off for good. She'd told him that George had started demanding more of her attention, taking little blue pills so they could be together. "I think he might suspect I've been, well, y'know."

"And you're agreeing to all this?" Donnie snapped. It was one thing having patience when he thought he was the only one sleeping with Grace, but this was something else. A picture of her on top of the old guy flashed into his head, or Big Boss George on top – good God, he'd crush her with that belly! Nothing like the rock-hard abs Donnie boasted, having hit the gym once he'd started seeing Grace.

She pulled her head away long enough to answer. "He's my *husband*, what choice do I have."

He let go of her and stood up, took a few steps away from the bed. From Grace. She was up seconds later, joining him, arms around his waist. "Please, baby. I'm in such a difficult position here." And he had to bite his tongue before he said something like: "What, cowgirl? Missionary? Doggy-style?" Nothing they hadn't done together themselves, and more; in fact during their time as a couple they'd done things that would make the authors of the Karma Sutra blush. Instead, he just slumped. Almost began crying himself.

"Please…"

"Please what?" he asked. "How do you *want* me to feel about this, Grace? Do you want me to beg? Do you want me to get down on my hands and knees and plead with you to leave him now? Is that it?"

He heard her behind him, sighing. "I can't do that, even if you did beg me. My family, I told you—"

"I'll look after your bloody family, Grace!" Donnie turned to face her.

"You don't understand. He'd not only cut them off, he'd ruin them. Ruin *us*."

Donnie opened and closed his mouth. "How do you mean? I thought you said he was a good man?"

"He is." Grace breathed out the words, they were almost a whisper. "But he's still a *man*, he gets jealous same as you do. Over this he'd be vindictive with it. I'd lose everything, I know that and it's okay – I'd do that for you. But my family, you Donnie. I can't do that to all of you."

Donnie had to admit that made him hesitate. He didn't want to be *ruined*, whatever form that took. Not just no money, but not able to make any more. Have to go back to… Shit, George might even go digging around in his past, could put him in that jail he so hated the thought of. "I—"

"Listen, he's not in great shape. His heart. If you give it long enough, I think…" Grace bit her lip. "You just have to be patient, my love. Give it some more time."

Patient, when she was asking them to cool things to put George off the scent. When George was pounding away inside the woman he loved – yes, loved damn it! – like there was no tomorrow.

But he had been, *tried* to be patient. Virtuous, sort of. Waited and waited… And George had hung in there, was still sleeping with *his* Grace, who – whenever he got to see her – was more and more miserable all the time. Just wanted to be with him.

"I wish…" she'd start saying sometimes, then turn away so he couldn't see the tears in her eyes. Donnie knew what she wished, though, what she wanted: a way out. But George was tying her hands. That thought made his lip curl too, wondering if the man was into the kinky stuff as well? He never asked her about all that, it just hurt too much.

There was patient, and there was patient.

Idle hands and all that.

"Come on! Why are we all still standing here!" A guy

dressed in cargos and a green jumper ahead of them was shouting; demanding. "I'm running out of patience!"

Something needed to be…

"You're quite right, this is intolerable!" A woman's voice, upper-class. Sounded like she should be a politician or something. "Something needs to be done!"

Something had needed to be done about George.

It wasn't as if Grace had asked him outright, wasn't fucking *The Postman Always Rings Twice* or whatever, and she wasn't some femme fatale. In the end Donnie's own patience had worn out, and he'd decided to get rid of the thing standing in his way again. If not now, then when? George could plod along with that dodgy ticker for years. After all, he could afford the best healthcare money could buy.

Had been able to afford the best security, as well. Donnie's security, which he knew inside out. Which he'd been able to bypass that one night and gain access to the man when he knew Grace was visiting her family. Knew all the codes for the cameras and alarms to dupe the system, knew the shift changes of the guards. Hadn't been difficult, not for someone like him – someone who could break into anywhere even if he hadn't had the advantage. Hadn't been difficult to bring on the attack either, if you knew what you were doing; had researched it all to make it look on the level.

Donnie would never forget the expression on Big Boss Uncle George's face when he woke up and saw him there by the bed, dressed head to toe in black, like a shadow. He'd been terrified, too scared to even move. And Donnie had almost stopped at that point, turned around and let him live. The fear on that face! But then he'd remembered where he was, the bed that man was in – the things George had done with *his* Grace in that bed! It had sealed the guy's fate, those thoughts, those images. Donnie wanted never to have to think about that ever again.

He'd stolen something else that night, maybe something even more precious than Grace's heart (the best quality gear! *Why not take…*). A life. Something that could never, ever be returned to the owner. Donnie had felt bad about it, of course he had. He was no killer – not like some of the fellas he'd known back in the day, some of them had even enjoyed it. Fred for one, with that scar on his chin.

In the end, though, it would mean Grace was safe – her family was safe – and they could finally be together.

Or so he'd thought.

Patience, more patience…

He was thrown out of his memories because it looked like the queue was moving. "Oh, here we go," said Grace, tapping him on the arm.

"About bloody time!" Donnie said to her, thinking again about all the things he was going to do to her once they were in that room in this posh joint. Away from prying eyes. Away from people and their judgements. Their…

"Accusations?" he'd said to her, once the funeral was done and dusted. Once the authorities had decided it was 'natural causes'. And it had been, sort of. Nature given a helping hand, if you like. Grace hadn't asked him outright, but she'd known from the look in his eye what he'd done. Knew him so, so well. But never said anything directly to Donnie. Only about how it would all appear to the outside world.

"Yeah, we have to give it time, baby. Just so people don't jump to the wrong conclusion." The right one, as it happened. "So they don't get suspicious."

"Why would they?"

Grace shook her head. "We've been seeing each other for a long time, in private. In secret."

"I know. And now we don't have to, do we? We don't have to hide. George is out of the picture. You're secure, your family's secure."

Grace's brow had furrowed. "Think about how it all *looks*, though."

"I don't give a shit how it looks!" he'd answered, thinking: nobody can prove a damned thing!

All of me… Why not take…

"You don't understand, I've already had that bitch of a daughter of his sniffing round. Never wanted a thing to do with him when he was alive, but now there's money involved…"

"Probably just wants to buy more drugs," Donnie replied, for in the time since the party he'd discovered daughter Rose had been in and out of so many rehab clinics she might as well live in one. That had been the major bone of contention between Big Boss George and her; as a consequence he'd left the girl practically nothing. "Can't you just bung her some cash?"

Grace shook her head. "Not that simple, she's got a real problem with George's estate going to someone who's not blood. Thinks it's rightfully hers and is prepared to fight me for it; she's hired a top lawyer and everything. Working pro-bono in expectation of a fat payout."

"Jesus." Donnie rubbed his face.

"So you see my problem, if she goes digging around into this… We have to cool things off again, at least for now sweetheart."

Grace had been right, of course. Rose might cause them a huge headache. People could speculate about what had happened till the cows came home, but that woman had an axe to grind – revenge against Daddy Dearest if nothing else – and if they weren't careful she'd use it to chop them both to pieces...

Which was what he wanted to do to this bloody queue! How long had they been waiting here now? *Too long* was the answer. Donnie craned his neck again, front and back, scoping it out, observing. But he couldn't even spot the desk, couldn't see how quickly they were dealing with folk – if at all! Then again, he couldn't see to the back either, how many irate people were behind them. Not that it really mattered how many were left after they'd got their key. That woman had been right, this was intolerable. The waiting, no movement at all...

No movement while Rose started legal proceedings, not being able to see Grace for weeks on end which, frankly, was killing Donnie. It was worse than when George had been alive! No, not quite. He didn't have to worry about that fat old git banging Grace in the meantime, just had to sit tight, see how all this stuff panned out. Sit tight, wait, and wait, and—

Then suddenly it was over. Word reached them that Rose had OD'd in her bathtub, Whitney-style. An accident, definitely. Probably. But Donnie had to wonder about the timing of it all, just as George's daughter was getting closer to the truth about him and Grace. Digging up just a little too much dirt for comfort. And with her newfound wealth, maybe Grace had decided to do something about it. Hired someone like good old Fred to do something about it.

Something had needed to be done.

"Something… We need to do *something*, complain to the manager or whatever? A member of staff. Has anyone seen a member of staff around, you know those guys with the maroon waistcoats?" This was coming from yet another 'satisfied' customer, a chap with a pencil moustache wearing a white jacket.

Someone was getting even more agitated behind them, towards the back of the queue – wherever that was. Babbling in some foreign tongue, shouting loudly. Donnie squinted, trying to see what the fuss was about. "Guy's going to have a stroke or something," he said to Grace, who nodded; just like his old mum had. Donnie could've sworn he glimpsed some kind of fur (the foreign guy with his beard, or was it his wife? But wearing a fur coat in this heat? Come on…), and something glinting in the distance. Something the man was holding.

"There's no point, it won't help," Grace answered.

"I'd like to know what *would* at this point in time. I thought we'd have a while in the room before dinner, didn't you?"

She nodded again. "I mean, I'd hoped. But it's okay, we're here for a while. In fact we have all the time in the world, baby, don't we?" Grace slipped her arm through his, gave him a kiss on the cheek. He turned for a proper kiss, but she'd already shied away, looking around her. "Not here," Grace whispered. Donnie could definitely understand it, the others in that queue gaping at them like fish in a bowl.

But *fuck!* If it didn't start moving soon, if they didn't get to that room soon—

What? The world wasn't going to end, was it? He sucked in a deep breath, let it out again. Grace was right, now they were together there was nothing stopping them. They had all the time in the…

"…world is watching. We just need to wait a little while longer." Her voice on the mobile cancelling their date for that weekend.

"But why? I don't understand. There's nothing stopping us, is there?" Not now both Rose and the legal action had died a death. He still hadn't asked her about that, whether it was something she'd arranged – but then did Donnie really want to know? She'd never asked him about George, when all was said and done.

"It's just… Just too soon after what's happened. We need to give it a decent amount of time, then nobody will care."

A long sigh from his end. "So when are we… When will I see you next?"

"There's quite a bit to sort out, but soon. Then we can talk about the future properly. I promise. You just need to hold on, just need to have a little more…"

"…patience, baby." Donnie was back in the present again, Grace cutting into his thoughts. "We got here eventually, didn't we? Like we talked about, together at last."

"Finally," Donnie answered. "Yeah." Somewhere romantic (he'd fucking show George!), somewhere warm like the Riviera. Where they could spend all day in bed if they wanted, or by the pool sipping cocktails.

A slow comfortable…

Why not take…

He pinched the bridge of his nose, squeezed his eyes shut. "I guess I'm just tired."

"Not *too* tired, I hope?" said Grace, and when he

opened his eyes he could see the concern in her eyes.

"No, I... It was just a long drive is all. Stuck in those jams at the airport."

"The scenery on the way was pretty, though," she pointed out.

Pretty when you're not the one doing the driving, he thought. *When you have the luxury of being able to look out through the window.* No one else to blame, however, he knew that. He was the one who'd suggested they hire a car rather than get driven to the hotel. Preferring to do it himself, handle things as usual. Idle hands... Had no patience with other people. No patience at all.

They'd got lost a couple of times as well, the phone signal rubbish on those arse-end of nowhere lanes. Those tight bends when you could barely see the—

Donnie looked around again, he could see the queue – in front and behind – but very little else. Probably because there *was* very little else, or what was present appeared blurred. Indistinct.

"Where... where did the foyer go?" he asked Grace.

"What are you talking about?" she asked him, removing her arm.

"The hotel, Grace. The one we're in, the one we drove to. I'm having trouble making out..." His attention was diverted though, because he was remembering now where he'd seen that bald guy before. The one he'd thought was a presenter or something, an actor on TV. Oh, he'd seen him on TV all right, in a news bulletin. "Grace!" he shouted, then lowered his voice. "Grace, d'you see that bloke over there? No, don't look!"

"Don't look? How am I supposed to—"

"I think... Yes, they were looking for him. The police.

I saw his face on the news that time, when…" Donnie was wracking his brains, trying to remember. When had that been? He was struggling to—

And that woman, she'd sounded like a politician because she was one. Or had been, before that scandal to do with the school that had caught fire because of corner-cutting she'd signed off on. "Donnie? Donnie, what's wrong with you?"

He was staring, eyes flitting from face to face, some of them so, so familiar. The facelift woman, an editor of some top magazine, an influencer who'd promoted the perfect body image which had led to all those suicides of young girls. And the bloke in the cargos and green jumper, hadn't he had something to do with a starting a war? Yeah, that's right, they'd sent troops in because of it. So many soldiers lost it was—

Serial killer! That's what that first guy had been. Had lured women back to his place and then—

Donnie looked back over his shoulder, again trying to make out the figure who was still shouting in that foreign tongue. The one with the beard, the furs. The shining metal.

Someone with an axe to grind.

Someone from the history books, someone brutal. Part of the convention they were having here? Fancy dress rather than medical. Cosplaying, didn't they call it?

Although the guy in the white coat with the moustache… He *was* a doctor, wasn't he? Or a scientist at any rate, responsible for that drug they'd rushed out to treat some disability or another – the one that had ended up killing more people than it cured. Vilified, he'd been. Hounded and driven to…

Driven.

Those tight corners, those country lanes. Sitting tight.

When he looked back round again, Donnie saw… Saw the man with the scar running along his chin. Someone from his past, who'd get rid of people for the right price.

"But you're good at this stuff, lad!"

Breaking in, yes. But not breaking out. Never wanted to end up in—

Donnie was whirling around, frantically trying to hold on to his surroundings. As the furniture, walls, his luggage, everything seemed to blur even more. "Donnie, you're scaring me. Donnie!"

He turned and grabbed Grace by the arms. "Do you remember how we got here?" he asked her seriously.

"Got here? The car, you mean?"

"Do you remember arriving, parking up?" He waved his hand in the air. "Coming in here? Joining this—"

This bloody queue. With no beginning that he could see, no end. No counter where people were being dealt with, given keys to the rooms.

"I demand to see the manager!" someone was shouting.

You *shouldn't*, thought Donnie. No, you really don't want to see the manager of this place, the Big Boss. Not like His underlings wearing maroon, but wearing the very reddest of reds. Suddenly, Donnie no longer wanted to be in a room – a cell – in this place. He was fine if he never reached it, whether he was with Grace or not.

Although the alternative was being here, not sitting, but *standing* tight. Waiting, not his strong suit, always wanting to get things done. To do them himself. Overcoming…

Overtaking. Trying to overtake on that bend, when he really couldn't see what was coming in the opposite direction until it was way too late. The lorry that would make mincemeat of their car. No one could've survived that, not him, not—

The end of the world? No, just *their* world.

A world watching...

He looked at Grace now. Was it even really her, or just someone who looked like her. Cosplaying, grinning. A shadow? Someone here to keep telling him to be:

"Patient, baby. You just have to wait and everything will come right in the end. It'll all work out." They'd be together, finally. Was this his Grace, though? It looked like her, talked like her. But *she* hadn't done anything wrong, not like him.

Can't prove a damned thing! Here, it didn't matter – they didn't need to. No more secrets, no more hiding. Just judgement of the worst possible kind.

Rose... there had always been that question mark hanging over Rose! The accident. The bathtub.

Tell me she didn't do it herself? thought Donnie.

Takes one to know one.

Maybe not so pure.

Made for sin.

...all of me, why not take...

Heaven-sent? Hardly.

Body, soul.

Their souls. Together forever.

Like there was no tomorrow.

Soulmates if you believed in such... All the time in the—

Remembering, starting to remember everything.

The pain, his body mangled up. Bits of metal like arrows entering (him, like Cupid's arrows striking) his heart.

It was killing Donnie...

Nothing around him now, no hotel, no luggage, no stairway leading tantalisingly upwards.

Living the high life... If only!

Good Heavens!

Heaven-sent? No.

A way out...

To the pleasures... pleasures of Paradise.

If not now, then...

Something needs to be done about—

There was nothing but the heat.

Bathe... cooking in its warmth.

Donnie felt like he was on fire, suddenly aware of just how hot it was in here. Hotter than...

Really needed to cool things off.

...Take someone out of somewhere, but couldn't take the place out of a person... No matter how much you pretended. Could take—

Why not take...

My heart, my soul...

What he'd become used to of late... The late Donnie Treadwell... carefully...

And the queue. The queue stretching back, stretching forward. Not waiting in a hotel, but the worst prison ever invented. Or maybe the torment was the queue itself? The hopelessness of it all.

Patience. Like his old religious mum used to say, 'Patience is a virtue.'

Fire and brimstone.

Would endure whatever tortures had ever been...

Expecting the skin to split when —

Donnie began to scream, everyone turning and looking in his direction. "Baby, baby what's wrong?" asked Grace. "Why are you… What's—"

Everything! he wanted to say. Everything's wrong! It's all wrong down here, a place of wrongs. Punishment for wrongdoing.

He closed his eyes, then opened them again. To find himself still in the queue, but the hotel lobby had returned. The luggage, the stairs. "What the…" he began, but already the memory of it not being real, not being there at all, was fading. Soon to be replaced by others, to go over and over in his mind what had happened, what he'd – they'd – done.

Donnie checked his watch again, tapped it, then held it up to his ear. The damned thing must be broken again (the damned…). Shouldn't be, the amount it had cost him. Now he had the money to pay for it, now they both did.

What the Hell was going on here? Why weren't they moving?

"Patience, love," said Grace, smiling sweetly. He really did love her so much. "Patience. We have all the time in the world." (*It's okay, we're here for a while.*) Donnie frowned. Why did that thought suddenly fill him with dread?

All of me… why not take….

All the time in the world. The waiting. The line, the queue. This bloody queue!

It never seemed to end.

Crumbs

The gnarled and twisted hand swept the last of the crumbs from the table, over the edge and into the grateful mouths waiting below.

She grinned, watching as the dogs caught them, fought over them – just as they'd done over the scraps of gristle that had been left after the cooking, the baking. As they'd done with the handful of bones she'd let them have afterwards: the rest buried outside, same as always. Observing those animals now, licking their lips, hoping for more, made her feel the same way. No matter how she tried to eke out the food, it simply never lasted long enough – this one little more than a couple of days – and she'd be left feeling hungry once more.

The thought of the succulent filling, the gravy it had produced, spilling out when she cut into the pie crust, it made her salivate almost as much as the dogs round this rickety, blood-stained table that admittedly had seen better days. But then what hadn't in the cabin?

All things in moderation, she told herself. *Never take too many and never too often,* that was her mantra. *Never be seen*, which wasn't hard out here.

Letting the dogs outside, her stomach rumbled – a reminder of the dish she'd polished off only a few hours ago, leaving the clean-up till now. Her shoulders slumped, sad. But, standing on the doorstep, she couldn't help sniffing the air – couldn't help smiling once more when she smelt what was already coming this way, revealing yellow-brown crooked teeth. She always knew whenever anyone was inside her forest (it wasn't officially hers), whether it was intentional or not; whether they'd wandered in by mistake and got lost or had come here on purpose (that didn't happen very often). The road a few miles away, on the outskirts of the dense foliage, was her usual hunting ground – tacks on the ground made a real mess of tyres – but it would seem that fate was bringing the next set of victims to her instead.

And they were young, no more than nine, ten years of age, so her senses told her. What they were doing in the heart of her forest was anyone's guess, but that didn't matter. It would be silly to ignore such an opportunity, moderation or not.

Besides, the meat of the young was so much more tender than that of adults. The power it gave to her so much greater.

Clapping her hands together, she did a little dance of joy. Oh, it was going to be so perfect! She'd get started with her preparations right away.

And, thinking this, she shut the doors – shutting out the dogs to go about their business.

So she could go about hers inside.

* * * * *

Harry Travis still wasn't sure this was a good idea.

It wasn't that he didn't agree with his older sister… only older by a year and a half, but a lot older upstairs in the brain department; 'An old head on young shoulders' was how their gran used to put it when she'd still been around, he'd been told. So when Gabby, Gabrielle, spoke, you listened, and this time she'd definitely had something worth listening to. She'd overheard their 'mother' talking to one of her dodgy friends on the phone, saying all kinds of things about them – the gist of it being that she wanted shot of them both, one way or another.

Bernice wasn't their real mum, of course. That woman – who Harry only vaguely recalled; a laugh here, a snatch of nursery rhyme sung to get him off to sleep there – had passed away when he was only very small. The big 'C' they said whenever it was mentioned, and for years he hadn't had a clue what that meant. Had she drowned? That's what it sounded like to him, although as he was the first to admit, he wasn't that clever. Definitely not as clever as Gabrielle.

"I'm frightened that witch is going to do something seriously bad to us," she'd whispered to Harry one night when they were in their bedroom – two single beds fairly close together, because everything was close together in their place, it was so small; a tiny flat in a huge tower block. Hadn't always been that way. Back when their mum had been on the scene, they'd had a much bigger place: a house, with an upstairs and everything. But then, well, Mum had gone, their dad had eventually lost his job and he'd met Bernice – which really hadn't helped matters in the slightest. The way she spent his money, especially on drink… So much for his promises when they were younger that one day they'd be rich! "She was saying how much better off they'd be without the ankle-biters around."

"What's an ankle-bi—"

"Us Harry, us."

"But Dad wouldn't let anything happen to us… would he?" Their father was a kind man, a good man. The problem was for some bizarre reason he was also totally devoted to Bernice, like she had him under some kind of spell. Hence the witch nickname. She'd had him wrapped around her little finger since they'd met, at a friend of a friend's wedding. Perhaps it had been the sense of occasion or something, or just the fact it had been a really good do – or that their dad was incredibly lonely, would cry himself to sleep most nights; they could hear him through the walls – but anyway, it hadn't been long before Bernice had a ring of her own on the third finger of her left hand. A registry office ceremony, because there was no cash for a lavish affair, but legally binding nonetheless. And you could tell that Bernice did actually care about the man, loved him in her own way. Loved him so much, she really didn't want to share him with anyone.

She'd been nice enough to the kids at first, mainly so it didn't tip their dad off as to just how nasty she could be – especially when she'd had a skinful. But very soon after the ring had gone on, she'd shown her true colours, particularly behind their dad's back.

They could do very little right, the chores they were given less about helping out around the home and more because Bernice was such a lazy cow. They'd even been threatened, had come in for a few drunken beatings, though Bernice made sure she left no marks on their faces. Bruises that could easily have happened when they were out playing, because their dad wouldn't believe a word of it even if they'd tried to tell him. So Harry shouldn't really have been surprised at the suggestion that she wanted them gone: reminders of a previous marriage Bernice could do without.

"Dad's not around a lot of the time, though, is he? Wouldn't be difficult for her to arrange an accident or something? Get us out of the picture. Push us down a flight of stairs or whatever. Or maybe even sell us off somewhere to make some money."

"*Sell us off!*"

Gabrielle had shushed him, Harry's voice rising at the very notion of being sold into slavery; that, to him, would be worse than the stairs. It sounded ludicrous, and yet Gabrielle said it with such resolve he found himself believing her. "You know the kind of people she hangs around with, her background," she'd told her brother. "I wouldn't put it past her."

Harry swallowed dryly. "So what do we do?"

"I don't know," she'd said then, because she didn't. "All I know is we can't stay here much longer. It just isn't safe."

The opportunity had presented itself not long after that, in the form of another one of their 'delightful' weekend trips out as a family. In reality a trip where their dad was going to do a bit of poaching, and would take them along as look-outs. They'd been with him many times before, always to a different spot, and sometimes – on special occasions – he'd even taught them a few of the tricks his father passed on to him about tracking, fishing; he'd set traps with bait small animals would find irresistible, shoot a bird or two, maybe even a deer if it was a good day.

All to put food on the table for them, to prevent the kids from going to bed hungry, yet still surviving on scraps, on crumbs. Naturally, they'd need less food if the children weren't around – especially with Harry's appetite!

Gabrielle had told Harry they needed to make their move before Bernice made hers. To pack a few things – items of clothing or whatnot – in a bag, so they could run away before the inevitable happened.

"But I... I don't want to run," he informed her, almost in tears. "Where would we go?"

"I'm not sure. I-I think Mum had some family on the coast, distant cousins. We can head in that direction? They might even be able to help with what's been happening, might believe us? But we can get by in the wild for a bit if we have to, we've watched Dad hunt enough times to get food, water. Set up camp. It'll be like an adventure, Harry – and you like adventures, don't you?"

He'd half-nodded, half-shaken his head. He liked *reading* about adventures in comics – usually in the newsagents, because they couldn't afford to buy them – or in books from the library. (Unlike most of their generation, they didn't live on their phones – the only person who could apparently afford one of those in their household was Bernice.) But Harry wasn't sure he liked the idea of being *in* an adventure, especially if it meant he had to live in a forest. "We won't be *living* there," Gabrielle had assured him. "It's only for a while till we can figure something else out. Harry, listen to me, it's really not safe at home anymore. And at least we'll be together," she promised.

"But Dad, he... Won't he wonder where we went? Won't he worry?"

Gabrielle looked like she wanted to cry then, but

fought it back. "It'll be okay. He has Bernice; it's all he seems to care about these days." And there was a fair amount of resentment in her voice when she said that, The kind of bitterness that could only come from a daughter abandoned by her father. Who'd been surviving on other kinds of crumbs – of affection, of whatever was left after Bernice was done with him. "It's you and me, Harry. Like always really, since Mum di… You and me."

Harry hadn't been at all sure, though: right up until the moment they ran off he hadn't been sure. He'd listened to Gabrielle and packed a few things, including some snack bars he'd recently taken from the canteen at school. However, when it came time to actually going – after their dad had brought them up here in his battered old banger – he'd not been at all certain.

Slinging his equally old rifle over his shoulder, their father had bent and said to them, "You two stay here for now, try not to cause your mother any grief. I won't be long."

Gabrielle had watched him go off with a snort, tucking one of her blonde curls behind an ear. "Cause *her* any grief? And she's *not* our mother!"

Bernice, for her part, couldn't have cared less. She was too busy getting blotto on wine and listening to the radio in the rusted old car, because she couldn't get a signal on her phone.

"Now's our chance, come on," Gabrielle told him. When Harry had hesitated, she'd grabbed his wrist and pulled him into the undergrowth, covering their tracks as she went. By the time Bernice even noticed – if she ever did – they'd be long gone.

But, as they were making their way through the

forest, Harry was less certain than ever. Back there, with Dad, he had a home – whatever it was like. Shouldn't they be fighting to keep it, fighting to force Bernice out if anything? He didn't want to be sold off anywhere, or for something to happen to him in an accident, but he didn't really want to be sleeping out here tonight, either. What he did know for positive was he was hungry, so he'd taken out a couple of those snack bars and offered one to Gabrielle – who'd refused it with a shake of her head.

"You should save those for later," she warned him, "just in case." But he ate his anyway. He'd never been one to wait, especially when it came to being hungry.

She'd been right though, because the further into the forest they went – the deeper into the green – the less signs there were of potential food. No rivers for fishing, no small animals around to catch. No suitable places to camp or shelter, like a cave or such; they hadn't even brought tents – didn't have any! And by the time the light began to dip, they were tired, cold and famished. "Maybe… maybe we should think about going back now Gabrielle," Harry suggested. "We can run away another day."

But when he saw her look over her shoulder, he knew – he was sure – there was no going back, in more ways than one. Gabrielle wouldn't be able to find her way even if she wanted to.

They were lost. Hopelessly and totally lost.

* * * * *

It had been slim pickings out there today.

When he returned, Mark Travis was pretty much

empty-handed. A couple of hares, that was about it – not really worth coming all the way out here, not worth the petrol. They'd eke it out, though, as usual; he'd take less, making sure the others got their share. Bernice, who was still where he'd left her in the car listening to her music – not much of a look-out, might be *attracting* attention apart from anything else, although this spot was pretty isolated…

And the kids. He'd tried to do right by them since their mother had passed, but was sad to say he'd left a lot of the day-to-day stuff to them after it had happened. No, face it, he'd fallen to pieces and left *everything* to them. The love of his life gone, his world turned upside down – he might as well have died too, that's how he felt. He'd barely been able to function, had lost his job at the factory when he was just about to get a foot on the ladder management-wise. Selfishly, he'd even thought about leaving the kids – possibly permanently, had picked up a razor-blade once or twice to do the deed. They'd be better off without him, he reasoned.

Then Bernice had come along, and she'd given him an incentive to keep on going. Might have been selfish again, but here was this other woman who was interested in him – and he'd only had that once before. Someone who was fun (folk might say a little *too much* fun) someone who made him feel good about himself. Someone who might even become a mother for his two kids, if he was lucky.

He wasn't blind, Mark realised that it was difficult: that the kids would always have that memory of their mum; and Bernice could never, ever take her place (it wasn't about that). But still, it was good to be a family again, no matter what their problems might be – a lot of them financial, it had to be said, stretched so thin there was hardly enough for food, in spite of all the wheeling and dealing he attempted. That was when he'd had the idea of starting up the poaching, just like his old dad had done way back when. It was at least a way for now to put some meat in their bellies.

It would take time, that's all. And one day, they'd find their way – earn their fortunes – he knew that as well.

One day, eventually, they'd be happy: he was sure of that if nothing else. They'd all be… Mark frowned, looking around. Where exactly were they *all*? Bernice was here, he'd already seen her, but the kids… Harry, Gabby (or as she always insisted since she'd hit ten, Gabrielle), where were they? He could usually hear if not see them, but on this occasion there was just the beat of Bernice's disco music filling the air.

"Bernice?" he asked as he approached his car, the bits of paintwork flaking off; he'd had the thing years, and almost got rid of it because it was so run-down (as it was it wasn't MOT'd, didn't have insurance). "Bernice!" he repeated, a bit louder, but she didn't appear to have heard him – was taking another drink from one of the bottles of wine she'd brought, the empties having been dropped on the ground next to the car. "Bernie…?" he tried again, before knocking on the half-open window.

She jumped, turned in his direction and squinted, like she was trying to focus. He opened the door and for a second Mark thought she was going to drop out, so he put a hand on her shoulder to steady her. "Bernie, you all right?"

Bernice nodded, a tangle of her dirty-blonde hair falling and dropping into her eyes.

Mark glanced around himself once more. "Bernie… Bernie, where are the kids? Where are Harry and Gabby?"

"What?" she said, slurring and frowning at the same time.

He reached in and switched off the radio, drawing a disdainful look from Bernice, then tossed the hares in the back seat. "Harry and Gabby. My… the kids. Where are they? I left them here."

Bernice shrugged. "No idea. They must have wandered off."

It wasn't inconceivable, they did like to go off and play their games; sometimes quite rough stuff, he'd spotted those bruises. Mark called out their names now, in every direction, not caring who heard. Then he checked the undergrowth; he was a tracker after all. No signs. No sign that they'd gone in any particular direction at all. How could that be, unless they'd covered them up? Gabby certainly had the rudimentary skills to do that. But why on earth would she?

Now Mark was starting to get worried.

"I-I'm sure they're fine," attempted Bernice – fine sounded like 'find', which was ironic because that's exactly what he wasn't able to do, find them.

Mark shook his head. "You were supposed to be keeping an eye on them!" And he couldn't help it: his voice rose, an edge creeping in.

"Keeping an… They're not fucking babies, Mark!" she snapped, getting to her feet. But they were, that was exactly what they were. Harry and Gabby were *his* babies, weren't they. Babies he'd already let down once. "They'll come back. They always do… sadly."

She'd mumbled the last part, and Mark whirled

round to ask: "What did you just say?"

Bernice looked at him blankly, as if she'd forgotten exactly what it was. "I… They'll be back, when they're hungry enough."

Mark wasn't so sure. "It's getting dark now, we need to look for them." It wasn't as if they could call the authorities, they'd want to know what he was doing here for one thing. "Come on."

He went to take her hand, but she pulled it away. "Shouldn't… One of us should probably stay here, in case they come back," Bernice told him with a nod. It wasn't a bad plan. But Mark had already lost two people he cared about; he wasn't about to take his eyes off the other.

"Bernie, please. Just come with me," he urged.

She sighed, but eventually relented, letting him take her arm and having another swig from the bottle of wine. "It *is* getting dark," she said, which he took to mean she was concerned for the children – but he also suspected she didn't want to stay here in the car when it was pitch black.

"Right, so the sooner we get started the better," Mark told her, pulling out his torch.

Then he led them both into the undergrowth in search of the kids.

* * * * *

She wasn't sure this was a good idea.

Hadn't been certain from the start, it was just all too… too perfect. Gabrielle was far from used to perfect; her default position was always suspicious. Always on guard and questioning – unlike her trusting brother, Harry.

Although he had trusted *her*, hadn't he, sort of. Enough to go with her, follow her out into these woods (like he'd had a choice!) when she didn't really have a clue where she was headed. The coast, eventually, but they had to get out of the forest first. In the end they'd just wandered around getting more and more lost, until she wasn't certain whether to go forwards or back anymore. Didn't know *how* to get back to the car, the bushes and leaves having apparently folded themselves around the pair of them, trapping them.

She'd started to feel empty around then – even emptier than usual – and had asked Harry for one of those snack bars he'd been noshing on earlier, only to find he'd scoffed the lot. "I'm sorry," he told her and she'd sighed. Should have expected it, whenever there was food in the offing he couldn't really help himself. Probably a consequence of never really having much.

Which was why when she began to smell it, she hadn't trusted her senses. Food, cooking. No, it couldn't be. But then Harry told her he could smell it too. Was off and following his nose before she could stop him. "Harry! Harry come back!"

She could just about see him through the trees, the light from the moon breaking through a bit more in this section of the woodland. Then, racing after him, Gabrielle almost fell over her brother – because he'd stopped, stock-still.

"What're you—" she began, then followed his gaze instead.

The brightness from that moon was practically illuminating the scene, like a spot-light trained on a stage. On a building, a cabin... actually more of a cottage than anything, out here in the middle of nowhere. It looked like the most welcoming place in the world and not just because they had nowhere else to go. No, it would have looked like that even if they'd had a mansion to go back to – even if they'd had both a dad and a mum (rather than a nightmarish step-mum) to return to.

It was a creamy-white stone cottage, with a thatched roof and chimney, which had smoke curling out of it that looked like it had been drawn in pencil. The door was made from varnished wood, and the windows – though too dark to see inside – were held in place by similar material. The whole thing looked like something from the front of a biscuit tin or a chocolate box selection, and in fact looked good enough to eat itself. *Not that you'd want to eat stone or wood or glass*, thought Gabrielle, blinking – but that smell! She'd looked sideways at Harry to see that his mouth was hanging open, taking all this in.

On the porch, which had a rocking chair on one side of it, lay two dogs – both labs, one black and another a golden colour. When they noticed the visitors, they got up, claws making a scratching sound as they scampered over the wooden slats and down the handful of steps to the ground. Gabrielle turned back in time to see this, reaching out and grabbing Harry's wrist again just as she'd done when she pulled him into the greenery in the first place. "Watch yourself," she warned, ever the worrier, always waiting for the other foot to fall.

But she needn't have worried. The dogs, wagging their tails and with their tongues sticking out of the sides of their mouths, bounded up to them and began racing round their legs. Then Harry's – the golden lab – jumped up him, almost knocking him over, and started licking his face. It must have tickled, because he was laughing so hard Gabrielle thought he was going to bust a gut. Hers was nuzzling her hand, insisting she stroke the top of its head.

Gabrielle reached out her fingers, then suddenly pulled them back. The dog whined, disappointed, and cocked its head.

"Lucy! Belle! Come back here at once!" The command was clear enough, but the voice was kindly and soft so the dogs completely ignored it. Gabrielle looked over at the porch again to see a figure standing there, in the now-open doorway, leaning on a stick. She was plump – that was possibly the best way to describe her – with rosy cheeks, white hair and glasses, and she was wearing a flowery dress and a shawl Gabrielle suspected she must have knitted herself all the way out here. The woman beamed at them, at the dogs playing around them, and at that moment she reminded Gabrielle of someone. Had a look of their gran about her, though she doubted Harry would be able to remember her. Then the woman continued, stepping forwards with a limp, relying heavily on that stick. "Our visitors don't want you slobbering all over them!"

She descended those steps, having a little difficulty with the final one – so much so, Gabrielle nearly rushed over to help her then stopped herself. Apart from the fact she didn't even know this woman, a lot of older people were fiercely independent (her gran certainly had been). They didn't want or need any help from other people, if they could avoid it.

And, yes, she made it down to ground-level just fine, then began walking across to the siblings, shaking her head. "Oh, look at them. They never listen. Might as well have cats, for all the notice they take of me!" she complained, as

Lucy – or was it Belle? – continued to lick Harry's face. The other one, the black dog, was still gazing up hopefully at Gabrielle. Not wishing to be rude, she finally patted it on the head and the animal gave a cheerful bark.

The woman drew up in front of them, panting for breath. Clearly just walking that short distance had taken it out of her. "Are you… are you all right?" asked Harry, in-between licks from the golden lab's tongue.

She laughed. "So thoughtful! I'm just fine, my dear. Just fine. Old is all, old and weary." Another laugh, followed by a smile which revealed such brilliantly white teeth. "But what about you two?" She turned to look at Gabrielle as well when she said this. "Are *you* all right? Where did you come from? What are you doing out here in the middle of this place, all alone at this time of night?"

"It's a good question," Harry told her.

"Oh, but where are my manners? I'm Cassy… Cassandra. Though people round these parts call me Grandmother Cass, or just 'Mother Cass. Well, that is to say, they used to. Don't get many people visiting around here these days. Which is what makes it so special now when they do." She winked and the boy chuckled.

"I'm Harold," he said. "Harold Travis."

The old woman seemed to think about this, then said, "My, that's a very grown-up name."

He laughed again. "Harry. I prefer Harry." Then, nodding over to his sister: "She likes Gabrielle rather than Gabby. Didn't used to."

"Well, each to their own, eh? Probably because your sister here's becoming a young woman. Girls grow up a lot faster than boys."

Harry scowled. "Do not."

138

"They do, you know." 'Mother Cass winked at Gabrielle now, but she didn't laugh. She was too busy thinking about what she'd just said.

"How did you know I was his sister?" she asked, point-blank.

This seemed to throw 'Mother Cass a little. "Well, you… I—"

"We could have just been friends."

"You look alike," responded the old woman. "Anyone can see the resemblance, young lady. Stands out a mile."

Gabrielle nodded, but she still wasn't convinced. "How did you—"

"Listen," said 'Mother Cass, "we can't stand out here all night nattering. You'll catch your death. There's a warm fire inside, and lots of food. I just whipped up a batch of chocolate cookies, they're fresh from the oven!"

"Cookies?" Harry repeated, the woman having said the magic word.

"That's right. And cakes too, muffins, gingerbread. Delicious with a glass of milk! Or even fizzy pop if you like, I have that as well, just in c—"

"You were cooking this late at night?" asked Gabrielle.

The old woman sighed and nodded. "I don't sleep much lately, not the way I used to do when I was younger. Gives me something to do. What can I say, I like to bake. Probably why I look like this!" She patted her stomach with her free hand, laughing again. Harry joined in once more. "You can tell me all about everything inside. Belle, Belle! You can put Harry down now, let the poor boy get a breath." So goldie was Belle then? "She likes you, I can tell," continued 'Mother Cass. "You can feed her too, if you want?"

Harry grinned; it was clear that he would definitely like that. They'd never had pets of their own – never been able to afford them – and the thought of spending more time with that friendly canine was just as appealing to her brother as the sweet stuff on offer. All so hard to refuse. This whole place so… *so* perfect. Harry looked at his sister and asked, "Can I?"

At least he'd done that much, but before she could even answer he was going with 'Mother Cass as she turned and limped back towards her house. Lucy stared at Gabrielle for a few moments more, then joined them heading off.

A few moments after that – once she'd finished looking around her, realising that she didn't want to be on her own out here, that she should probably go where her brother was going – and, even though she was sure it wasn't a good idea, Gabrielle followed them all inside too.

* * * * *

Those bloody brats!

Bernice puffed and panted, having finished the dregs of the wine some time ago, though she refused to let go of the bottle. The effects of it were wearing off now – the buzz from all those bottles beginning to wear off, as a matter of fact. And this was *so* not fun anymore, not that it ever had been.

If it hadn't been for those two ankle-biters – she liked that name for them, could demonise them then, imagine them gnawing on her – they wouldn't be out here in the first place. Not because they'd disappeared, but because they were a drain on the both of them. Parasites, nothing more.

She'd never wanted any of her own for exactly that reason, figured it wouldn't be fair on either them or her if she brought children into the world. Wasn't as if she was exactly mother material anyway; her friends and relatives had them and she steered clear wherever possible. Of course, accidents happen, especially with the amount of men Bernice had been with in her time, but it was easy enough to fix. She thought no more about getting rid of an unborn child than she did one that was running around in the world. Running around in the world interfering with her business, at any rate. With her life.

Her life with Mark.

Oh, she loved him. Had loved him from the moment she first clapped eyes on the guy, knew he was different from all the other men she'd known, she'd been with. He had a kind face, kind eyes. He was just... kind. So she'd made that move at the wedding, going over to talk to him, getting on so well until he'd brought up the subject of those two. Bernice had to admit, she'd almost walked away at that point. A couple of kids from his previous marriage, a marriage to someone he spoke about with such adoration, was it really worth the hassle? But by then she'd fallen – always did fall quickly, and hard, usually for the wrong ones. The ones who delighted in nothing more than knocking her around. Mark would never do that, she could tell. Didn't have the balls, apart from anything else.

Bernice had shrugged, figured she could put up with it for a while until she thought of something. Had even played nice with them to begin with, all the time thinking that at some point they *had* to go. These walking, talking reminders of his past. Of his ex. That was the biggest problem for her, if she was being honest. How would she and Mark ever be happy, ever have any privacy when those two were hanging around all the time?

They had their uses, sure. Set them to work doing chores, like cleaning the toilet or just tidying up – cooking, when there was anything *to* cook. Running errands for some of the people she still knew from the streets. But the more time she spent with the pair, the more she began to resent them. If they were gone, there'd be two less mouths to feed for a start, less of a need to keep coming out on these stupid hunting expeditions. At first she'd fantasized about them being kidnapped or something, not necessarily any harm coming to them. Maybe taken by a family who actually wanted them?

But those fantasies had soon taken a darker turn. In one of them, she'd imagined just throwing them out of the window of their flat and saying they'd tripped. She might get away with it for one of them, but probably not two – and if the other had an 'accident' after that it was sure to make the police suspicious. If she got thrown in jail, what would happen to her life with Mark then? Anyway, she'd done nothing about it lately, apart from have a good old bitch with a mate on the phone, so when Mark came back after foraging and found they'd wandered off, it seemed like fate might have stepped in and done the job for her.

Bernice hadn't been taking any notice of what they were up to, had been more interested in drinking her wine and listening to her tunes. She wasn't the bloody babysitter, who cared what they did?

Mark. Mark cared, she reminded herself. Which was why she had to be a bit more careful with her comments. She'd been so drunk back there she'd almost said something about it all, about how perhaps it wouldn't be such a bad thing if they'd wandered off somewhere. But it would have been too soon; Mark wouldn't understand. In time, though, he'd get used to the new dynamic. He'd be sad, would miss them (it was more than she would; good riddance to bad rubbish!) Bernice understood that, but he'd get through it… with her help. They'd both be able to move on, move forward.

Which was why the more time they spent out here, the more chance there was they'd actually find them. Imagine that, being offered a glimmer of hope just to have it snatched away from her! No, she had to do something – and she was more or less sober now, so she'd be able to put it tactfully, slant it in a way that would benefit her. She'd become used to doing that during their marriage.

"Mark… Mark?" she piped up, stumbling through the undergrowth after him as he moved forwards, waving his torch left and right. She didn't want to lose sight of him and become lost out here herself; wouldn't have a clue how to get back to the car. Did Mark even? "Mark, are you listening to me?"

He turned. "What Bernice? What is it? I'm trying to look for signs of my kids out here." There was a desperation to his voice – the kind of desperation that only came from someone who'd been searching for something important for hours.

"I…" *Careful, Bernice,* she told herself again. "It's dark. Maybe we should go back and start again in the morning." That would work. Get him to go back, and by then they might be even further away. Put it to him in a way that showed him she cared what happened – even if she didn't.

"I-I can't do that, Bernice. I have to keep looking right now. Heaven knows what's happened to them!"

With a bit of luck, thought Bernice. *With a bit* more *luck...*

"I can't just abandon them."

"I never said that. I said we should try again in the morning." By which time she would hopefully have talked him around anyway. "We might just be going in circles, Mark!" She couldn't help snapping; she was so fed up of being out here now.

"They're my children," Mark replied.

I know, you said that already. Your *children. Not mine. We'll be better off without them.*

"I know, but—"

"But what? You were supposed to be keeping an eye on them, Bernice."

This again. The accusations. "I told you, they must have gone off to play somewhere. If we'd stayed by the car, they might have come back," Bernice retorted.

"They might have..." Mark shook his head. "I wonder if... I think maybe they intended to go. Run away."

"Why ever would they do that?" Bernice suspected: perhaps they'd got a whiff of something. If so, then she'd gladly claim credit for it, just not publicly.

"I don't... Everything's okay at home, isn't it? I mean, they're happy, right?"

Jesus, he really was good at deluding himself as far as they were concerned, wasn't he. "Sure," she replied.

"I mean, I don't think that—" Mark stopped, frozen

solid like someone had just pressed the pause button on the TV. His eyes were drawn to something on the floor and she followed his gaze as he flicked the light onto it. Bernice had to confess, she couldn't see anything at all. But Mark had, and virtually in the dark.

He moved towards whatever it was, crouching at the same time with a crack of his knees. It was only when he pointed to the spot with his torch-beam, and Bernice moved closer, that she saw them.

Crumbs.

Crumbs from something like a biscuit or a bar. That bloody greedy shit of a son of his! If only he hadn't eaten that, then—

Mark was smirking now. He'd picked up a trail. "Look, there are more over there. Clever boy."

Nothing clever about it at all, the lad was as thick as pig-shit. It was the girl; the girl she'd always had to be wary of. Regardless, Mark was up and moving forwards once more. No longer blundering around blind. Now he had a direction to go in.

Moving on, moving forwards – and she had no choice but to follow.

Those brats, she said to herself. *Those bloody brats!*

* * * * *

If only he hadn't eaten that.

Eaten anything, drunk anything. Then he wouldn't feel like this. So helpless, so weak. Then he might have been able to help.

Harry shook his head again. Gabrielle had known,

hadn't she. The clever one, not like him. He was as thick as—

Always in a hurry, especially when it came to filling his belly. When he'd seen the delights on that table – 'Mother Cass' descriptions really hadn't done it all justice: the cookies, golden and dark brown; the cream cake; the gingerbread – he hadn't been able to help himself, let alone anyone else. Harry had rushed past the roaring fire, attached to a huge range oven, taking a seat and shoving one thing after another into his mouth. Gabrielle had warned him, as well. Slow down, be careful, you'll make yourself sick. Well, he was sick all right: sick to his stomach!

But 'Mother Cass had seemed so, so nice – hadn't he learned anything from Bernice? Telling them to just tuck in, that they must be starving. She had no idea – or maybe she had. She'd seemed to know a lot of things about them, though Harry had been very slow on the uptake there as well.

As they'd sat at the table – Gabrielle somewhat reluctantly – and he'd eaten, the dogs winding around their legs underneath, the old woman had encouraged them to open up about their problems. Harry had been more than happy to get the ball rolling, telling her about Bernice and their homelife.

"That must be so hard," 'Mother Cass had said. "No wonder you ran off!"

"We thought she might do something to us," Harry informed her, talking with his mouth full, spitting crumbs everywhere. "Gabrielle thought, anyway."

"She *was* going to," argued the girl. "Something horrible. It was only a matter of time."

'Mother Cass had nodded sagely. "Then you

probably did the right thing. We wouldn't want something horrible happening to two such sweet children."

Harry had smiled at that. Not many people had ever called them sweet.

"Not ankle-biters at all. I mean, where does that witch get off calling you that!"

"I know, right?" Harry had said, spitting more bits of food out and ignoring the way Gabrielle was pulling a face. He washed it all down with more fizzy pop, tossing scraps to the dogs under the table.

"How..." his sister interrupted at that point.

"Yes dear?" said 'Mother Cass.

"How did you know she called us that?" asked Gabrielle.

"What?"

"Ankle-biters. Harry never mentioned anything about that, he doesn't even know what it means. And how did you know I call her the witch?"

"I..." 'Mother Cass smiled again, but there was something wrong about it this time. Her teeth yellow instead of those oh-so white ones Harry had assumed must be false, they were so perfect. "I really wish you'd have something to eat, dear. To drink. Like your brother. It would make things so much simpler."

Gabrielle folded her arms over her chest. "Who *are* you?" she asked then, suspicious as always.

"I told you, 'Mother Cass. Grandmother Cass."

"I know, but who are you really?"

The old woman sighed once again. "I used to help people. Heal people. Could even heal the big C, as they call it."

The big C? That's when Harry had started to become

uncomfortable himself. Not an unusual turn of phrase in itself, but added to the other stuff…

"A Healer?" Gabrielle had asked.

"Why yes! I thought I could do some good with the gifts *He* gave me."

"God," said his sister.

The woman simply grinned. "But, well, when folk eventually found out what was actually doing the healing… Let's just say they were none too happy. Would have done something seriously bad to me if I'd stayed around them."

There it was again, another of those phrases Gabrielle had used about their situation.

"So I ran, same as you two. Out here into the middle of nowhere. Where nobody could find me, but *I* could find people if I wanted to. Might as well embrace who you really are." The smile widened. "Nobody could find me that is, except you two. Not even sure how you did, must be something in your blood. On your mother's side maybe, or—"

Harry had let out a howl at that point, clutching his stomach. Gabrielle had warned him, told him he'd make himself ill from all that food and pop, but he hadn't listened.

"Oh my," said 'Mother Cass, getting up and going to him. "Are you all right? That sounds nasty. Maybe you'd better lie down over here on this." For some reason, and he hadn't spotted it before, there was a small single bed in the corner of the room. It reminded him a little of his own actually. Harry had nodded, gone with her and laid down gratefully, his stomach doing summersaults.

'Mother Cass had stepped back then. "Now, doesn't

that feel better already?"

No, he'd tried to say. No, it really didn't.

"Harry," said Gabrielle. "Harry I think it's time we left. I don't think it's saf—"

"Nonsense!" the old woman had snapped. "You can't go yet. We're not finished." She looked first one way at Harry, then over at Gabrielle again. "Such *sweet* children, shouldn't go to waste. You're not appreciated at home, not loved. Not wanted. But *I* want you. I want you *so very* badly." When she said the last bit, her voice changed from the softly spoken one she'd been using since they arrived to a more guttural sound.

Then she grabbed Gabrielle by the arm, pulling her from the table and swinging her around. "Ow! Get off me!" shouted his sister.

"Far too clever, you are. An... an old head on your shoulders. But you might as well embrace who – what – you really are, my dear," Grandmother Cass told her. "And what you are is food. Crumbs from life's table, but sustenance for me."

Harry got to his feet then, regardless of the pain. "L-Let go of her!" He staggered forward, but was stopped by something he couldn't see. Something in front of him, an invisible barrier.

"I suppose there's no more need for this pantomime," said the old woman, waving her hand.

The first thing Harry saw were the bars he'd walked into. The bars all around him. He was in some sort of cage, a cage that hadn't been there before. A trap! And, try as he might – hands on the bars, shaking them, weakly it had to be said, as he didn't have much strength all of a sudden – there was no way out of it. When he paused, he'd taken in more of the changes that were happening all around, changing the whole of that cottage.

It was much darker for one thing, the gas-lamps that had illuminated the room they were in replaced by flickering candles with what looked like veins going up the side. Made from some kind of fat? The wooden – not stone – walls were filled with holes and stained a kind of red colour, like they'd been splattered with crimson paint. In fact the whole of the room looked like that, not just the walls but the floor, the door, everything. And on those walls were the most hideous tools Harry had ever seen: curved blades and saws; knives of all sizes and shapes; and chains, lots of chains. All were similarly stained scarlet.

When his eyes flicked back across to the table they'd been seated at, Harry had seen the awful truth about what they'd been eating. Plates covered in flies – of which there didn't seem to be any shortage – and writhing maggots. Parasites of all varieties. Cups full of dirty water, or even blood? How could they have been made to look so tempting, so irresistible?

One word flashed through his mind: *Bait.*

Harry had almost thrown up on the spot, but something kept it all down. Was that part of her plan too, Grandmother Cass? To fatten them up somehow?

As for the woman herself, she'd undergone a transformation too – or had she always been that way and made them see what they wanted to see? Instead of a friendly, round woman with white hair and spectacles, there was a much thinner and much older figure. Her skin was leathery and wrinkled, especially at her face, with bags under her eyes and hair like matted string. Her clothes were practically rags hanging off her, and where she had hold of Gabrielle her nails were like claws.

When she threw the girl down on the floor, more claws were suddenly visible, however. The dogs ventured out from under the table, and a breath had caught in Harry's throat. One still golden – or more accurately pus-coloured – the other black, they were more like something out of a hellish nightmare now. They were sniffing at Gabrielle, teeth bared.

"Lucifer! Beelzebub!" snapped 'Mother Cass, and unlike outside the creatures had obeyed instantly, leaving the food and coming to heel. She guffawed. "I'm so glad they're not cats."

Gabrielle, as terrified as she was, made to get up, to head across to Harry and set him free. And that's when 'Mother Cass had stamped on her leg, breaking it with a cracking sound. His sister had screamed at the top of her lungs, tears filling her eyes.

Towering over her, the woman had looked to the wall – looking directly at a cleaver. Then she stopped, paused. Was sniffing the air.

"It seems that more food is coming," she'd said then. "More fillings for my pies. I do so love to bake!"

And that's when Harry had collapsed, his legs no longer holding him up. Wishing he hadn't been so impatient, hadn't eaten or drunk any of that vile stuff from the table.

Then he might have been able to help.

* * * * *

There was nothing Mark Travis could do to help.

No sooner had they broken through into the clearing, having followed the general direction the crumbs had taken them – even after they'd run out – and they'd spotted the run-down old cabin, than the door had opened and the dogs had been released.

Though he wasn't quite sure he'd actually call them dogs, more like monsters really. Sinewy and glistening in the light from the moon here, their teeth barely fit inside their mouths – were like something that should have belonged to a sabre-toothed tiger! Bernice, off to the right of him, had let out a wail, then a scream, as one of the dogs leapt up and went for her throat.

Mark had wanted to help, but the lighter-coloured one had gone for him – clamping onto his leg instead, his thigh to be precise. Trying to bring him down. Ignoring the pain – it felt as if the animal was biting through the meat and bone – he gritted his teeth and had rammed down the butt of his trusty rifle, smashing into the skull of the thing. Once, twice, three times: he could not get the beast to release its grip.

Suddenly he was falling over, and the dog was climbing up him. It opened its jaws once more and Mark could do nothing but wedge the rifle sideways into the open gap, shoving it backwards. Could it bite through the gun? It was having a good old try.

He risked a look to his left, saw that Bernice, though felled, had smashed the empty bottle she'd been cradling for so long like a baby, and was stabbing it sideways into the dog at her throat. Glassing it, tearing chunks of flesh from it just as it was doing to her.

Mark shoved harder, ramming the rifle back and up into the attack dog's mouth. He heard a splitting sound, a tearing as the jaw on one side began to rip. He told himself to keep on pushing, pushing, and then at the last moment he wrenched the rifle sideways, taking the dog's head with it. There was the snap of bones, something in the dog's neck giving way. It kept on trying to bite the rifle for a few more moments, as if the information simply hadn't reached its brain – or perhaps it was just plain indestructible – but then it slumped onto Mark, its breathing shallow. Finally, the creature stopped breathing altogether.

"Beelzebub!" The screech almost hurt his ears when it came, and Mark rolled the creature off, to see a woman – at least he thought it was a woman – standing in the doorway, holding a cleaver in one hand and a knife in the other. She was crying, screaming at the top of her voice at what he'd done – which was when he worked out that must have been the name of the dog. Quite appropriate really. The woman glanced across at Bernice then and screamed again: "Lucifer!"

Mark looked as well and saw that, though Bernice was barely twitching, the dog that had attacked her was slumped across her too. Both of this woman's 'pets' were dead.

Returning his gaze to her, he saw the old lady scowl, then cock her head right back and howl at the moon like a dog herself; like some sort of werewolf. But this wasn't one of those kinds of stories. When she brought her head back down, her eyes were glowing a strange azure colour – and she was mouthing something, words he couldn't make out. The only thing Mark did hear was: "Rise my children. *Rise!*"

There was a rumbling, he felt it through his hips. The ground undulating, vibrating. He scrambled to his feet, almost falling back over again because of his wounded thigh. But just as he'd righted himself, he saw the first of them emerge.

Bones, poking out of the ground. Jutting up like icebergs initially, then coming together, snaking into each other and melding. The first of the bone-things stood up, and had almost as much difficulty as Mark. It wasn't a skeleton as such, because the bones were from lots of different sources it seemed, but it formed a rough 'body'. And it wasn't alone. More bone-monsters were rising up, this hideous woman's 'children' as she'd called them, even though some of the bones were definitely from adults.

And then they began to lurch towards Mark, all making for him. He blinked once, twice, but yes this was actually happening. He was about to be set upon by a skeletal army of the dead!

He raised his rifle to shoulder height and let off a shot. It chipped the head of one figure, which was actually two or three skulls forming a whole. But that didn't slow it down. Mark aimed for the legs next, shooting out a kneecap here, a shin there and toppling the things – which just continued to crawl towards him, their orders clear.

One of the monstrosities reached him, and he batted it away with the end of the rifle. Another attempted to grab the barrel, snatch the weapon away from him. Something embedded itself in his shoulder and he nearly dropped the rifle anyway. Flicking his eyes to the left again, he saw the knife the woman had been holding sticking out of there. Now it was his turn to howl.

The woman started towards him herself next, cleaver raised high. He was about to pay the price for killing one of her dogs – thought perhaps Bernice, his dear wife Bernice, had paid that price already for the other.

Then the woman stopped in her tracks, let out a scream – but of real pain this time. Pain because… as Mark gazed across, he saw his daughter Gabrielle – Gabby – on the ground, crawling like those skeletons in front of him. Had crawled right up to the woman's leg and bit into it. At the ankle to be precise.

It was enough to distract the woman, make her look away. Mark hadn't needed Gabby to break off and shout, "Shoot her! Kill her, Dad!" but it had definitely been an incentive. He shrugged off the bone-things closest to him and raised the rifle, aiming as best he could with one arm, one hand. His first shot caught the old crone in the torso, but she hardly seemed to feel it. The second, more through luck than judgement – fate, his lucky day – zeroed in on her head, exploding out the other side in a shower of blood and brains.

She dropped to her knees, and as she did so the bone-things fell too: shattering back into their individual pieces. Then she keeled over sideways, dropping the cleaver.

Mark limped towards the woman, rifle still raised. But he needn't have worried. The crone was dead.

Especially after Gabby had snatched her cleaver and cut off her head at the neck.

* * * * *

It had certainly been a tale to tell.

A tale none of them were sure about telling at all, after they'd waited in the cabin till morning – freeing Harry, their father holding both children in his arms, one in each

– and then made their way up towards the car, Gabby still in her father's arms, picking up the crumb trail finally and taking it from there.

In the end, they'd had no choice. They'd all needed medical attention, and the people at the hospital had called the police. They, in turn, had questioned Harry and Gabby's father and he'd told them about the mad woman's place. How she'd taken his children, killed his wife, and they had been left with no choice but to kill *her*.

The cops had turned a blind eye to the fact Mark Travis wasn't supposed to be hunting in that forest, because they'd been able to clear up so many missing persons cases from over the years – some dating back almost a century – that it had made both them, and him, heroes. They ignored some of the stranger stuff, put it down to the fact there were mercury sulphite gas springs in the area that could easily have caused hallucinations. Something their dad, especially the more time that passed, began to believe as well; he'd always been quite delusional in that respect. It was probably easier to live with than the truth.

Book and film deal offers had eventually followed, which he'd been reluctant to take, but Gabby – not Gabrielle now, she'd decided – had convinced him otherwise. A way to a better life, and one without Bernice, she'd thought to herself – good riddance to bad rubbish (the spell broken, though she was never really able to cast them – not like some people: the *real* witch). Her dad would get over it, move forward, move on, with them. His children: just Gabby, Harry and him. He'd proven by saving them that he cared, that he loved them with all his heart. No more crumbs of affection, crumbs of anything.

They'd have a happy life now, would never go

hungry, would never be beaten again. She'd never have to run away, never live in fear of something happening to herself or Harry ever again.

At least that's what Gabby told herself as she grew up. *Until* she grew up and discovered there were worse things in life than cannibalistic witches, than hellhounds and bone-creatures.

But that, as they say, is another story entirely.

Pure Evil

'The road to hell is paved with good intentions.'
Proverb

<u>Lasko Facility for the Criminally Insane - 11:00 p.m.</u>

Professor Elizabeth Warren sat back and waited.

She waited for the inevitable string of obscenities to waft through the halls and greet her here in the isolation wing. It would only be one voice of many at the facility. *Too many* for her liking. Time was growing short indeed.

Elizabeth looked at the hands extended in front of her on the table. The skin was starting to loosen around the knuckles and wrinkles had appeared where there used to be none. She was getting old, slowly but surely. And it may have been a well-worn adage, but she had so much to do and so little time in which to do it.

There was a timid knock on the door and the locks clicked open. Hal Cowen, her research assistant, came in with a bundle of papers under his arm and a steaming plastic cup in his hand. He placed the black coffee on the table beside her.

"He's on his way," Hal told her. "Thought you could do with a drink before you got started. It's decaff."

"Thanks Hal." Their eyes met. She saw genuine affection there for her. Or was it pity?

If she were only fifteen years younger Elizabeth would show him how she really felt; he might be able to fill the gaping void inside her left by years of hard work and loneliness. No time for love – it was one of her many regrets. Then again, if she were still a young woman she probably wouldn't have employed Hal in the first place. She would've carried on the work herself as she had done most of her life, making the same mistakes all over again. Sacrificing her own enjoyment for the good of humanity. Christ, that made her sound like some kind of superhero or something; she shuddered at the comparison.

Elizabeth knew that Hal would do anything for her, anything she asked him to. Including *that*: he'd probably even jump at the chance. But she couldn't take advantage of his hero-worship to bed a man almost half her age, as much as it kept her awake at night.

Elizabeth broke eye contact and stared at the coffee cup instead, the liquid inside swirling round and round. Thick and black.

"The cameras are all set up next door." Hal pointed at the two-way mirror that monopolised most of the interview room's opposite wall. It wasn't fooling anyone, that thing. Patients knew there would be psychotherapists holding clipboards, jotting everything down, and possibly even the Governor himself hiding behind that reflective glass – observing them as they answered pointless questions, trying to get a handle on what made them tick.

What made them do the things they did. None of the so-called experts could ever possibly understand. Not fully. Not like she did.

Hal passed her the papers he was warming in his armpit. Case notes, police files. Anything and everything on their next subject: one Edwin Sloane. Rapist, murderer. Psychopath.

Evil. Pure evil.

The photograph said it all. His snarling pose, sweaty forehead and unkempt hair. The very picture of insanity. Just to emphasise this, there were also stills of his victims. All young women aged between nineteen and thirty, violated then slashed to bits as if some ferocious animal had beset them. It wasn't far from the truth. Yes, insanity was the only word to describe it.

But insanity is such a subjective thing after all. Sloane probably felt that he was the only sane person alive, and that the other people he encountered – those women, the cops, his jailers – deviated from his definition in some way. They couldn't see things with the clarity he saw them. Desires and impulses influenced Sloane, the same ones affecting everyone to some extent, even if folk didn't admit to them. The only difference was, he acted upon these regardless of the cost. He could no more help it than people could help their sexual persuasions. Sloane had been born this way, with more than his fair share of evil boiling away inside – in spite of what specialists might tell you about background and childhood. Freud would probably have said he'd been taken away from his mother's teat too soon, or that he'd accidentally walked in on his parents copulating: the primal scene both repugnant and encapsulating.

Elizabeth Warren didn't subscribe to any of that. She looked at Sloane, and others like him, and saw someone who could be treated. But only she could do it. Only she knew how.

She took a sip of the coffee, the profanities growing louder. This was the part she hated most. The confrontation. It never went well to start with. There was resistance, hostility, violence – or the *threat* of it. Nevertheless, she'd learnt to cope. Elizabeth had to endure this to get to the other side. There *was* light at the end of the tunnel, another old aphorism. Besides, it wasn't their fault. They weren't in control. She had to keep telling herself that or *she'd* end up checking into one of the cells here at Lasko.

"Are you sure you'll be all right?" asked Hal. "We could always reschedule."

She was touched by his concern, but there had been enough hold-ups already. "I'm fine, Hal. Stop worrying. We have to get on with this; it's the only way we'll ever be taken seriously. Sloane is the last, then we can go public."

Elizabeth couldn't wait for that. All this sneaking about, conducting her experiments in secret, was getting more than a bit tiresome. As a reputable scientist – well, she liked to think so at any rate – part-neurologist, part-physicist and biologist, part-*inventor* really, it went against the grain. Put her on a par with people like Josef Mengele, when in reality she was so far removed from maniacs like that it was laughable. Elizabeth wanted only to help, to be remembered as someone who strove for peace. It *would* happen. Eventually.

She had to prove herself first and teach Hal as much as he could possibly learn. Elizabeth wouldn't trust anyone else with her legacy.

It should be easier for him, she hoped, once they'd come out of the closet. No more bending the rules. All the groundwork had been laid; the prototype was already in operation. When the government saw what they'd accomplished at Lasko they would get all the backing they needed for the future. And in Hal's lifetime perhaps he'd see the last of these dreadful places.

God, that would be *some* day.

But she'd had to fight tooth and nail just to get this far. All the months spent 'convincing' Governor Hadfield to let her conduct her little trials. Greasing the wheels, she believed it was called in these circles, a mixture of bribery and calling in favours she'd amassed over the years. Even then her arrival had been met with no less than contempt. Elizabeth hadn't expected to make friends here – no, definitely not here – but she had hoped for a modicum of professional courtesy. They were all working towards the same goals at the end of the day, weren't they? Sometimes she wondered.

However, she could understand their caution up to a point, because her reputation as a forthright campaigner preceded her wherever she went. The investigation she was carrying out at Lasko may have been top secret, but Elizabeth had never been one to keep her opinions to herself. She'd rubbed a fair few people up the wrong way during her career with outspoken ideas about the management of the mentally ill (more specifically the criminally ill; that distinction was paramount) and the causes of said ailments – medical, not mental.

She'd also been involved in a number of heated TV debates, the last one being only a month or so ago. Of course her old sparring partner had been there, harassing her for the full fifty minutes of the show: The 'Reverend' Aaron Myatt, representing *The Church of Divine Enlightenment*. Whilst it was true that she didn't believe in God personally, she could usually respect the views of his spokespeople. Usually. They had their beliefs. She had hers. But this guy Myatt and his group were something else, giving both evangelists and fanatics a bad name.

Elizabeth wouldn't mind so much if they could argue rationally instead of just shouting people down. The spiky-haired moron who called himself their 'leader on Earth' looked more like a boxer than a preacher, barely squeezing into his black quasi-Catholic outfit, complete with dog collar. And on that particular night he'd been worse than usual, interrupting whenever she spoke, making insulting – and possibly slanderous – comments about her and her vocation, and contradicting everything she did manage to say.

His point of view was a unique one, she'd given him that. Myatt posited that these misunderstood unfortunates should be left alone because it was all part of God's plan. His will. He had created them that way for a reason, and any tampering with this great design was the Devil's work.

Presumably then, Elizabeth had countered, Myatt would be much happier if such people were allowed to run around on the streets doing whatever the hell they liked because The Almighty had ordained it. This provoked a slight ripple of laughter from the studio audience and Myatt had growled openly at her.

But that was nothing compared to the unease she'd felt when he accused her of conducting inhuman tests on the piteous, harmless sheep. For a minute or two she actually thought he'd found out something and would expose her before she could even start her trials. It soon became clear, though, that he believed she was developing a new kind of electro-shock treatment, a practice she'd already gone on record as condemning. Myatt didn't have a clue what she was up to, so she let him ramble on. It was good television if nothing else. But Elizabeth decided she'd definitely check the guest list before agreeing to do any more shows, and if Myatt's name was present she'd back out tout suite.

Still, as much as it pained her to admit it, there was one thing they saw eye-to-eye on. Evil *did* exist, she'd known that all her life, and could speak from personal experience. But it wasn't an incorporeal thing, it wasn't demonic or Devil's work – or God's either for that matter, as Myatt asserted. No, it was real and it was inside each and every person on Earth to varying degrees.

Ironically, many thought she was insane herself; Governor Hadfield being the latest supporter of this wildly held belief. But she knew on approach to Lasko with Hal that first day, escorted down the driveway towards the converted Georgian house, that she would finally show them she was right.

Her results would speak for themselves, she felt, and that's exactly what they did. Nine patients in a little over two and a half weeks, three sessions apiece, had walked out of the interview room changed men. Elizabeth would never forget the look on Hadfield's face when the first one went back to his cell as quiet as a church mouse. He saw what she'd done. She'd even tried to explain it to him in the most basic possible terms (terms which required a Ph.D. to understand). But still he looked for the raving lunatic, Gerry Fulton – the High-street Bomber – who'd met with

Elizabeth the previous day. Hadfield looked for him in his cell, looked for him in the man's eyes. But it was too late; he was already gone. Supplanted by someone who looked and talked like Fulton, yet was nothing like him. Not deep down. Something was… *missing*. The Gerry Fulton now residing in B wing wouldn't hurt a fly if his life depended on it.

What behavioural specialists, psychiatrists and the strongest medications had spent years trying to achieve, Elizabeth Warren had completed in a day or so. She'd turned him into an honest, law-abiding citizen who might one day re-join the community he'd sought to obliterate with his explosive devices. But not yet. People wouldn't understand – especially the families of all those dead shoppers. If they saw him walk free without any explanation it could do more harm than good. Maybe when this was all out in the open, though. When they could grasp what had been done. Would they understand even then? She'd *make* them somehow.

"I said get the fuck off me!"

Sloane was at the door now, brought in by two massive orderlies. Normally he would have been doped up to be moved, but Elizabeth had had more success with those inmates who weren't as high as kites. It didn't take as long for some reason. And with Sloane it would be better for all concerned if this were over quickly.

The two men wrestled Sloane past Elizabeth and Hal. He looked even worse in real life, a dangerous volcano ready to blow. Sloane spat at Elizabeth, the globule landing next to his own records on the desk. Like something alive, it worked its way to the edge and dribbled off.

"I got something for you, lady," he rasped.

"Something nice and tasty. Later, later."

Elizabeth tried not to shake, but it was hard. She felt Hal's hand on her shoulder, glad of the support as always.

Sloane struggled as the orderlies pushed him down into the seat. He was tightly encased in an off-white straitjacket, but they strapped him to the chair to make sure, around the stomach and at the ankles. He wasn't going anywhere.

"Thank you. Would you mind waiting outside, please, until we're finished?" Elizabeth said to the men. Their presence would only agitate Sloane further, and they'd just be a shout away if anything happened. She was in no danger now.

"Did you hear what I said?" Sloane bellowed after the orderlies had left. "I got something for you!"

Elizabeth looked at him sternly, meeting his gaze and refusing to back down. "And I, Mr Sloane, have got something for you."

Hal left her side and went to the far corner of the room. He came back wheeling a trolley with a cover over it.

"Do you know who I am?" demanded Sloane. "Let me tell you what I done."

"Did you enjoy defiling and murdering all those innocent women, Mr Sloane?" Elizabeth asked him, getting to her feet.

"I wanted to hear them scream. I'm gonna hear you scream soon, lady. Do to you what I—"

"Yes, but *why* Edwin?" She used his first name now that they were acquainted. "Do you even know why?"

"I wanted to hear them scream," he repeated.

"That's not a reason."

Sloane shrugged. He didn't know what else to say to her, she knew that. He just liked it.

"Shall I tell you why you did all those things, Edwin?" Sloane didn't respond. "It's because you have something inside you—"

"Let me go and you'll have something inside you, as well," he said, sneering.

"—something you can't control." Elizabeth pinched a piece of the sheet, ready to pull it off. "And I am going to take it out."

Sloane looked at the machine. A long metal box with switches and dials on one side and readouts at the other. Set inside it was a glass square with dual tubes the thickness of electric wires running from it.

"Don't need no lie detector. I'm proud of what I done. Wanna tell everyone."

Elizabeth took no notice. This wasn't the real Edwin Sloane; she would meet *him* soon enough.

Hal helped her attach the clear tubes to Sloane, holding the sides of his head straight so he couldn't bite her. Sloane spat at Elizabeth a couple more times, one missile landing in her silver-blonde hair, another glancing off her cheek. It didn't deter her from fastening the ducts to his temples.

"Don't struggle, Edwin. It will only hurt for a moment, then everything will be all right. I promise." Elizabeth flipped a combination of switches. There was a humming sound like a pair of electric clippers, and Hal let go of Sloane's head.

Then he felt it. Oh, Jesus, how he felt it!

The ends of the tubes vibrated. They seemed to be

tunnelling beneath his skin. Something was entering his head, digging deep. And it hurt! The machine cranked up a notch and Sloane was aware of a terrible force on either side of his skull, as if his head was going in two opposite directions. The flesh was taut around his eyes, which swivelled left and right; watching as a dark-grey and red jelly oozed down the tube. But he was feeling something else, too. Something he'd not felt in a long, long time. Not since he was very little.

Edwin Sloane was afraid.

The bitch is sucking my brains out! he thought, working himself up. *There it goes. Look at that shit! Like fucking milkshake through a straw...*

Elizabeth nodded to herself as it was collected, the indicator rising inside the glass, adding to the rest already inside; nine patients' worth. This was the best part. Observing as the subject changed.

She was watching it so intently now, the slime that looked virtually harmless and was anything but. That which she alone had found a way to locate – in the prefrontal cortex, the moral centre of the brain – and make visible with a special combination of dyes. To identify and extract, like siphoning out a cataract from a cloudy eye. She was so focused, so caught up in the moment that she didn't hear the door opening behind her.

Elizabeth was vaguely conscious of Hal saying something like, "Hey, we're not ready yet!" then stopping abruptly.

The next sound she heard was that of a baseball bat connecting with her shoulder blades lengthways, knocking her to the floor. There was a brief elapse of time, a second –

two at the most – before shock dissolved into pain and her eyes gave birth to tears.

Shouting: Hal's voice. Then an incredible *WHUMP!* like someone beating a carpet on a line. Now winded groans and coughing filled the air.

Elizabeth blinked. The room was full of people who shouldn't be there. Five, no six men. And the one at the front... her eyes still too misted to see properly. Was that a mess of spiky hair?

"Myatt! Wha—" She couldn't say much, her mind wouldn't let her. It was too busy asking questions: What were Myatt and his followers doing here at Lasko? Where were the orderlies? Dead? How had Myatt gotten past security? Got into a locked room? What did they want? To kill her? If she shouted for help would anyone hear her above all the other voices?

The questions went unanswered; that white-hot burning across her shoulders taking precedence.

Sloane was squealing in his chair.

"Take those things off him," ordered Myatt. Then he turned to the Neanderthal with the bat. "Destroy this equipment," he ordered, indicating the machine. "There has been enough suffering here today."

"No!" Elizabeth yelled at him. "Myatt, you can't—" A boot lodged itself in her belly, silencing her protests.

"Oh but I can, Professor Warren. And I *will* end this now before God punishes us all. You must see that what you're doing here is wrong. He has been merciful thus far, and I just hope I have arrived in time to appease him."

One of Myatt's disciples pulled the tubes from Sloane's head. They came out at least an inch, spilling dark-grey fluid onto his fingers. The stench was terrific, like a pile of dead bodies stuffed in a greenhouse on a summer's day. He wiped it down his trousers and began to untie Sloane's straps – taking Myatt's orders too literally. Freeing him from *all* his bonds.

The thickset man was striking Warren's machine with his bat. *Clank, clank!* So hard the wood was splintering. And one by one the others joined in with the 'weapons' they'd brought. A crowbar, a lump hammer, a piece of copper piping.

Myatt watched it all with satisfaction, crying at the top of his lungs: "Thy will be done. Thy will be done!" over and over; wallowing in the destruction of a lifetime's work. *A lifetime's sacrifice!* The device looked like so much scrap from a wrecker's yard by the time they'd finished with it.

And with one final blow the thug with the bat smashed its glass casing.

Elizabeth saw it first. Trickling onto the floor like Sloane's spittle, her 'discovery'. Slurping around Myatt's feet and the feet of his followers, climbing up their legs, spreading out to touch her where she lay. Elizabeth tried to edge away but somebody took hold of her neck and squeezed.

Sloane was leering down at her, his other hand over her mouth – revenge on his mind. She knew what came next. She'd seen it in the photographs from his file. But she wasn't scared.

She'd never be scared again as long as she lived.

* * * * *

Governor Albert Hadfield trod the squeaking surface

of the corridor with his men just behind, nightsticks at the ready.

It was just gone twelve.

Myatt and his gang would be finished by now. Long gone. What a stroke of genius that had been on his part, to let that nutter do his dirty work for him. Calling the Reverend up, letting him know where Warren would be (no one else knew of their whereabouts). Giving him access to Lasko.

Myatt had been reluctant initially, worried it was a set-up. Everyone knew how he felt about Warren. Hadfield had convinced him otherwise, outlining the terrible experiments she was performing, making things up because he didn't understand them himself.

Bullshit, all of it! How could you take the badness out of someone? It was downright ludicrous, her and that bastard machine. She was frying patients' brains, that's what she was doing. Turning them into vegetables. And all the crap that came out of them was just smoke and mirrors, a magician's act. An act that might just fool those arseholes in power.

If she got the go-ahead to do this on a regular basis it would put them all out of work. He'd seen the other nine, he'd seen Fulton. It could happen. Hadfield wasn't about to take any chances.

They came to the interview room and the Governor told two of his men, the same two who'd brought Sloane in an hour ago, to go next door and retrieve the cameras. He knew they'd be in there; she'd recorded every one of the sessions.

Then Hadfield took three more orderlies and unlocked the interview room.

Red.

That's what he saw when the door was pushed back. Red. Everywhere. On the walls, on the ceiling, on the two-way mirror.

His first thought was: *Sloane did this.*

But Sloane was there on the table, head snapped back, tongue out like a Labrador, trousers round his ankles, and a big gaping hole between his legs where his genitalia used to be.

More bodies lay beneath him on the ground. One had a crowbar sticking out of the top of its head, used to split the skull in two; another had been beaten down so hard it was almost flat – like in the cartoons when a steamroller comes, except in cartoons they always get up again, and they're never ever covered in bumps and blood like that; and one particularly unlucky sod looked like he'd been turned inside out and dragged bodily around the walls.

Hadfield began to whimper, trying to step back behind his protectors, one of whom was dropping to his knees. The lump hammer swung again, pounding what was left of his cranium into his shoulders. The crunching sound made Hadfield nauseous. A naked Cowen, Warren's assistant, raised the hammer again, taking out the other man on the Governor's right.

At Hadfield's left The Reverend Myatt rammed a piece of copper piping into the final orderly's guts with such force his stomach collapsed on impact.

Finally Hadfield saw Elizabeth Warren herself at the back of the room. She stepped out of the darkness wearing nothing except an interesting necklace 'borrowed' from Sloane. Nail marks covered her arms, torso and legs, which he suspected were self-inflicted. Two of her new followers walked with her like lapdogs, one the caveman with the bat, the lower half of his face plastered with crimson grue. They were at her feet, worshipping her.

But there was something wrong with those feet, with all their feet. A grey-blackness covering them like boots. It was all over the floor, too, winding in and out of the blood like serpents through grass.

Pure Evil.

Hadfield nearly passed out from the smell alone.

Elizabeth came forward as young Cowen and her apparent second-in-command Myatt held the Governor fast. She looked crazed, but in a calm, eerie sort of way. Then she kissed her assistant hungrily, tongue darting in and out of his mouth, before breaking off again with a grin.

The plan was simple, she explained. Set the inmates free and spread the Evil far and wide, fed on a diet of carnage and unfettered emotion. Lasko was only the start. She had so much to do in so little time.

"Thy will be done," Elizabeth intoned and the others repeated.

"L-L-Let me go. You're all fucking mad!" Hadfield was trying to break free, the acts they'd committed finally filtering through.

"We will, Albert," said Elizabeth, stroking his cheek, her fingernails scraping the skin, "but first I have something for you, something nice and tasty." Her face was shiny-grey now, masked by a thin layer of Evil. Hadfield panicked, attempting to turn his head away as if reading her mind. It wasn't hard; her intentions were clear. Elizabeth's hand reached his neck.

And when she spoke again he couldn't even see her mouth. "Don't struggle, Albert. It'll only hurt for a moment, I promise.

"Then everything will be all right."

Mortis-Man: Origins

He was no stranger to the darkness.

He'd experienced it at an early age. Not just the kind most kids are afraid of – ironically that didn't really bother him much. This was deeper, the kind of darkness that comes from the loss of a parent. Painful, internal, but also enveloping. Affecting the whole household.

It had definitely affected Blake Wagner's father when his wife died, leaving the man to bring up a child on his own. Blake had been told that she'd died of natural causes, not that he really understood what that meant either at the tender age of four. Natural? What was natural about someone not being there anymore? Around one minute, the next—

"Death is not the end," that's what they'd said at her funeral service, he'd always remembered that.

Wasn't until he was much older that Blake found out the truth, that she'd taken her own life: the depression that had plagued her most of her life finally getting its way; a very different kind of darkness. His dad had done his best given the circumstances, and Blake certainly didn't want to give the impression that it had all been doom and gloom.

He remembered being taken to ballgames, the cinema, spending time playing football with his dad in the park. Special times, precious times. Because his father worked so, so hard: a miner who spent a lot of his time underground, in the shadows. Blake was a small kid, didn't really blossom until he got into his teens, so he'd been bullied a lot at school. In fact, it was a pack of particularly mean kids who'd first told him about his mother.

"Why don't you just off yourself like she did. Do us all a favour!" a nasty pale-faced youth with tight, curly hair once said to him, and Blake had to go and ask his father what that meant. He could still remember the big man rubbing his face and sitting Blake down to talk to him. About her state of mind, about the pills she'd taken to go to sleep because she felt like she really couldn't cope, couldn't face the world anymore.

"At least now she's not suffering, Blake," he said with tears in his eyes. "She just slipped away into the darkness."

In the end his father had been buried by it, had died in the dark when the cave-in had happened. But that was much later on, when Blake had been thinking of going to the academy. He guessed it had been all those cop shows on TV that had done it, the boob-tube like a surrogate parent to him when his dad wasn't around. The police taking down bad guys, good always winning against evil – their moral codes – it made sense of a senseless world.

He'd already made a start, by standing up to those bullies – God, he couldn't stand bullies! – taking boxing and self-defence lessons, getting stronger and bigger at the same time. So that when the pasty-faced youth tried it on one day with his mates, Blake was ready for him. Was gearing up to take them all on, when all it had really taken was bringing down the ring-leader. Once the boss was on the ground, all the others lost their nerve. It taught him more than any of his lessons at school ever had.

So, when his dad passed – alone, suffocating and terrified in that mine – there was nothing to stick around for in that rural area Blake called home. He signed up for the academy and headed off, to learn properly about the law and how he might uphold it. It had been hard work, but also fun; his fellow classmates all with the same mindset as him. Full of the same certainty, that they could make a difference. When he graduated, it was the proudest day of his entire life so far. And Blake liked to think that his mum and dad were proud as well, wherever they were.

Now he was rising up out of yet another darkness. The blackness of his sleep, when he'd managed to get to sleep, that was – because of the mixture of nerves and excitement. Waking up in the small apartment he'd moved into just the other week, assigned to this particular city as his first post. (He'd told them he was willing to go anywhere, had no particular ties – the bank had long since repossessed the family home – as long as it was somewhere he could make his mark.) Waking up in the bed he'd put together himself, which was still a little rickety but was all he could afford on a beat cop's wages. Blake had some savings from various jobs in his teens, but was, well, saving them for a rainy day. Which didn't look too far off, judging from the scene out of his grimy window. Yawning, he climbed out of bed and wandered over to that window, looking over this new place he called home. Everything had led him here. The city he'd seen on approach, riding his bike past the nicer estates on the outskirts, the graveyard that looked pretty much abandoned.

Glaive City, with its spires and tall buildings stretching out into the distance. The streets that ran in and out of those, streets he'd been patrolling for the last few days with his partner Ellis, someone who had a few more miles on the clock than him and had been tasked to show Blake the ropes. So far already they'd looked into a burglary – "Not much chance of ever getting the stolen items back," Ellis had said, shaking his head as they left the distraught woman's place – a stick-up at a corner store, a case of domestic abuse – Blake had just wanted to go out and find the guy doing that, but his spouse wasn't ready yet to press charges ("Chances are she never will," Ellis informed him, "she'll probably turn up dead someday…") – and a guy who was flashing schoolkids on their way home; there had been no sign of him by the time they showed up, so all they'd done was take a few statements.

Not the best of starts, granted. Hadn't made much of a difference… yet. But Ellis seemed like the kind of guy he could definitely learn from while on the job, a 'seen it all' veteran. And Blake had been welcomed to the station by the big Chief himself, McDonald – who everyone just called Mack.

"Ah, our newest recruit!" he'd said in that booming voice of his, catching Blake in the corridor just before his shift the other day. The rotund man with the red cheeks had clapped him on the shoulder with one hand and shook the other. "Heart and soul of this precinct, you lot are. The front line troops. I hope Ellis here isn't leading you too far astray?"

Blake had chuckled. "No, sir."

"Not yet anyway." Mack laughed himself, winking at Ellis, then said: "But seriously, if you ever need anything, son. If you're ever worried about something, my door's always open."

"I'll… Thank you sir, really appreciate that."

One more clap on the shoulder and he let them go off for their shift. Not the worst thing to have the ear of his boss, to have the guy who could get things done on tap. Would stand him in good stead moving forwards, Blake figured.

He drifted away from his bedroom window now, got down on the floor and started his exercise regime with one-handed push-ups. Part of being a cop as far as he was concerned was staying in shape; not just visiting – or glancing in the direction of – the gym once a week like Ellis said he did, but committing to it every day. (Commitment in general.) What if they had to run someone down, climb over fences or whatever?

Blake switched hands, placing that one behind his back and taking the strain on his other arm, pushing himself up and down. He was looking forward to his day, to hopefully doing some good, finally. Nailing a criminal or two, not just leaving loose ends.

It was what he was doing here after all, chasing away the darkness.

Protecting people from it.

* * * * *

Right now, he was in the dark.

Not just literally, because the men in ski-masks

who'd grabbed him had placed a hood over his head, but because he didn't know why. Why anyone would snatch him from the streets, bind his hands in front of him and bundle him into a van to whisk him off somewhere. He'd made a couple of attempts to pull the hood off, to escape, and each time been punched or kicked in the back of the van as it trundled along.

Finally, one of the men had jammed a gun in his ribs and told him to behave himself.

"But… I mean… I don't understand…" A whack across the jaw with that same gun had shut him up and he hadn't said anything since.

Not even as they'd pulled up and he'd been dragged from the van, up a series of steps to someplace. Dragged inside, shoved, where he'd stumbled to find his balance and failed. Dropping to the ground so hard it hurt his knees. He started to remove the hood again and heard a voice say "Leave it!" so he did, waiting to find out what this was all about. He was still wracking his brains when the hood was suddenly torn off a few minutes later, his bonds cut.

It was not much brighter in this room, he had to say, and he blinked once, twice. Attempted to focus. In the light from the one bare bulb, he could see ahead of him that he wasn't the only one who'd been relieved of his facial covering. The masks that had been obscuring the men's faces were gone, revealing what they looked like. He took in a guy with jet-black hair and a white stripe running almost dead-centre over the top of his head, another one with a bald head and a handle-bar moustache, and a pair of identical twins, blond with buzz-cuts.

Blinking again, his mouth dropped open. He knew

these people, had heard of them anyway. There wasn't a person alive who hadn't heard of this crew: the Badger; Strongman; and the Twins. Trusted generals, right-hand men. Loyal servants of a particular person he'd also heard of, someone who'd been making waves over the last couple of years. Someone in line to take over the top spot, crime-lord of the whole of Glaive City.

There were footsteps now, coming from somewhere behind these men. The 'wall' parted and at last he saw their leader, stepping forward in his expensive suit and tie. Striking-looking, that was the only way to describe him; not quite model or film star good looks, because there was also a meanness present. Possibly even a hint of insanity.

"Mr Moore," the man said as he approached.

"M-M-Mr Miller, sir," Moore replied, still on his knees.

The man's eyes tilted downwards. "You look like you're begging down there. *Are* you begging?"

"M-M-Mr Miller?"

The mob-boss smiled and it was a chilling sight. "Because that won't help you, you know."

Moore looked from Badger to the Twins and then Strongman in turn, searching their faces for an answer, and couldn't find one. In the end he returned his gaze to Miller. "I-I don't—"

"The pawnbrokers on the corner of 12th. Ring any bells?"

Moore's mouth fell open again and he shook his head. Miller nodded to Strongman who came round the side of Moore and smacked him in the head.

"How about now? Those bells ringing yet?" They definitely were, had been as soon as Miller mentioned the place. The faint memory of a bell hanging over a shop doorway. "I expect there are a few little birds flying round your head as well, tweeting." Miller whistled then, doing a bird call, and laughed. "There's no point lying to us, Mr Moore. We know exactly who you are and what you did. Bit off your patch, wasn't it? Petty thief and all that."

Moore swallowed dryly. He knew exactly what this was about too, and brought his hands together again even though they were no longer bound. "I... Mr Miller, please. I had no idea that was... If I'd known it was... then I'd have—"

"Praying now, is it?" Miller interrupted. "That won't help you either. There's only one god around here and he's not in a very forgiving mood."

"I'll... I can pay it all back. Tell you where the money is." Moore was beginning to regret his ambitions, eyes too big for his belly. Should have stuck to picking pockets, to hitting marks on the street. What the fuck had made him think graduating to robbing a place like that was a good idea?

Because he knew it bought and sold quality items, knew there'd be a decent amount of money on the premises. And there had been, in the till. In the safe under the counter, which he'd made the man with glasses open and unload at gunpoint. Plenty of cash all right, but laundered; the place a front for Miller's other operations. One of many, Moore suspected now. Oh, he was bargaining with that money, but a lot of it had gone already. He'd splashed out on drugs – there was a new one on the market, 'Trip', which offered exactly that, the *ultimate* trip, but cost a bit – and various other pleasures. His tastes were quite singular in that department, and again that took bucks.

"Light-fingered, isn't that what they call it?" There were mumbles of agreement from Miller's men. "Although yours look a little chubby there, a bit on the heavy side, Mr Moore. Perhaps we can help you with that."

In seconds, the Twins were on Moore's other side. One held his arm, the other grabbed his hand. The second twin was holding something and when Moore looked down he saw it was a set of very sharp gardening shears. "*No!* No, please! I'm sorry, Mr Miller. I'm—"

His scream filled the room as the second twin cut off the little finger of his right hand. "Snip-snip, Mr Moore. That's how it's done," said Miller.

Another finger was separated from the hand and fell to the floor, accompanied by a further scream.

"Oh, do cut it out," quipped Miller. "Do you get it? Cut it out?" He chortled at his own joke, but was drowned out by more cries. "Or should I say off?" Moore was in agony, almost on the point of blacking out, but Strongman slapped his face to keep him awake. Surely someone could hear him? But he knew better than that; Miller's men had driven him somewhere they couldn't be heard. This room was probably soundproofed.

The twin switched to the other hand, in search of more digits to detach. If he was lucky, and right now Moore didn't really feel very lucky at all, they'd leave it at that. Fingers, a warning. And for a few moments, when Miller held up a hand for them to pause, it looked like they might be done.

Then the man bent down, gazing at Moore, and said: "I think it's time to get started, don't you?"

At some point during what happened next, Moore did black out a few times, then finally for good.

In the dark once again.

* * * * *

Night-time had fallen, darkness descending over the city.

Not that you'd know it because the lights from the squad cars were illuminating the scene. Yellow tape separated this side-street from the road, from rubberneckers desperate to see what was going on. What had been found.

If they were to get a better look, they might not be too fond of what they saw, thought Adlard. Newly-promoted Detective Henry Adlard, called to the scene, called away from home, actually, just as Emily was dishing up a delicious pie for dinner. He wished he was back there at the table with her, looking at that beautiful face instead of this ugly mess.

Relishing how good that pie looked, breaking into it, with meat and juices spilling out. Though he guessed that if he was back there now, he'd have lost his appetite. Not least because of the similarities between that pie and this guy's head. This unidentified guy's head.

Adlard pulled his longcoat a bit tighter around him, pulled down the brim of his fedora. "So, what're we thinking? Suicide?" said someone beside him. His partner, Davis, scratching at that pockmarked skin of his, which always looked vaguely diseased. Adlard said nothing back. "Anyone who lived around here would want to top themselves. I'm thinking suicide," repeated Davis, looking up at the rooftop where the body had come from.

"Suicide?" Adlard turned when he heard the other

voice. Saw a fresh-faced young officer standing there. "Are you kidding?"

Adlard looked him up and down: a prime example of straight from the academy rookie. Reminded him of himself a few years and a handful of pounds ago. "And you are?" he asked.

"Wagner, sir." Adlard thought he was going to salute. "Officer Blake Wagner. Myself and my partner here…" He turned and waved to indicate the beat cop behind him, who simply shrugged. "We were first on the scene, called it in."

"So you're to blame for me missing dinner with my wife, Wagner?" said Adlard. The young guy looked like he was going to apologise, but Adlard batted it away; he hadn't been serious anyway. *Of course* this needed to be called in. It was a dead body, suicide or no suicide. "You don't agree with Detective Davis' assessment of the situation, I take it?"

Wagner shook his head. "Anyone can see that's not what happened here. The guy didn't just throw himself off that roof."

"Oh? Care to tell us how you reached that conclusion?" asked Adlard.

"Well, for one thing he had fingers missing on his right and left hands." Adlard looked again. He'd been so focussed on the face, that mashed up pie of a face, he hadn't even noticed the hands. But now Wagner came to mention it, this fellow *was* missing some of his fingers.

"Might have been born like that for all we know," Davis chipped in. "A disability, industrial accident or somethin'."

"They look like fresh wounds to me, sir," Wagner

continued, though Adlard wasn't sure whether he was addressing him or his partner. "And if someone had, say, roughed up the vic, what better way to try and conceal the fact than tossing him off a rooftop?"

Adlard looked from Wagner to Davis; the kid had a point. Definitely reminded the detective of himself when he first started out, full of energy and principles. Before this city got its hooks into him, seeped into his blood. Before he learned to look the other way, especially when people like Diseased Davis were taking kickbacks. Not that Adlard got involved in all that, he still had *some* principles, it was just that there was nothing be done about it. You couldn't really get away from shit like that, and it was best to just keep your head down rather than try and fight it. Pick your battles.

"Or the opposite could be true," the young cop added.

"How so?" asked Adlard.

"This could have been staged. A serial killer maybe?" It was Wagner's turn to shrug. "Dunno."

It sounded like he did know, sounded very much like he knew exactly what he was talking about – had some good instincts. A detective's instincts, which was something to encourage, wasn't it? Nothing to apologise for.

Davis chuckled. "A serial killer? Come *on!* I still say this was a suicide."

Now Wagner was addressing Adlard and Adlard alone: "Will there be a post-mortem at all, sir?"

Adlard opened his mouth and closed it, then nodded. There was bound to be, dotting the i's and crossing the t's. The department was nothing if not thorough with its procedures, on paper at any rate.

"Would it be possible to attend? Or failing that maybe take a look at the results?"

"A look at the..." Davis nudged Adlard with his elbow. "Is he for fucking real?"

Wagner said nothing, just waited for the answer, which was, "I'll see what I can do."

Davis let out a grunt, then muttered, "Suicide, I'm telling you!" The young cop said something himself then under his breath. "What was that?"

Another shrug, and Wagner pretended to cough. "Just clearing my throat."

But Adlard had heard him clearly enough. It hadn't been a swear word, calling Davis a name or anything. He'd said: "Wasn't suicide. This was a message."

And the more he thought about it, the more Adlard was inclined to agree.

* * * * *

Everything had led him here.

His investigations, in his own time of course, and because nobody else appeared to be looking into all this. Nobody else seemed to care. Blake entered, ignoring the bell that rang above him, looking left and right. He hadn't been stupid enough to come here in uniform, same as he hadn't been asking around on the streets wearing his blues.

That had been interesting, and he'd almost come unstuck – when he'd been jumped by that gang of thugs after he'd been asking questions of the homeless people warming themselves by some flames in a barrel.

"I smell bacon!" a guy who with no discernible neck had barked, before lunging at him.

Blake hadn't been prepared to deal with so many at once, not even with his skills, and they'd got a couple of lucky punches in which had floored him, then proceeded to start kicking the prone figure.

Blake had searched around for the leader, because taking him out would make the others fold, he was positive of that – but he just couldn't *tell* who was in charge. Mention of the vic's name had apparently been enough, and it was only then that the true leader of this pack revealed themselves.

Herself.

"Moore? What about him?" she'd asked. Her name had been Gail, hair woofed up and wearing a leather corset that wouldn't have looked out of place at one of the strip joints in the place they called 'Little Vegas' around here.

"I'm..." Blake sucked in a breath or three. "I'm trying to find out who killed him." Moore, the petty thief who'd been ID'd later on, a post-mortem showing that his system was full of a drug called Trip that Blake hadn't even heard of. Detective Adlard had been as good as his word, making a point of catching him at the precinct – same as the chief had done when he started – to fill him in. Blake liked to think he was a good judge of character and this fellow seemed okay, which was more than could be said for his prick of a partner who'd spotted the exchange and barged in.

"What the fuck, Henry? Why are you even bothering with this runt?"

"It's called the sharing of departmental information, Davis."

"None of his business," the pockmarked man had growled.

"He asked to be kept informed. I'm just giving him the broad strokes," Adlard argued.

"So, some lowlife creep got high and took a walk off a building. So what?"

"Cutting his own fingers off first?" Blake had queried.

"Guys whacked out like that, they don't know what they're doing. You're not still carping on about your serial killer theory, are you?" Blake said nothing. "If he was killed – and I mean if – then whoever did it was doing us a favour. Hey," he said, nudging his partner again – he was fond of doing that – "maybe Glaive City has its very own vigilante ridding the streets of scum!"

"That'll be the day," said Adlard.

"They'd put a freaking statue up of him!" Davis said, chortling, nudging Adlard a final time. Blake had thanked the detectives anyway for keeping him in the loop, then been told by Davis as Adlard was wandering off: "Now you leave it be, okay?"

No. Not okay. This Moore character might have been a thief, but he hadn't deserved what had happened to him. What had been done to him. It was up to the law to decide his punishment, not ordinary civilians. And why was Davis so keen on him leaving this be in the first place? That just made Blake even more suspicious.

Which had led him to the streets, to the thugs, to Gail. "You're trying to find out who killed Moore? Why?"

Blake wobbled as he got to his feet, jutted out his jaw and told her, "Because it's the right thing to do."

They'd all laughed, including Gail. "Moore brought

this on himself," she said, hands on her hips. Then she looked down sadly. "Though I'm not sure what little Flint is going to do now."

"Little… Moore has a son?"

Another laugh. "I'm not sure you'd call him that, but he sorta looks out for him. In return for certain favours, if you catch my drift."

Blake's lip curled. Maybe Moore *had* deserved his fate, after all. Maybe he'd deserved worse? Had this been the work of a vigilante after all, as Davis had joked? Still, Blake needed to follow this wherever it went. See it through. "I can give you money for information." He'd brought some along, what was left of his meagre savings. And yes, it had chosen that moment to start raining; though to be fair it did that a lot in Glaive.

"Honey, we'll be taking that anyway," Gail informed him. Then she paused, and gave him the address. It was a place Moore had robbed recently; it appeared that the community here, no matter how crooked, still looked out for each other. Honour amongst thieves and all that. "But you might not want to go poking that particular hornet's nest. If you take my advice you'll steer clear. Pretty guy like you could get real messed up."

"That a threat?" asked Blake.

"It's a warning, sweetheart," she told him bluntly, then nodded and her underlings had given him another beating as a parting gift, relieving him of the money he'd had in his pocket. But he'd got the address. An address which led him to this pawnbrokers on the corner of 12th.

Blake examined a few items on display: an electric guitar, a couple of ornaments – picking them up and checking out the prices. Out of his range, definitely.

"Excuse me." Blake turned and saw a thin man in glasses standing not far away. "Can I help you?"

Blake smiled. "Oh, I do hope so," he replied.

* * * * *

As he left, looking up at the bell which rang again, Wagner didn't see the man in the car opposite.

The man who'd followed him here, who'd been watching him for a while and watched now as the young man got back on his motorbike, securing his helmet and gunning the engine. The man continued to watch as Wagner rode away, then picked up the car-phone – a relatively new device in this day and age – and dialled a number.

"Yes, hello," said the man with the black hair and white stripe. "It's me. I think we might have a problem."

* * * * *

The bar was heaving.

Adlard had told the lads he'd just stop in for a couple, and only because he had a few bucks riding on the home team. It was game night and this bar was probably the safest place to be right now, mainly because it was a cop bar; Brubaker's was the closest drinking hole to their precinct, a sports bar, so it was only natural that the boys in blue would gravitate towards it in their off-time. And especially tonight.

"Henry! Henry, come and join us!" This was Davis, already a handful of pints down and starting in on the vodka shots.

"I can't stay too long, I promised Emily."

"Henpecked!" shouted Davis, jostling his arm. "That's what you are. Need to put that little lady in her place."

Adlard said nothing. Emily knew her place, and that was beside him. Same as his was beside her. A partnership in every sense of the word. He was lucky to have her and he knew it, would definitely rather be at home with her than here in this noisy, sweaty establishment with Davis breathing fumes into his face. That said, him and his better half had fallen out a few times lately, mainly because they'd been trying for a baby for several months and nothing was happening.

"You can't rush these things," Adlard kept telling her, all the while thinking that maybe it was the universe trying to tell them not to bring a child into this world. Into this city. It was no place to bring a kid up and in their hearts they both knew it.

Davis nudged his shoulder. "Relax, relax. Have a drink!" He gave Adlard a pint glass which was slopping over with amber liquid.

"Thanks," he told his partner, who after all this time still apparently couldn't get his head around the fact Adlard preferred to sip a nice whiskey and maybe have a game or two of cards in good company.

Davis turned back to the group he'd been chatting with before Adlard walked in, waiting for the game to kick off. With a bit of luck he'd forget that Adlard was there at all. Casting his gaze over the scene, the detective spotted faces he recognised, including their chief, Mack, who always liked to spend time with his troops.

Then there he was, a young man he hadn't seen in a little while but who he'd been meaning to catch up with: Wagner. Officer Blake Wagner, in the corner booth – a part of this, yet so far apart from it he might as well have been sitting outside in the middle of the street. Quietly detaching himself, Adlard pushed past his colleagues and made his way over to the other side of the bar, squeezing between a couple of cops who were still in uniform – either had just finished, or were just going on their shifts. He hoped it was the former.

There were noticeable spaces on either side and opposite Wagner. Might have been because it was notoriously hard to see the screens from that angle, or more likely it was because he had a face like a wet weekend. Hardly getting into the spirit of things, just gazing down at the tumbler clutched in his hand, a generous amount of brown liquid sloshing around in the bottom as he swirled it.

"Brandy?" asked Adlard, raising his voice slightly so he could be heard over the crowd.

It took Wagner a second or two before he noticed the man was even standing there, then he said, "What?"

Adlard nodded at the glass. "Brandy, or—"

"Bourbon," replied Wagner.

"Ah, man after my own heart. Although I do love a nice Irish single malt." He caught Wagner looking at the beer in his own glass. "Oh, Davis," he told him, which was explanation enough. "Mind if I…" Now he nodded at the seat opposite the young man, who nodded himself, then thought about it and shook his head, extending his hand in case his meaning was unclear. "Cheers. Haven't seen you around lately, Wagner."

"Been keeping my head down, getting on with the job."

"Keeping yourself busy, certainly," said Adlard. "Making a few waves in the process, so I hear."

Wagner's eyes narrowed. "You checking up on me, Detective?"

"No need. You've not exactly been discreet." He took a swig of the beer and pulled a face. "Been doing a bit of digging, off-books so I heard."

"There's no…" Wagner laughed. "No law against it."

"If there was you'd have to arrest yourself." Adlard laughed now, but Wagner didn't join in. "Depends on how much you dig. How hard you push things."

Now Wagner grinned. "How about as hard as you need to?"

"Look, I get it. I was your age once; you want to make an impression. Just be careful it's not the wrong one."

Wagner drank some of his bourbon. "By trying to get to the truth, looking into what happened to your man Moore."

Adlard scratched his head. It had been a couple of months or so since he'd heard that name; the case had stalled as far as he could recall. "Why the interest in some drugged-up bum?"

"Because, regardless of what your partner kept insisting, it wasn't suicide. He was killed, revenge for turning over a pawnbrokers."

The detective frowned. "What?"

Wagner lowered his voice, so Adlard could just about hear him. "You heard of a guy called Miller, sir?"

Of course he had, everyone in Glaive City had heard

of that maniac! One of the biggest mob-bosses around, tipped for the head job one day. "You're telling me it was Miller who shoved him off a building?"

"Not before pumping him full of Trip and cutting off his fingers," Wagner informed his superior. "See, the pawnbrokers I was talking about is just the tip of the iceberg, part of a money laundering racket that takes in prostitution – which relies on human trafficking, by the way – illegal gambling and the distribution of Trip."

Adlard held up his glass, tipped it in Wagner's direction. "I suppose they told you all about this at the pawnbrokers?"

Wagner shook his head. "Like I say, just the tip of the iceberg – and I *have* been busy."

"Listen kid, a lot of that is common knowledge. Maybe not the whys and wherefores, but anyone with half a brain knows to leave things like that well enough alone."

"Especially if they're getting paid to look the other way?"

Adlard touched his chest. "You're barking up the wrong neck of the woods there."

"But it happens, I've discovered. It's happening right now, sadly. How many of the cops in this bar are on the take? Owned by who knows who? How about Detective Davis, where do his loyalties lie?" Wagner asked, looking around the room just as a cheer went up for a touchdown.

Waiting until the noise died down, Adlard said, "You've been here, what, a couple of months, three? You don't know how things work in Glaive yet."

"And you've forgotten how things work," Wagner replied. "How they *should* work."

"Hey, now wait just a—"

"Do you know what was left in my locker the other day, Detective? A big bag of money, just sitting there in my private locker at work."

Adlard rubbed his forehead. "Christ Almighty. What did you do?"

"What do you think? I ran it up to the top. Handed it in to the chief."

That was the other possible reason he was sitting alone then; the rumours Adlard had heard were true. Not only was this kid stirring the pot, making accusations about corruption in the force – whether they were accurate or not was neither here nor there – he'd also very publicly handed in a bribe. A bribe that had more than likely originated from Miller. "Do you think that was wise?"

Wagner shrugged. "It was the right thing to do." And in spite of what he thought of Wagner's actions, Adlard couldn't help admiring them too. "As police officers we need to be beyond reproach, we need to make a difference. To *be* different. Otherwise what's the point of us?"

"We also need to pick our battles, kid." Adlard sighed. "All this because of some piece of gutter trash!"

"That was only the start, like I said. And it's about what's right."

The detective took another gulp of his beer, his mouth suddenly very dry. "Think about the escalation. You don't just declare war on someone like Miller, not without backup."

Wagner leaned over the table. "Then help me, sir."

"I'm *trying* to help you. Trying to warn you that—"

"Help me by being my backup. Remember why you got into this in the first place."

"You know nothing about me," Adlard replied.

"I'm—"

"Well, isn't this cosy?" said a voice beside them, making them both start. Someone leaning over the back of the booth. "Watchya talking about, fellas?"

"Nothing, Davis. Just modern policing methods."

"Sounds like a laugh-riot. Hey!" He nudged Adlard's shoulder, almost causing him to spill his drink. "You should come and check out the game. Could be in for a win tonight!"

Wagner looked at him then. It was just a bet, an under the counter wager, but the disappointment in his eyes was palpable.

Prostitution… Illegal gambling. We need to be beyond reproach.

Adlard sighed again. "See you around, kid. Take care."

Wagner held up his glass as a goodbye. But even as he was being led back over to the main screen showing the game, Adlard couldn't help looking back at him. At the young man with more balls than he'd ever had. Who was willing to stand by his morals no matter what. No matter where it led.

But that was the problem, wasn't it. Where all this would lead, the escalation.

Where it would all end up.

* * * * *

It was so dark in there, he could hardly see.

Blake edged forwards, Ellis bringing up the rear – having mounted the steps to get to this level. But it would be worth it, *so* worth it. Finally, a chance to catch these people in the act…

He'd been in the process of grabbing coffees for him and his partner when the call came in. Blake had been right about that guy, a family man with real values and someone he could really relate to – he'd not only learned a lot from him, the pair had become quite good friends. "Wagner," Ellis had shouted over to him. "Wagner, get your ass over here!"

Blake had rushed across the road, still carrying the takeaways in both hands. "What's going on?" he asked.

"We just got a heads up on a major Trip operation over at the old waste plant."

"Trip…"

"Multiple units are heading that way. Come on, get in!"

Blake didn't need telling twice; he'd dropped the cups on the ground and clambered in. They were heading in sirens off, so it didn't give anyone a chance to get away. This was exactly what Blake had been waiting for, a chance to take down one of Miller's ventures and it had fallen right into his lap. What's more, they'd be going in en masse. There was no way the authorities would have been able to ignore something this big, no way those who'd been bought off could get out of the raid. That's why it had been last minute, he figured, to avoid any tip-offs and catch the culprits red-handed.

Ellis had drawn up round the back of the ageing industrial-looking place: the perfect location to set up a Trip 'factory'. And Blake had been out seconds after that, popping the boot to grab a shot-gun. "Wait, hang on, Wagner. We can't go in yet. We should wait for the rest of—"

"They'll be here soon. They can always catch up!" Blake had told him, tossing the man a shot-gun of his own. "We need to get in there, right now." He suddenly realised he was talking to a superior officer rather than just his partner and added: "Don't we? Before it's too late? At least check it out?" It was crucial that they move in, stop anyone from destroying evidence that could tie this place to Miller. It was a dream op, a dream come true! And he wasn't about to let it slip through his fingers. Ellis nodded, somewhat reluctantly.

So, they'd gone in, beginning their search on the ground floor, and finding nothing but rusty piping, old conveyor belts and empty barrels. Not a soul around, but then this place was supposedly abandoned, and it would be the perfect cover in case anyone just wandered in. Blake had pointed upwards, for them to ascend the steps. That's when it started to get dark, moving up and along the corridor on the upper level. Blake had reached for the torch on his belt, flicking it on and flashing it around ahead. The corridor leading towards what looked like offices. That had to be it, the centre of this operation.

He cast a glance over his shoulder to see Ellis still following, but shaking his head. Wanting to hold off, maybe even go back.

"What?" whispered Blake.

"I don't like this. Where's the damned backup?" the older man said in hushed tones, looking nervously over his own shoulder.

Blake would have been lying if he said it wasn't a concern, but the thought of swooping in on these bastards was overriding everything. Stopping him from seeing straight. He gripped his shot-gun tighter, the torch clacking against its barrel, then made the decision to push on ahead, through those doors into the offices. He kicked them open to find—

The remains of an operation: tables covered in empty test-tubes and trays; plastic baggies and needles. If there'd been Trip here, and the people who made the stuff, they were long gone. It was only then that he heard it, the noise from behind. The loud crack of a gunshot.

"*Ellis!*" Blake called out, turned and—

Was struck on the side of the head by something, sending his cap flying. The butt of a pistol maybe? "I wouldn't worry about him," said a gruff voice. "He's been taken care of." Then he was hit again: hard. Blake lowered his shot-gun, and tried to raise it, but the weapon was kicked out of his hands along with his torch.

Darkness again. He reached for his side-arm and was kicked once more, this time in the stomach, knocking him backwards into the offices where he collided with the edge of a table. "There's... There are more of us coming!" he tried to say, but it came out as a series of wheezes because he'd been winded.

A light came on, a small bulb, and he saw that there were men in the room with him. Three... No, *four* men. Two were identical, boasting a revolver apiece, both with pearl handles; another had black hair with a white stripe running through it; and the last – bald with a moustache – rushed him, even as Blake was still attempting to get his gun out of its holster. He grabbed Blake's wrist with one hand, hauled him into the air next with the other. Jesus, the guy was *strong!*

Blake managed to free his pistol but couldn't hold on

to it; the gun fell uselessly from his grasp.

He was slammed down onto the floor again with such force he thought the huge man might have broken his back. Blake let out a moan, rolling and then moaning again in pain.

"Officer Wagner, we meet at last," said another voice, a lighter altogether more playful one.

He looked up through watery eyes to see a further figure, a newcomer in the room, standing there in an expensive suit with his hands behind his back. The man was grinning, stepping forwards, but only slightly. Letting the others cover him, protect him. The leader of this little band. The leader he'd been on the trail of for some time.

"Miller," Blake spat.

"I'm flattered, truly I am. It's not often uniformed officers take a special interest in my activities. Following your little clues, putting two and two together, working things out. How exciting! And so, here you find yourself at the waste disposal plant, where I get rid of all my unwanted rubbish." He laughed and the sound was like a million of those needles on the tables sticking in Blake at the same time. "I would say unwanted shit, but it isn't that kind of place. It's… My family started off in this game, did you know that? Oh, they didn't own a plant or anything; they worked in one, night and day to scrape a living. So it's kind of familiar territory for me… Now, where was I? Oh yeah, your Nancy Drew-ing. Impressive. Irritating but impressive. Here's the thing, though, I kinda like you. You're tenacious. That's how you've lasted this long, that's why I sent you that token of appreciation. How sad that you rejected it."

"Go to hell!" said Blake.

"Wait, *wait!*" Miller barked. "You didn't let me finish! That's better. You're lucky I'm such a tolerant man."

"Tell that to Moore."

"Moore?" Miller looked confused and one of his men had to remind him who that was. "Oh, that parasite! Why are you wasting time worrying about *him*?" Miller looked around. "Actually, it was in a room just like this one down there a ways that we had our fun with that particular piece of garbage." He laughed out loud, clapping. "Such fun: snipetty, snip! Now, let's *cut* to the chase, shall we?" Another chuckle at his own warped sense of humour. "There's a place here for you, Wagner, in my merry little band. Should you so wish."

"I-I'd rather die!" Blake told him.

Miller cocked his head. "That can be arranged. But not before a little more fun, eh?" He brought one of his hands round to the front, and it was holding a metal canister. "You know what this is?"

Blake frowned, then replied: "Trip? You going to dose me up like you did with Moore?"

"Again with the Moore bullshit, you're obsessed!" Miller held the container up higher; light from the bulb reflected off its shiny surface. "No, this is a little something they used to use here back in the day, to dissolve the more stubborn substances. Works a treat on flesh as well. Makes quite a mess, so I'm told." He nodded to the twins, who moved forwards – tucking their weapons away in their underarm holsters. "Gentlemen, if you'd be so good as to strip Officer Wagner for me. It's nothing kinky, I promise."

When they were close enough, blocking off the larger man who'd taken him down initially, Blake spotted his opportunity. He rose quickly, kicking out the knee of one of the twins and bringing the flat of his hand up and into the chin of the other. The two remaining men acted quickly, rushing to take the place of their companions – but it was the leader Blake was lunging for. Always the leader! Almost reached him too, before the strong guy and white-stripe got hold of him.

Miller, who'd appeared shocked for a moment, almost scared, regained his composure. "Ha, you'll pay for that!" he warned.

Then he spotted the gun. One of a pair with matching pearl handles Blake had stolen from the second twin as he'd been striking him. Two shots, but instead of hitting the chest he'd been aiming for, because white-stripe was pulling down Blake's arm, they went high.

Hitting Miller in the head, one penetrating his cheek, the second an eye on the other side. He let out an almighty howl, dropping the metal container in the process.

"Shit! The boss!" growled the strong man, rushing to his side and crouching.

Blake, meanwhile, was relieved of his weapon – which was handed back to its owner, who promptly shot him in the stomach. For the first few seconds he felt nothing, then came the pain. Waves of agonising pain.

"H-He's still alive." This was the second twin. For a second Blake thought they were talking about him, but it was Miller they were gathering around. "What do we do?"

"Get him out of here, get him some help!" shouted white-stripe.

"Wait… Wait," said the bald guy with the moustache leaning over their prone leader. "He's saying something. What? I can't—" He rose slowly, and one of the twins asked what he'd said. The strong man looked down at the canister. "He said to fuck him up."

One of the blond twins bent and snatched up the container, while the other one went over to Blake, began tugging at his clothes, pulling them off. The young policeman tried to stop him, but they put another bullet in him and the pain was simply too much.

He was vaguely aware of the strong man carrying Miller off, before white-stripe hoved into view. "This," he said, "now this is for our boss. And it's going to be your worst nightmare, pig!" The blond twin with the canister handed it to white-stripe, who finished unscrewing the top, revealing a nozzle.

Then Blake realised that the pain he'd felt before was just a shadow. Because soon he understood what real pain was.

What real darkness was, too.

* * * * *

It was dark when he woke.

Was disturbed by the shrill ringing of the phone, his wife stirring beside him and asking who it was.

"Give me a second and I'll find out," managed Adlard groggily, rolling over and snatching the receiver off the cradle. "Yeah, this is he." The detective listened to what was being said, then sat bolt upright, hanging up. Swung his legs immediately out of bed and was getting dressed by the time Emily asked him again:

"Who was it?"

The only answer he gave was, "I have to go."

And before she could say any more, he'd already

206

gone.

Adlard drove with the siren on top of his new Mustang blaring, breaking the speed limits to reach his destination.

He'd been told that a badly wounded Ellis had played dead and called in what had happened as soon as the people who'd shot him departed. He'd been mumbling something about backup apparently, which hadn't arrived.

It had all the markings of a trap. Not to get to Ellis, but to take out another person. Someone who'd been poking his nose into things he shouldn't have done, someone who'd paid for that with his life. Jesus, hadn't Adlard tried to warn the kid! Hadn't he told him how this would pan out eventually?

One ambulance passed him as he got there, heading out, probably whisking Ellis off to the hospital to be looked at. Another one arrived not long after Adlard pulled up. He was out then and making his way through the sea of cop cars and uniformed officers, wondering where they'd all been when this was going down.

"Help me by being my backup. Remember why you got into this in the first place."

"You don't want to go any further, Detective," a black officer informed him. "It's a bad scene up there. Shot him a bunch of times, sprayed him with some kind of acid. Sprayed him in the face!"

Adlard tried to swallow, but found he couldn't. That poor kid...

He waited there while the ambo guys went in and it wasn't long before they emerged with the corpse, on a gurney and covered over with a blanket. But not all the way. The closer they came, the more Adlard could see that the face – what was left of it – wasn't covered. When he pushed past more uniformed officers, flashing his badge around, he asked one of the paramedics what the situation was.

"Faint pulse. God knows how, but it's there." The woman looked down at the victim's face and Adlard thought she was going to throw up on the spot. He couldn't say he really blamed her. "Are you a relative of his, Detective? A friend?"

"I'm…" Adlard realised he didn't quite know how to answer that. He didn't know anything about Wagner's family, wasn't even sure he had any – certainly not in the city, not near enough to get here quickly – but as for whether he was his friend? He'd chatted to him maybe two or three times, liked the kid, had got the shout because he was one of the plainclothes officers on call and it had looked like homicide. Turned out that was premature, at least for now.

"Detective?"

"I'll ride with him, if that's okay?" said Adlard. The female paramedic nodded and when she and her colleague had loaded Wagner in the back, Adlard climbed in with the woman and sat next to his 'friend'. Figured that if he didn't have long left, somebody should at least be with him.

Then they'd slammed the doors and gotten underway, with more sirens blaring.

The kid had made some weird noises along the way, struggling to breathe Adlard assumed – and he was given oxygen several times by the paramedic, in-between trying to clean his burns. But at one point Adlard distinctly heard a name. One that he immediately recognised; one he wasn't surprised at all to be on this man's lips.

"M-Miller," he whispered, almost inaudibly…

"Miller."

It had been a long wait.

Adlard had called Emily up and let her know the score, told her what was going on because this was going to take some time.

"Oh… Oh Henry, I'm so sorry. Poor boy. Were you two close?"

"We… Not especially, but something's telling me I need to be here, sweetheart." Guilt perhaps? a little voice said and he stomped on it.

"Then you do what you need to do. Do what's right." Too late for that… She asked if he wanted her to come down there as well, but Adlard told her to try and get some sleep instead. No point the both of them being awake all night. As it transpired, it was the middle of the next day before there was any news. A hand shook him where he sat in the visitors' lounge, slumping, having dropped off sometime after they'd informed him Wagner was in surgery.

Standing before him was a small guy in blue scrubs and a white coat, hands in his pockets. "Detective Adlard? Sorry to… I'm told you're here with Officer Wagner?"

Adlard rubbed his eyes, nodded, and got to his feet.

"I'm Doctor Yost," said the man extending his hand, which Adlard shook.

"What's happening, doc?" he asked.

"We finished operating not long ago, managed to remove the bullets and stabilize the patient. There was considerable damage to the spinal column, however."

"And what…?"

Yost looked at the ground. "It means it's highly unlikely Officer Wagner will ever walk again, I'm afraid."

"Christ," breathed out Adlard, rubbing his face. As if the kid didn't have enough fucking problems. Thinking that, he asked suddenly: "And the other… His skin?"

Yost looked him in the eye again. "We washed off the corrosive substance until it was all gone."

Not for the first time since he'd received the call, Adlard found himself having trouble swallowing, his mouth like the Sahara. Corrosive substance. For the love of—

"We'll continue to treat the wounds, the burns – and will cover them with the appropriate dressings when we're able. He'll be on a high dose of painkillers for some time to come, pretty much out of it and not up to visitors yet. The next twenty-four hours will be the most telling though; if he gets through those then he stands a fighting chance of waking up. All things considered and after what he's gone through, he's been pretty lucky so far I'd say."

Adlard's eyes went wide. "Lucky? You're kidding, doc. Crippled, his skin… Shot so many times…"

Yost still nodded. "We almost lost him at several junctures during this procedure alone, Detective. In fact, technically he died for over six minutes once back there, but we managed to pull him back from the brink."

Even as he thanked the doctor, shaking his hand once more, Adlard couldn't help thinking, and he immediately felt ashamed as it passed through his mind, that it might have been better – for everyone, but for Wagner especially – if they'd just let the poor fucker go headlong over that brink.

If they'd just let him die.

* * * * *

The first week was touch and go.

Wagner had to be resuscitated a few times, once when Adlard was visiting – because he came in as often as he could, fitting it around work, and every day back then. Wagner had crashed and Adlard had been asked quite firmly to leave, so that the team could come into his private room and work on him.

They'd pulled the kid through that one, and the others. Back from the brink any number of times. And it crossed the detective's mind again during those early days that they should just call it and leave the guy alone. It was almost like he was trying to get back to that state, trying to find peace – eternal peace? – because even with the amount of painkillers he was on he must have been in agony.

Nevertheless, he hung in there. Later on, Adlard would be grateful for that and when he looked back was even more ashamed of wishing young Wagner would just depart this mortal plane. Because when he was more with it, when he finally woke up – covered in bandages, with a long road of skin grafts ahead of him they'd been told – the pair of them had become quite close. Chatting and playing cards when Wagner was able, shooting the breeze and avoiding the obvious mammoths in the room.

It wasn't just that Wagner had no family in the city, he had none left at all. Perhaps that was why Adlard kept on coming to the hospital, or maybe it was because he was frightened that the person who'd done this would send others to finish the job off – and after Wagner had fought so hard to hang on to life, as well.

"M-Miller."

That said, word must have gotten back by now to that outfit about the state this kid was in. The damage the acid had done, the fact he was crippled for life – confirmed by this time, Yost telling Wagner, "I'm afraid it's pretty much definite, the trauma was just too severe. I'm really sorry. But you'll never walk again." – the amount of times he'd already died, something that had left him with only a vague recollection of the events leading up to what happened.

"It's all… Every time I try to remember, it just slips away from me," he'd said time and again to anyone who'd listen. Adlard had to wonder if that was entirely the truth, or was Wagner thinking the same thing as him: that any hint he might remember would result in another attempt on his life? He'd remembered enough in the ambulance to utter that name:

"M-Miller."

But only Adlard had heard it, had kept the information to himself for that self-same reason. And one of the first things Wagner had asked about was Ellis, whether his old partner was still alive.

"He's doing… okay," Adlard told him, leaving out the 'better than you' bit. "Stopped a couple. Will be on desk duty for a good while, if not for the rest of his career. But at least he managed to radio in. That's what probably saved… saved your life."

Davis had cropped up one time when Adlard had been there as well, but he hadn't entered the room. Had the decency to wait outside till Adlard surfaced. "How's the kid doing?" he asked.

Adlard felt like replying, "Why do you care?" because his partner hadn't asked on the job about Wagner once. "How do you think?" had been his actual reply.

Davis nodded sombrely, then grinned. "Could've been worse though, eh?"

"How d'you figure?"

"Well, it could've been one of us, Henry, eh?" He nudged his partner and Adlard gave him a look that said, 'I think you're done here' which was probably why he fucked off out of it not long afterwards.

Chief Mack also paid Wagner a visit, apologising profusely for what had happened. "We let you down son, the department as a whole. And, well, there aren't the words…" There were tears in the man's eyes as he went to take Wagner's hand, then thought twice about it. "Rest assured there'll be an internal investigation into what happened, why the backup never arrived. Oh, and compensation. A tidy little sum!' Getting that in first before Wagner even thought about suing them, a pre-emptive offer that was more money than Adlard would see in several lifetimes. Wouldn't make up for what had been done to Wagner, though.

The department had definitely let him down. But so had Adlard.

"It wasn't your fault," Wagner told the detective, though it sounded more like he was letting him off the hook than anything. Making him feel better, because he'd asked – actually asked Adlard! – for his help. For backup. And he'd told him to fucking 'take care'. Take care when he had the biggest bloody target on his back that—

Some might say that Wagner had brought it on himself, all that digging. But it wasn't something Adlard would ever say himself, not anymore. He'd only been trying to do the right thing, make a difference. Was as green as grass and had gone about it in a ham-fisted way, yes, but didn't deserve this. *Nobody* deserved this.

Adlard had visited after the first of the skin grafts, enough to know that neither this nor any in the future would make much difference given his particular affliction.

"We're not sure why, but it didn't take," a different doctor – this one a woman called Simonson – told Adlard. "Doesn't bode well, moving forwards. But new treatments are coming along all the time. You just never know."

Wagner had cried when he'd been told the news and Adlard's heart went out to him. Nobody wanted to hear they'd be disfigured like that forever – and Adlard couldn't help flashing back to when he first saw him, the mess he was in. He probably didn't look quite like that now, under those bandages which made him look like the Invisible Man, but close enough.

Then one day, once Wagner had received his pay-out, Adlard had arrived at the hospital to find the bed empty. At first he feared the worst, rushing to find a nurse.

"Has he… Did he…" Finally, and after all this time. After getting to know the kid properly, becoming if not a father figure to replace the one he'd lost, then a big brother… after all of that had they now lost him?

The auburn-haired nurse shook her head. "Don't worry, he's okay. Checked himself out this morning."

"Checked himself…?" Adlard had to wonder how, and where, Wagner might go. He definitely wasn't at home because the kid had let that flat go, had barely any possessions in it anyway and they'd all been put into storage. So…

"Did he say anything else?" Adlard asked.

"Just that he was planning on leaving town for a bit."

But then the kind of cash he now had bought a lot of privileges, could take you anywhere. Maybe he just needed to get away from the place where all this happened, and maybe that was for the best. A holiday somewhere perhaps? He'd see the kid again, Adlard was sure of that. He'd definitely see him again.

He just wasn't sure when.

Three Years Later

He knew the darkness now, intimately.

It was hard to describe, like being dragged backwards through water. Through that blackness. Not a tunnel, no light at the end of it. Or floating up out of your body, being aware of what was happening around you. Floating upwards and heading towards your loved ones. Though they were there, Blake had felt their presence; somehow knew they were around on the periphery of this, watching, keeping an eye on him.

His mother, his father.

But he'd been somewhere else, not in Heaven or Hell or whatever you believed in, whatever place you figured was waiting for you when you died. Whatever you deserved, good person or bad. And he'd led a reasonable life, he liked to think. Tried to do the right thing, which was how he'd ended up in this mess in the first place. No good deed and all that.

He was aware that he'd died, not just once but quite a few times – and over a period of time – kept being dragged back. Just until *it* was sure he was ready, the darkness. Until *it* was certain he knew what he had to do when he returned.

The mission? An agent of that darkness?

In the same way that he was aware of his parents somewhere not far away, like they were in another room or something, he'd also been aware of a presence that wanted him to do something. Wasn't very clear to start with; it was muddled, foggy, but some kind of deal had been involved. Wasn't his time yet, he had a purpose. If he was sent back, there was something he had to do.

Then he'd heard the voice from somewhere, "We're losing him again. There's no way he's coming back this time!"

Which was all the incentive Blake needed. Telling him he couldn't do something, like come back from the dead, was the one sure-fire way of getting it to happen. No way he was coming back? He'd show them. Commitment, see?

That was when he'd woken up and stayed awake, stayed alive. Back there in the hospital. When he'd been able to talk, he'd told them he couldn't remember what happened to him. It was bullshit, of course. Blake remembered every single harrowing second of it.

Being shot multiple times, then the acid on his bare skin. On his face. Oh, the torture of that! If what happened after he died was hard to describe, try getting across the anguish of something like… The burning, the smell of his own flesh dissolving. Of his humanity being stripped away, just like his clothes had been ahead of the punishment.

Words, just words. There'd be no way of making anyone understand unless they'd been through it – and nobody had. Not in exactly the same way. None who'd come back after all that, who'd been *allowed* to come back.

For a reason, a purpose. A tool, an instrument. Because whatever had been with him could see further than Blake, than human beings. Time had no meaning in the darkness, the future an open book.

What he'd become, *who* he'd become.

A lot of it had faded naturally, once he'd returned. Was bound to do, because he was alive again. Back in the world, existing. Trapped in this weakened body, in this scarred flesh. Back with Adlard, who'd been there when he opened his eyes for the first time. Who'd come back to visit again and again. Who'd become his friend, in spite of himself – because if you were going to do what he was going to do, not that he had the first clue how to make it happen, then friends were the last thing you needed. People you cared about could be used against you, and yet Blake hadn't been able to help it. He'd been… touched. Knew that it was just a guilty conscience on Adlard's behalf, at first anyway, but couldn't help liking him.

The conversations, the games of cards.

He'd missed that when it was time to leave, time to go on his journey. *Another* journey. He had things to do, things Adlard would never be able to understand. Research that would give everything away, his plans. Blake had to do this alone, or mostly alone; there would be people who'd assist him along the way, but wouldn't be able to see the big picture. Just bits of the puzzle he was piecing together, same as when he was piecing together clues about his murderer's empire. An empire in the making, one which was now complete as far as he could tell.

His enemy hadn't died, regardless of Blake's best efforts. But he had changed, become the person *he* was always meant to be. Just like Blake would be in the end. And just as that man's kingdom had grown, getting rid of the competition, so would Blake's.

It was almost time now. Almost... Then they'd see. Then they'd understand, as much as they ever could.

The darkness. He'd brought that darkness back with him.

A darkness that was about to change everything.

* * * * *

He was escorted into the darkness.

Into the black of that room, walked inside by the man at his elbow. Badger took in the person he was escorting now, the person in charge of making sure their supplies of Trip were plentiful. Making sure it reached a wider audience than just the people in Glaive City. It had been key to their taking over, that drug. Getting people hooked on it, forcing them to rely on it. Do anything for it.

"Just inside here," Badger told the stooping man.

"Why is it so dark?" asked the visitor, the person who'd been summoned.

"That's the way he likes it." There was no need to go into the whys and wherefores. "Here we are." Badger extended a hand, though wasn't sure whether the man could see it or not.

"H-Hello?" said the fellow tentatively. "Mr Miller? Are you there?"

He was there, otherwise what would be the point of bringing him?

"Mr Claremont," said a voice in the darkness that couldn't quite pronounce the name correctly. "And please, call me by my real name."

The man looked at Badger, as if asking his permission. Badger nodded. "M-Maniac," whispered Claremont.

"Better," said the voice. It was what the papers were calling him now, 'The Maniac'. Mainly because of his brutal methods, the way he'd eliminated the competition in Glaive City by massacring his opposition. The blowing up of inner-city gangster Chris Everett and his family – children and all – in their home had been a particular eye-opener. "I expect you're wondering why I called you here?"

"I…"

"The shortfall in production, Mr Claremont. You need to do better. The new facilities are adequate, I trust?" These were way out in the scrublands, away from prying eyes.

"They're… Yes, but—"

"But nothing."

Claremont sighed, stepping forward. "The workers are exhausted, you're asking too much of them."

"They can always be replaced, Mr Claremont. Anyone can be replaced." The threat wasn't lost on this man, but still he argued his case. *Brave,* thought Badger. *Stupid, but Brave.*

"They're reliable people, people we can trust."

"Are they, though?"

"They know what they're doing and they're doing their best."

"All right, all right, enough. Talk to me about the distribution problem."

Another sigh. "The security at border control is tightening up, the overheads, the bribe money you're paying is just about covering the—"

"I don't want to hear excuses, Claremont!" The 'mister' had gone now, Badger could virtually smell the anger in the air. "I want solutions!"

"I-I'm sorry, we—"

"Apologies are just as bad!"

"I'm sorry, but do you think we could have some light in here?" Badger wasn't sure who Claremont was asking, him or his boss. It didn't matter, because he got his wish – and now was probably wishing he hadn't. The lightbulb came on, showing The Maniac in all his glory. Literally, because apart from a pair of red boxers with white polka dots, he was naked as the day he was born. But that wasn't the first thing that drew attention. The first thing most people saw was that lop-sided grin, a result of being shot in the cheek. The other was the black hole where his eye had once been on the opposite side, the result of another wayward bullet. Badger remembered the day well, remembered where it had happened – in this very place where his boss insisted on spending most of his time nowadays.

Sitting on his throne, as he was now. A throne not of gold, but made up of random objects, junk to anyone else: bits of old bicycles, washing machines, a couple of tennis racquets, a TV screen at the end of each arm.

Instead of expelling a breath now, Claremont sucked one in at the crazy sight ahead of him. Especially when he saw what the man was holding. "Okay, okay. Let's get down to brass tacks. I could give a shit about the rest of it, honestly, but do you have any more of that batch you cooked up for us last month?"

Claremont was still staring and Badger coughed to snap him out of it. He'd been the same the first time he'd seen his boss, after the surgeries. "But sir, that was a bad batch. It killed the test subjects. Or sent them mad."

"Yes...?" said The Maniac, as if waiting for the punchline to a joke. "And?"

"And you want *more* of that?"

"Of course!" snapped the man on the throne. "What did I just say?"

"I-I'm not sure I—"

Now it was The Maniac's turn to let out a big sigh. "This is getting boring, it's simply no fun at all!" He got up and covered the distance between them. Claremont attempted to back up, but Badger placed a hand on his back to stop him. The meeting wasn't over yet. The Maniac raised what was in his left hand first, then his right. "Today's programme, Claremont," he said, wrenching his head back towards those TVs embedded in the 'throne', "is brought to us by the words katana and Uzi."

Because those were the objects he was gripping in his fists: a sword and a gun. And before Claremont could say another word, The Maniac struck. The Uzi pumped bullet after bullet into the stooping man, causing him to dance like some kind of puppet, whilst at the same time his blade swished through the air. It not only lopped off Claremont's head in one swift movement, it apparently cut his strings because the body dropped to the ground with a thud.

Badger and The Maniac watched as a round shape flew though the air. "Now that's what I call an overhead!"

said the latter, quick as a flash, and guffawed at his own quip. The object hadn't even landed before Badger was being addressed. "Sort this mess out, would you?" It wasn't clear whether he meant clean up the mess on the floor, or the mess Claremont had apparently made with the Trip business. Possibly both.

Badger nodded. Someone at the facility in the scrublands was about to get promoted, and he hoped they made a better job of things than Claremont.

He looked down at where the round thing had ended up, coming to a rest just shy of the throne. Saw dead eyes staring back at him.

Otherwise, he thought to himself, more heads would definitely roll.

* * * * *

It was almost as if a weight had been lifted.

He felt better the more miles he put between himself and that city. It was a lovely spot, couldn't have picked a better one actually, just outside of Glaive: within the city limits, but not really part of the city. It was brighter here too, more open air. And Adlard found himself wondering why he'd never thought about moving out here with Emily, instead of remaining where they were in the heart of that beast behind him.

Because you're not an old fart, a voice threw back at him. Nowhere near retirement age. Maybe if they'd had a baby, then… (don't think about that). *What the hell would you do out here? Play golf?* Wasn't an old fart, wasn't incapable of looking after himself.

Wasn't disabled.

Because that was the other choice, wasn't it. For folk who couldn't keep up with the pace of life in Glaive, these kinds of communities were a blessing. Medical assistance on tap, at the push of a button, the pull of a cord. He'd looked at various places like this for his old mum back in the mid-west, for when the time came. But she was a stubborn old bird, and she had her sister of course. The two of them made quite a comedy double-act, grumbling about this and that, like a female version of Statler and Waldorf.

The man he was on his way to see, who he'd only found out was back because he kept his ear to the ground, didn't have any siblings. No-one to grow old with and moan about this or that. Not that the future Blake Wagner was looking at was particularly pleasant, whether he had company or not.

He'd waited, for such a long time. Waiting to see if Wagner would get in touch, let him know how things were, how he was doing. Maybe it was his own fault, perhaps he'd seen a friendship developing where there hadn't been one; just a captive audience. Nobody else around to pass the time with apart from doctors and nurses who were always busy.

But still, he could have just let Adlard know whether he was alive or dead. He paused and thought about that for a moment, about how on earth anyone could let you know if they were dead. Wasn't as if he hadn't been before, though was it? Dead, alive; alive, dead.

Now Wagner was back, had moved into a bungalow on Hazel Avenue – modified and kitted out to suit the man's unique needs, he'd been told. Just like the car Adlard spotted on the driveway of that house, a kind of silver mini-people carrier affair with a high roof and a large door on the back, which he assumed had a ramp.

Adlard pulled his Mustang into the curb, setting the handbrake. He paused before climbing out, wasn't quite sure of the reception he'd get. Wasn't sure whether Wagner now blamed him for what had happened a couple of years ago, for not helping when he'd reached out. Not being that backup. He hadn't said anything along those lines when he'd been in the hospital, but that didn't mean a thing. Might have had time to cultivate that hatred, that anger. Something which had clearly forced him to leave in the first place, so he wasn't constantly reminded of those bad memories. Of all that pain.

Which begged the question: what *was* Wagner doing back? It was something Adlard was too curious about to stay away, regardless of the greeting he'd get.

Then suddenly he was up and out of the car, jamming his hat on and walking up the drive past the neatly trimmed gardens with the flowers blooming (another benefit of this kind of assisted living community, a handyman and gardener on call). Adlard raised his hand to knock on the door, but hesitated once again. Almost turned back, when the door opened without him having to do anything.

In front of him was a man dressed in scrubs similar to the ones Adlard had become so familiar with during those months Wagner was in hospital, only this uniform had the logo of a private firm on the chest. Paid for with money that must surely still be left over from the pay-out. Even in Wagner's condition, you'd have a job to spend all of that cash in, well, forever. Adlard had long since tamped down the jealousy about that, because whatever this man did with that money it was to make the time he had left bearable. Hell, he wouldn't even begrudge him having dancing girls in his living room twenty-four seven.

"Oh, hey!" said the man. A handsome guy who looked so much like Wagner had before the… 'accident'. No, call it what it was: an attack. There was nothing accidental about what had occurred. Nothing at all.

"Hey," Adlard said back.

"I was just…" It was obvious the nurse was leaving, but as Adlard looked beyond him he saw a couple more. Just part of the care package that this firm clearly offered. "Did you want to see Blake?"

"If… Er, yeah, if he's free."

"And you are?"

"He's an old friend," came a voice from inside. "Thanks guys, much appreciated," it said next and the other nurses – a man and a woman – joined their colleague, nodding both a greeting and a goodbye as they filed past.

"No worries," the woman called back.

"He's had his wash and physio now," said the third to Adlard, though they didn't owe him any kind of explanation. Then all of them were gone, heading over to another car parked a little down the road.

"Well, come on in then," the voice wafted through once more, so Adlard cautiously crossed the threshold and removed his hat again; it had hardly been worth putting it on.

And there he was, sitting on what looked like a throne: Blake Wagner. Only it wasn't a throne, it was an electronic wheelchair built up at the sides, an oxygen tank fixed to the back with a tube that hung down where Wagner could reach it. He was dressed in loose-fitting trackie bottoms and a sweatshirt, and the detective had to wonder whether those burns were still causing him pain after all this time? It was obvious from the hands resting on the arms of the wheelchair that if he'd had any more grafts, then Simonson's prediction had been an accurate one. They hadn't taken. If he'd needed any more evidence of that, all Adlard had to do was look at Wagner's face, not that he could see it properly – which he guessed was sort of the point.

Because Wagner was wearing a kind of 'human' mask. Adlard didn't know any other way to describe it. Made from some kind of plastic, it was painted a flesh-colour that was just slightly… off. An attempt to make people less uncomfortable, Adlard suspected, but if anything it was more creepy-looking than what might be beneath (bearing in mind, he hadn't really seen that face for a long time). Wagner tilted his head slightly as Adlard approached, hands still behind his back.

"Henry," said Wagner through lips that didn't move.

"You recognised my voice then," Adlard queried. "An old friend. Are we?"

"What?"

"Still friends?"

There was silence for a moment or two, then Wagner said: "Of course! Why wouldn't we be?"

Adlard let out the breath he hadn't realised he'd been holding, then suddenly felt quite angry. "Because you left without saying a word. Because you've been gone…" He shook his head.

"Henry, I'm so very sorry. I'm terrible at goodbyes, and besides I thought you might talk me out of leaving."

"To do what? To go where? You could have let me know whether you were okay or not, written a letter or something. Would it have killed you to pick up a goddamn phone?"

Another pause. "I can only apologise again. I was… busy."

"What could have been so important that—"

"I was trying to fix myself," the man stated simply. "I don't expect you to understand, but something like that… There was a lot to process, and as much as I appreciated our little chats – in fact they kept me going, Henry – they were stopping me from coming to terms with all this. Getting my head straight."

"All right," said Adlard. "Okay ki—" He stopped himself, because looking at this person in the wheelchair he understood that he was no longer a kid at all. He'd changed, grown up in his quest to 'come to terms with things' as he called it. Was more a man than a kid, more self-assured than cocksure. At peace with himself, if you like. "Wait a second, how do you mean 'fix yourself'?"

"Find ways of dealing with the pain for starters, maybe even find a way to walk again." Adlard pulled a face and Wagner laughed softly. "I know, I know Henry. Stupid. But I had to try."

"So where…?"

"All over really, following leads again. Anything that might help. Herbal medicines, acupuncture, meditation…"

"And did you… Did anything…?"

Wagner shook his head. "Afraid not. But like I said, I had to try. It gave them time to sort out this place at least, fix it up so I can be as self-sufficient as possible. Here, I'll show you around." Another pause and the man looked down, nodded at Adlard. "What's that you've got?"

The detective had forgotten himself that he was

holding something other than his hat. "Oh, right. Here…" He held out the box for Wagner to take. "A housewarming present."

"Henry, you didn't have to…" Wagner opened the box up, took out the bottle and gave a chuckle. "I'm not sure Irish single malt will mix very well with my meds, but…"

"Christ, I'm sorry. I didn't—"

Another laugh. "It's fine, honestly. I'll save it for a… I won't say a rainy day. A special occasion, then." Boxing up the bottle again and placing it in his lap, he started the wheelchair and began to steer it towards the nearest room. "We'll begin in the kitchen, then I can put the coffee on."

Adlard spent a pleasant afternoon being shown around Wagner's new abode, adapted for his needs. Then the pair of them sat in the living room and chatted like they'd done back in the day.

It was only a matter of time before the conversation turned towards what had been happening in Glaive City while Wagner had been away, though. "If only that *place* could have been fixed," Wagner said conversationally. "I'm quite glad I'm all the way out here."

"I-It's not so bad," said Adlard, the words more bitter than the dregs of coffee he had left in his cup.

"Henry, I read the papers. I know just how far it's slipped. This guy, Maniac? Isn't that what you used to call… Miller?" Wagner had trouble even getting that name out.

Adlard said nothing in reply. "So why come back here at all? And why now? I mean the timing's—"

"To face my fears," said Wagner. "What better time to do that with the anniversary coming up of…" His trailed off for a moment. "As for why here, it's my home." But it had only been his home for a short time, hadn't it. Why not go back to his real home? thought Adlard, and then asked the question.

"There's nothing for me there," said the man in the wheelchair. "Wasn't even before I came here. Besides, I'm still hopeful things will come right in Glaive. On that note, how's work, how're things in the department? Any headway with weeding out the bad apples?"

The detective's brow furrowed. How did Wagner know he'd been trying to do that? Not getting very far, but at least trying. "It's… an ongoing process," was all he would say.

"How many of the cops that frequent Brubaker's are owned now?" asked Wagner flatly.

How many of them are above reproach? Again, Adlard remained silent.

"Perhaps you could do with a little help," Wagner suggested, and when Adlard pointed at him the man laughed. "Hardly. I'm not really in a fit state to…" And just to emphasise the fact he sucked on the oxygen. "Besides, I wouldn't go back into that line of work if you paid me another fortune. I think I'll just take it easy for a while. Sit back and smell the flowers." There were certainly enough in the garden out there. "But no, I meant someone who could cut through the bullshit. Make the streets safe again."

"We're the ones doing that," argued Adlard.

"Are you?"

More silence from the detective, because he really didn't know what to say.

"Let me ask you this, Henry, do you feel safe on the streets of Glaive City?"

He gave Wagner a weak smile. "I think maybe it's time I was leaving, let you get on with taking it easy like you said." Adlard rose, picking up his fedora and jamming it on his head. "I'll see myself out, Blake."

"Maybe... Well, I hope to see you again sometime," said the voice trailing after him.

Adlard looked back over his shoulder as he opened the door. "Yeah, I'm sure you will."

Then he was gone, slamming the door after him.

Blake waited a few moments, before opening the secret panel in the side of this wheelchair.

He took out the syringe filled with a yellow liquid that looked like custard. Barely hesitating, he brought it down into his thigh and depressed the plunger. It took a second or two, but then he felt it. Felt *everything* – in limbs that weren't really supposed to.

Next Blake placed a foot on the floor, levering himself up and out of the chair. His first steps were always like a baby, and he practically tottered towards the window, just in time to see Henry Adlard reach his Mustang. He pulled back momentarily when Henry glanced at the bungalow, at the window. He'd almost given himself away once that afternoon, didn't want the policeman to see him walking around as large as—

All that talk about needing help, about them needing someone to cut through the bullshit. But the fact remained the cops here were rotten to the core (more bad apples than not), so much worse than they'd been even years ago. That needed to change, then maybe people like Henry could start to make progress.

But the process of fixing that, of fixing everything, did need a helping hand now. Someone to do the job the police clearly couldn't. It was part of why he'd come back, not just from that other place, but to Glaive City. Part of his mission.

It was time now; he could feel it. Blake looked up and saw the sky darkening. Time to introduce a few people to the *real* darkness.

"Tell me, Henry, do you feel safe?"

Soon there would be no safe place for *them* to hide. Not from what he'd brought back from the void.

And definitely not from him.

* * * * *

He felt safe.

God, who wouldn't with the police escort they were being given. But then, it was warranted, the amount of bullion they were escorting from the National Bank. Yes, Will Percival felt safe. Safe driving this van, with his partner Zeck beside him, both of them dressed like they were on their way to some kind of riot. The third and fourth members of their team were in the back, Quesada and Gross, in with the gold itself. Fucking hell, the things Percival could do with that money, the dreams he could make a reality for him and his family.

But it didn't belong to him, he knew that. He was just paid to look after it, to keep *it* safe, and sometimes he thought to himself that he really wasn't being paid enough for that.

Like now for instance, as he checked his mirrors again to comfort himself, checking that fleet of squad cars were still with them as they made their way along this road out of the city. Only they weren't there. Well, they were, but they were peeling off for some reason. One by one, vanishing, like a giant invisible hand was sweeping them away. Maybe there was an emergency somewhere, but they'd been guaranteed a police escort all the way to Fort Mathilda, where they'd be unloading all this. Even if something constituted as an emergency, and Percival couldn't think what would take the officers away from this assignment, they'd leave some black and whites flanking them surely?

"Er…er, Zeck," he said to his partner, who looked across.

"What?"

"Something's—" Before he could say any more, witnessing car after car disappearing, until the security van they were in was left pretty much alone, Percival happened to look ahead of him again – and it was then he was sure.

Not just that something was very wrong indeed, that they were in some serious trouble, but that nobody was paying him enough for this – not even if they were taking it directly out of their haul in the back. Because in front of them now, Percival could see that the road was blocked.

Had been purposefully blocked, actually, by cars and vans parked across it.

Zeck followed his gaze and said: "Shit! Where are the cops, why aren't they overtaking? Sorting this out?"

But of course he didn't know, because Percival had

been in the middle of telling him when— "They're gone," he explained.

"Whadya mean, gone?"

"What do you think I fucking mean? They're not here, Zeck! Not behind us."

"What?" He changed tack. "Where are they, then?"

"Somewhere else," Percival stated. "I don't fucking know, do I? They've just gone. Fucked off!"

"All of them?"

Percival nodded. "More or less." He risked another look, then confirmed it.

"Okay, all right." Zeck clutched his rifle to him like a mother nursing a child. "Ram them, then!"

"What?" asked Percival.

Zeck shifted about in his seat, pulling on his seat-belt, which he hadn't bothered with till now. "Those bastards up ahead. You're going to have to ram them."

"But—"

"It's either that or turn back." That would get Percival's vote in all honesty, but when he looked in his side-mirrors he saw more vans and cars, similar to the ones in front of them, blocking off that route as well. The embankments on either side of them were too steep to climb, so they had no option but to try it Zeck's way. Percival strapped himself in too, speeding up. There was no way of warning the pair of guards in the back, he just had to hope they'd be okay.

"Come on," snapped Zeck. "Faster. Put your foot down!"

Percival did so, driving the van onwards. He could see men now flitting about around the barricade, all brandishing machine-guns of one kind or another, and all of them wearing ski-masks. This was a professional operation and no mistake, planned ahead of time. He just couldn't work out how they'd got the police to abandon them. He hadn't seen anyone taking them out, but then there were those vehicles behind so…

Faster, faster. Percival hunched over the wheel, coaxing more speed out of the van until—

There was a loud bang. Several loud bangs in quick succession, as a matter of fact. He thought for a second or two that the men outside might have started shooting at them to put them off, but that's not what had happened at all. The van dropped, just an inch or two, but enough to force Percival to lose control. Then he realised what had happened when the back of the van dropped as well.

They must have used a stinger, a spike strip, rolled it out before they got here – hardly detectable at a distance and if you weren't really looking for it. Percival wrestled with the steering wheel, could see sparks as the metal of the actual wheels connected with the road. "Hold on!" he shouted, tugging left hard. It was a miracle he didn't roll the vehicle over, but they managed to stay upright and ended up crashing unceremoniously into the verge.

"Jesus," breathed Zeck, who was now bracing himself against the roof of the van with one hand.

Percival was breathing in and out quickly, slowed himself down so he didn't pass out. Then managed: "What now?"

But that was answered for him when the men in ski-masks set off, making for their van with guns raised. There was a big guy at the front, clearly the man in charge as the others were following him.

"Yeah, good luck with that!" barked Zeck, meaning

good luck getting into their bullet-proof van, with the triple lock on the back. They both jumped in the front at another bang, this time definitely a gunshot – yet it still hadn't originated from the gang in front. Men from those vehicles at the back then, trying to break in?

No. Because as Percival watched, he saw figures make their way round to the front of the van, past the front: Gross and Quesada with their hands on their heads, being led at gunpoint towards the biggest figure.

"How the fuck did they—" Zeck began, then stopped. Quesada was shouting something, wrenching his head backwards. The big guy waved to get their attention in the front cab.

"What's he doing?" asked Percival. Then he saw, when the large guy tore off Quesada's helmet and held an automatic pistol to his head, miming with his free hand for them to open their doors. Next he put up three fingers, folding one down immediately. The second went down not long afterwards.

"He's bluffing," said Zeck, but his mouth dropped open when Quesada was shot and dropped to the ground. "Christ almighty!"

The big man laughed and grabbed at Gross' helmet now, pulling that off and doing the same mime. They clearly had access to the bullion in the back now, which they were probably unloading, so what did they—

"They're tying up the loose ends," said Zeck, reading his thoughts. "Getting rid of any eye-witnesses." Not that they could see much because everyone was masked up. Three, two…

"Fuck!" shouted Zeck, then opened the door from the inside before Percival could stop him. Almost immediately, he was dragged clear of the cab by men who were waiting – who simultaneously relieved him of his rifle and helmet.

And put a bullet in his skull.

The same gun that had just done the deed was pointed in Percival's direction, and he was told to get out. He looked from that to Gross out front, frowning when he saw his colleague joining in with the big guy and laughing; when he saw the big guy place a hand on Gross' shoulder. If he'd had time to think, he would have probably worked it out – that's how they'd got into the back in the first place, Gross had *let* them in. It's why Quesada had been so agitated, looking back so pleadingly at them to try and convey that the man was a traitor.

And Percival, if he hadn't already started to, no longer felt safe at all. Felt less safe than he ever had in his life, and that included the time when he'd got lost in the woods on a field trip as a schoolkid and had to spend the night in there with all the weird noises, the strange animals. The darkness. Back then he'd sat on the ground, pulled his knees up to his chest and prayed for something – for some*one* – to save him, to make him feel safe again. Back then it had turned out to be a ranger, hood up against the rain that had started, who stumbled upon him by accident. A stroke of luck, his lucky day. The opposite of today.

Percival wanted to do that again, just pull up his knees to his chest and wait to be—

Only he wasn't a kid anymore, he was a grown man – and nobody was going to save him this time. Might as well pull up those knees, bend his head, and kiss his ass goodbye, because the man with the gun was getting impatient. Was barking at Percival to hurry up and get the fuck out, so he could suffer the same fate as Zeck.

It was then that he heard it, once the man had stopped shouting. A noise, a kind of droning sound like an insect. The man in the ski-mask heard it as well, and turned. The droning was growing louder by the second. The others out there were turning around as well, the big guy, Gross.

"What the f—" But the man with the gun on Percival didn't get a chance to finish, because there was a flash of light, an explosion, and suddenly the roadblock had a massive hole in the middle, smashed through as if that same invisible hand which had swept the police cars away had punched right through it.

Percival gaped ahead of him, trying to make out what was happening through the smoke. Then all of a sudden there was another figure, a hooded figure. Wearing a hood just like the ranger who'd found him back in those woods.

Except this one was leaping into the air through the gap in the vehicles it must have created. The men in ski-masks fired at it, but that didn't seem to deter the figure. In fact, it put itself between two men then moved at the last moment – causing them to shoot each other!

"Fuck…?" the man who'd been threatening Percival finally finished, and he couldn't have agreed more. Because that's what this person was doing to the thugs in masks: fucking them up, ducking and rising, punching as he did so; leaping and kicking, systematically taking them down. He wore some kind of black cape… No, the closer Percival looked, the more he felt sure it was some sort of cloak – which also explained the hood. In spite of this, he – because it was almost certainly a man – moved faster than anyone Percival had ever seen. Had the dexterity of a champion gymnast, coupled with the fighting moves of a martial arts expert. It was a deadly combination, for this mystery figure's opponents at any rate.

But it didn't end there. The men kept on firing, so he pulled something from that cloak, the material of which seemed to flow around this newcomer like a living thing rather than hindering him. The object was some kind of weapon, with curved blades either side of the handle, which he gripped in his fist. And he swiped it left and right, spinning the sharpened metal and cutting through gun barrels with the same ease it dug into flesh. Percival's jaw dropped as he witnessed it hooking into one goon's shoulder, who was then dragged around and flung at a couple of his friends. All three went down like skittles in a bowling alley.

It didn't matter if the men were quite some distance away, either, because the intruder could apparently send this weapon out from his hand – slicing into thighs and arms alike – then summon it to return with a flick of the wrist, like a trained animal answering the call of its master. Was it on some kind of wire?

More troops came from behind the security van, from the vehicles Percival had seen blocking off the rear. They charged at the cloaked shape, some of them hitting him dead-on yet he didn't go down. Instead, he extended the handle of his weapon so that it turned into a staff – the lethal blades still at both ends. He jabbed it left and right, blocking attacks and countering them. One thug was sliced right up the middle, spinning around with a shriek to reveal a red groove the length of his torso. Another was sliced across the backs of both ankles, severing the hamstrings and forcing him to keel over.

This new wave of men lasted about as long as the first one, but already some of the others were getting to their feet and rallying again – even as it began to spot with rain. That was when the hooded figure pointed at the big man, who until now had just stood back and watched the battle. A general, more than happy for his troops do his dirty work. For the cannon fodder to tire out their opponent. Though if that was the plan, it wasn't really working because their enemy was showing no signs of slowing down.

Gross mistakenly thought the hooded figure was pointing at him, and tried to run away. A coward as well as a turncoat. The big guy put two bullets in the back of his head; he'd served his purpose anyway.

Rain began to pelt down. The general took a step towards the figure in black, pulling off his own mask to reveal a bald man with a moustache. The direct challenge had been accepted, it seemed. Actually the big guy was grinning, as if he was looking forward to this fight. He stopped smiling when he got close enough to see what was under that hood, the face Percival couldn't see properly from this distance.

The big guy, the strongman – because that's what he resembled, a circus or carnival act – held up his pistol, but not to fire it. He showed it to the hooded figure, then nodded towards his opponent's staff. The figure in black retracted this, tucking the weapon away into the folds of his cloak again – and waited for the strongman to toss away his gun, which he did.

This was going to be settled hand-to-hand.

And it was the strongman who lunged first, boots kicking up water from the ground, swinging a punch that would have knocked most men into next week. The hooded figure just blocked it with a forearm, returning the favour and smashing his own fist into strongman's face. His nose exploded in a shower of blood and cartilage to add to the rain. He staggered back, shaking his head, looked like he couldn't believe what was happening – because it probably hadn't ever happened before. This was not a man used to people who fought back, let alone caused him any harm. That shock didn't last long, turned quickly to anger – and the strongman was attacking again, delivering more blows to the hooded figure. Most were blocked, but a couple got through, which the strongman seemed happy enough about.

Didn't affect the outcome in the end, however. Because as the moustached muscleman threw his next punch the cloaked figure sidestepped it easily, then grabbed the exposed wrist. The bald man looked sideways at him, tried to wrestle out of his grasp, but then there was an almighty crack as that wrist was snapped backwards, exposing the bones both there and at the elbow.

The strongman screamed like a baby, crying at the pain. But his hooded nemesis wasn't finished quite yet. The figure grabbed him by the throat, and though he was smaller than the man he was facing, lifted him easily off his feet. Percival heard a strangled "W-What are you?" before the hooded man flung him to the ground with a thump, splashing water everywhere. He finished off by kicking the big man's jaw sideways and knocking him unconscious.

Percival exchanged looks with the guy in the doorway, still holding the gun on him. He didn't bother asking again, just reached in and grabbed Percival, hauling him out of the cab as the cloaked figure approached.

The driver's helmet was ripped from Percival's

head, and he felt the pitter-patter of rain replace it; then felt the gun barrel pressing against his temple. "I'll kill him, I will!" There was no reply from the hooded figure, but he did stop a few metres away which made the goon with the gun think he'd got the upper hand. "That's right. You stay where you are, bitch!"

Thought he had the upper hand, but then came that *thwipping* sound – and Percival felt the breeze as a blade shot past his face. Suddenly the thug had no hand at all, because that and the gun were flying off into the distance. Another *thwip!* and the blade was pulled back, leaving the man to gaze at the stump he'd been left with. He shrieked, but thankfully passed out only moments later.

The rest of the gang was either down for the count or making a break for it, the defeat of their bald-headed leader enough to convince them to stand down, let alone this final act of horrific violence. Percival stared at the figure who'd saved him, through the rain, and it was only now that he got a good look at the 'man'. Only now that he saw his face, and felt like crying, felt like screaming himself. Instead, he nodded his thanks – not only to his saviour, but because his prayers had been answered yet again – and the figure nodded back, before turning and striding away, cloak billowing out behind him. Turning and heading back towards the gap in the blockade he'd created, where Percival could see a black motorbike waiting.

The hooded shape climbed on, rode away; accompanied by that droning sound Percival had heard before.

And though he was still in the middle of what had recently been a warzone, though he still wasn't sure who he could trust but would call it in anyway – nobody would be able to sweep this away – he felt safe. The safest he'd ever felt in his life, just knowing that whatever that thing had been was out there. His prayers given form.

The darkness given form.

* * * * *

It was dark at the back of the shipping container.

He could hardly see inside there, let alone right to the far end. That's where the cages were, at the rear, behind the official cargo which were boxes and boxes of paperclips. "Clear some of this shit away," the man with the blond buzzcut ordered, and the underlings with him started to do just that. Hefting the boxes to create a channel he could walk along, to examine the merchandise. Merchandise he would personally vet himself.

Merchandise, he saw as he walked down the length of the crate towards the cages, flashing a torch inside them and seeing lots of eyes, that was already quite malleable because of the drugs they'd been given. Drugs they'd taken freely because they thought they were being vaccinated for the trip, rather than being *given* Trip. Getting them hooked on it so they'd be even more compliant once they got them back to Little Vegas.

He ran a tongue over his lips, moistening them. The blond man couldn't wait to both use and abuse these women, fresh from overseas. He waved his torch around again, taking in what they were wearing. Hardly anything, was the answer to that one, some of the silk or lace ripped where those who'd loaded them up had got a bit carried away. There were bruises as well, a few cuts. That didn't matter, they would fade. And these girls had better get used to the rough stuff, because they'd be experiencing a whole lot more of it in the future.

A whole lot more of it at his hands, for starters.

He cast his mind back to when he'd had to share shipments like this one, with his sibling, his other half. His twin. Back before the incident with the young cop and the gun. Once Mr Miller… sorry, *The Maniac* as he now insisted on being called, had recovered enough, the first thing he'd done was execute that brother for such negligence. Or what he'd thought was the correct brother. Before either of them could say anything, his twin had found himself on the wrong end of a katana. He still recalled the look of shock, even as the man slid down the blade – but it was already too late. Speaking up at that point would only have resulted in both of them being executed. It was a wonder The Maniac hadn't done that anyway; it wasn't like he was in his right mind. Hardly stable before, there were rumours there was still a fragment of one bullet still lodged in his brain. It wouldn't have surprised anyone.

The remaining twin had been angry, of course he had – it was like a part of him had died that day, someone he'd grown up with, shared thoughts with – but what was to be done? And it did have its compensations, like a bigger cut of the money, more of the women. Not having to share women like the ones in front of him, although occasionally he and his brother had literally shared them in the same bed. That would never happen again, sadly.

Ah well, it was always better to concentrate on the here and now, on the wretches who'd give him such pleasure soon. Some of them crying, looking like they were coming round a bit. Time to get them into the vans and move them. "Hey! Hey, out there! Some help here!" Nothing. Not even an acknowledgement of his command. "Hey, you assholes! Can you hear me?" The twin with the buzzcut peered down the length of the crate, this time at the open doors. He couldn't see anyone there. "Don't make me come and fetch you!" he warned.

Still nothing.

"For fuck's sake!" he grunted, snapping off his torch and pocketing it, then made his way back along to the exit. "If you lot are sitting around playing with yourselves, I swear I'll—" He shut up when he saw the bodies. A handful scattered around just outside the crate, unconscious or dead he couldn't really tell, but definitely the morons he'd left there, who'd been moving those boxes only minutes beforehand. Stepping cautiously outside, he spotted more prone figures – their weapons lying as uselessly on the ground as they were. They hadn't had a chance to get off a round, any of them!

The closer he drew, the more he could see of the devastation. Of what had been done to them, the slashes across faces, the missing limbs. It had all happened so quickly they hadn't even had time to scream, by the looks of it! What could do that?

The blond twin looked left and right, along the docks. They were empty, which you'd expect at this time of night, overnight, and what they'd paid good money for. A little privacy… Only now the twin was wishing there was at least one dock worker around, to go and call for help – because the phone in his own car was too far away.

Slowly, he pulled out his gun; the pistol with the pearl handle he still kept holstered under his arm all these years later. The real cause of all that trouble with the young cop, that had cost him the life of his innocent brother; its own matching twin had been tossed in the sea, along with the body.

He took out the weapon but wasn't quite sure who he should be shooting at, because there wasn't a target. The twin still had no idea who'd done this.

No, wait. He did have *some* idea, didn't he? Strongman was in a cell right now, his busted arm in a cast and nursing a broken nose. Because he'd encountered something – someone – although he hadn't been making an awful lot of sense by all accounts. One guy, he'd said, had fucked up that entire takedown the other night. *One* guy! They'd thought he was talking out of his ass, maybe high on Trip himself. How could one man in a silly Halloween outfit have possibly brought down that crew? Some of their best men had been present!

Now he wasn't so sure it had been a tall story. Not sure in the slightest.

Especially when he felt something wrap around his neck, felt the ground falling away from him as he was hoisted upwards, dragged up and onto the top of the metal shipping crate. Whatever had wound itself around him was detached with a tug, and he watched as it zipped back into its housing, the end of it a curving blade. Watched as the person holding that weapon moved towards him.

The twin was up in seconds, ignoring the soreness of his throat. He still had the gun in his hand, so he opened fire. The figure ahead of him, the figure in that Halloween costume – a black cloak with a hood, some kind of weird white-cream mask – didn't even flinch as the bullets struck him, one after the next. Even at this close range, and closer, they appeared to have no effect whatsoever – and by the time the dark shape reached him, the remaining buzzcut twin had already discharged his gun, emptying the entire clip into this fucking thing. He stood there just holding it, not knowing what to do next.

But he didn't have to do anything, because the figure was cocking its head, reaching out and grabbing the pearl-handled gun, wrenching it from his grasp. In case he was quick enough to reload? What was the point? Wasn't like his bullets had done any damage the first time round. Nevertheless, the gun vanished into the folds of that black cloak, the same hand that had done it now reaching out to grab his shirt. The curved blade still resided in the shape's other hand, and he held it aloft.

Wasn't the most terrifying part of the ordeal, though. That was when he saw the 'mask' up close and personal. When he saw that face, or what was left of it – and he could swear those eyes that looked at him, looked into him, were glowing vaguely.

"D-Don't," begged the twin. "Please don't!" Begged, because he'd never been the strongest of the twins; not the dominant one, that had been his brother. His brother who'd been slaughtered for *his* mistake. And he wished his sibling was here today, facing this… this creature. Not because he wanted him to die in his stead, again, but because he might have stood a chance against the monstrosity holding him, about to cut him in half.

He closed his eyes, felt a warm wetness now below – but the figure hadn't even got started yet. No, the acrid smell told him exactly what that moisture was, as did the fact it was spreading across his crotch.

Nothing happened. He felt the hand dropping, releasing its grip on him. The twin risked opening one eye, just a slit, saw the figure stepping back, lowering the blade. He was being spared, his begging had worked.

Would it just let him go now?

He got the answer to that question when the thing's free hand balled up into a fist. And when that fist struck him, as hard as a sledgehammer, he wished he *was* dead. It felt like he was anyway. Not being able to see, the darkness…

The darkness that enveloped him totally.

* * * * *

It was dim in the room. Dark. But then that matched his mood perfectly.

The office was lit by just the single lamp; it was really late, or really early depending on how you looked at it. And the man with the white stripe in his hair sat behind his desk, leaning back in the leather chair and putting his feet up – crossing one over the other as they rested on the wooden surface. Badger poured himself a generous measure of clear liquid from a bottle that was already mostly empty, then knocked back half of that in one go. Almost immediately he got out a fresh bottle and topped his drink up, taking a cigar out of his jacket pocket and lighting it for good measure.

It had been a week.

Scratch that, it had been a fucking awful *couple* of weeks or so. And that was on top of the months preceding them. Not only had he been tasked with sorting out a mess Mill— The Maniac had created himself with their Trip production and supply line, but the bullion heist they'd planned to subsidise a lot of the upkeep of their operations had gone south. They'd get Strongman out of jail eventually, of course they would – they *owned* the jails, owned the police for that matter – but he'd been left in there as punishment for his failure more than anything.

Ranting on about some guy who'd single-handedly stamped on the robbery, and after they'd gone to all that trouble of making sure the van would lose its escort. Made sure the road would be blocked at both ends, the gold practically in their coffers already.

Then this one man. One guy, dressed like—

Fucking hell, it made no sense! Strongman was, well, he was the strongest of all of them. How had this fella handed his ass to him? Steroids? PCP? It didn't explain the ease with which he'd also taken out the entire crew on that job, and so quickly? Some had escaped before the authorities arrived – who'd had to be seen to be doing their job, once the media had gotten involved (there was only so much that could be covered up). They'd backed Strongman's version of events about this cloaked and hooded figure. But still, it made no sense.

Then, only a couple of days later, the remaining twin had been overseeing a shipment of potential whores, bound for a facility located right here in Little Vegas – with its illegal casinos, its drug dens, its clubs like the one Badger was in right now, sitting in the back office. A hedonist's dream, and all theirs. Inherited from the various mob bosses who'd been vying for control of this city – bosses wiped out by The Maniac's rampage, rising up like a phoenix from the ashes more determined than ever to take control.

Once he'd seized that control, though, he'd begun

to exhibit certain questionable characteristics. Rooting himself in that shithole of a waste plant, sitting on that throne in his underwear all day, was only the tip of the iceberg (Badger much preferred his own throne here). Some of the things the man had done verged on outright terrorism, and if Badger didn't know better he'd swear that his superior was trying to just fuck everything up. Cared more about his own fun, more about chaos, than the business empire he'd built through fear.

Take his obsession with those bad batches of Trip, for example. Mistakes, by-products that hadn't worked out, and yet The Maniac wanted more and more of it made. What he was going to do with it was anyone's guess; poison the lot of them perhaps? Badger hoped it wouldn't come to that, wouldn't come to a situation where they'd have to de-throne the king for all their sakes. As it was, in order to fix all this he'd been running around like a headless—

He paused, took the cigar out of his mouth, and rubbed his throat. Thought about Claremont, what had been done to him, unnecessarily in Badger's opinion though he'd kept that to himself. Wasn't it bad enough that he had to deal with this fucker who'd come out of the woodwork to challenge them, who'd released those bitches from their cages and left the twin inside one instead. Unconscious, in the ICU at present, it was debatable whether he'd ever wake up again. Same story there, the men taken out, taken down. The only witnesses, those slave-girls who'd told the media and police their story. Whacked out on drugs, yes, embellished definitely, but too similar to Strongman's tale to be ignored. One man again, the *same* man without a doubt.

But who? And why? He puffed on his cigar greedily,

asking himself the more pertinent question:

What would their new enemy do next?

Distracted as Badger was, and more than a little drunk – though not nearly drunk enough, he reckoned – he was only just noticing what was happening on the CCTV screens to the side of the desk, throwing back images of the club. Rotating through the dancefloor, the bar area, the strippers and lap-dancing section, all still heaving regardless of the hour; *because* of the hour probably, as these were activities best practised under the cover of darkness, after all. The only lighting in there was of the disco variety, flicking on and off, giving everything that weird stop-start effect like an old black and white movie.

Heaving, lots of bodies, all enjoying themselves – helped along by generous amounts of Trip which was freely available. Or at least they had been enjoying themselves the last time he looked. Badger almost choked on his drink when he saw the panic on those people's faces now, the stampede that was happening to get out.

"What in the name of—" He took his feet off the desk, sat forward in the chair so he could see better. The bouncers – guards by any other name, which had been tripled in light of recent events – were trying their best to funnel people through the exits, and failing. There were just too many of them.

Then Badger heard it. The wailing sound of a fire alarm going off, in the club and inside this office. But shouldn't that happen first, the alarm *then* the panic? Or had someone spotted something, caused the disruption and smashed an alarm? Either way, that was all he needed, another fucking headache. Literally, if that wailing noise didn't end soon!

Badger's eyes narrowed as one of the cameras zeroed in on a guard. He looked like he'd pulled his gun out (they were all armed, as standard) and was about to fire at something. The image flicked off before there was time to see what had spooked him.

More crowd shots, people being trampled on. This wasn't good for business, either. Then it rotated to show another couple of guards, both with their guns drawn as well. Something moved past them, almost like a shadow, Badger thought to himself. By the time it was gone again, so were the guards. Then the screen threw back one of the strippers, half-naked and screaming at something. Pointing.

But for the life of him he couldn't see why that alarm had been pulled. There was no sign of anything... More scenes of people stampeding, climbing and clambering over each other to get out of the club. Then someone flying – that's what it looked like at any rate – over the heads of the crowd. Badger rolled the cigar to the other corner of his mouth and blew out a stream of smoke, eyes narrowing even more. Not flying: that person had been thrown! There was a shot of them landing, rolling over the bar and disappearing. Badger couldn't be sure, it had all happened so quickly, but he thought he recognised the figure as another one of the guards.

Quickly, flashes of light appeared. Someone was using a machine-gun, and inside the club itself! What the hell were they thinking? They could cover up a few deaths, sure, but not a mass shooting! Not even they had the clout to—

More guards firing randomly now, into the air rather than at the crowds. Bursts of concentrated fire, trying to hit something, and then stopping suddenly, the guards vanishing from view.

He watched this for some time, mesmerised by it – when he should be rushing out there himself to see what exactly was going on. Trying to coordinate the evacuation, attempting to keep a lid on the situation.

But then he didn't need to, because the situation came to him. The door of his office crashed open and two of the guards who'd been out there were tossed inside. They landed awkwardly, folded up like origami, moaning and groaning for a second or so before laying silent and still.

Badger rose quickly, craning his head and squinting into the blackness down the far end of the office. It was as he was staring into this that he saw movement, barely detectable: the darkness coming alive. Or rather something detaching itself from the dark to stand alone and separate, yet still connected to it.

Pulling his own gun, he shot into the nothingness. Pumped bullet after bullet into the black, just like his guards had done beyond his office. Were there any of them left? he wondered, anyone coming to his aid? And still he had no idea whether he'd hit anything. Any*one*.

"Show yourself, you yellow piece of—"

So the person showed himself, striding forwards. Rushing at him with that cloak on and hood up, the same figure Strongman and the twin had encountered. The same figure who'd been doing their level best to pick their operations apart. Now it made sense, the panic, the confusion, the shooting. Now it made *perfect* sense; there had been no fire, just the alarm.

Badger pulled the trigger again, but realised too late

he was out. He reached into his pocket for another clip, ejecting the first one but not having a chance to reload before his attacker reached him and slapped away the weapon. Badger looked up and saw for the first time what was under that hood, and like the strippers he felt like screaming as well.

"W-What are you?" he asked instead.

"Your worst nightmare," came the guttural reply.

Badger paused, something half-remembered from the past. Then the figure was walking away from him, leaving him at the desk. Snapping out of his trance, Badger shouted, "But it can't be. You're… we—"

The figure spun around, and Badger understood that he'd simply wanted to disarm him so he could get his own shot in without inference. However, instead of a gun the figure was holding some kind of curved blade. And this he sent out towards Badger, his intention to gut him, surely?

But no. The blade was on some kind of wire and just as it was about to embed itself in Badger, it was pulled back. Another tease! Why didn't this creep just get on with it and—

Badger regretted his musings then, because he looked down and saw what the hooded figure had really been aiming for: the bottle of alcohol smashed, exploding and splattering all over the desk, the CCTV monitors.

Him.

Before he was aware of what was happening, his mouth was opening, the lit cigar falling from his lips. Touching the alcohol, igniting it with a *whoof!*

Now there was a fire all right! A raging one that engulfed not only him, but whatever it touched, lighting up his side of the office. And it would spread, Badger knew that as well. He didn't feel the pain at first, then the white-hotness of the flames reached his skin, having melted his clothing to him. Burning him, just like they'd burned—

Payback. His worst nightmare indeed, he just wasn't sure how it had come about.

Badger hung on a little while, finally letting go and screaming, shrieking a name though nobody could hear him over the alarm. Just the person in front of him.

The person stepping back into the darkness, the person with no face.

Then, mercifully, the darkness took Badger as well.

* * * * *

Adlard remembered a different night, long ago, but sitting in the same place.

Not exactly the same place, he'd been across from where he was right now nursing his whiskey. Blake Wagner had been sitting in this seat, alone even back then. No game on tonight at Brubaker's, but rather a fight. A boxing match that was bound to be rigged, not that he'd bet on the thing. He hadn't placed any of his 'harmless' bets since that night over three years ago.

We need to be beyond reproach.

Certainly not since he'd heard Wagner was back, since he'd visited him at his modified home and seen the state he was in. Still unable to walk, reliant on that oxygen when his breathing got too bad. Had seen what the corruption in this city had done to him first-hand, and refused to be even a little part of that anymore. Or to ignore it.

We need to make a difference. To be different. Otherwise what's the point of us?

Sometimes he had to wonder. But it wasn't enough just to be different, you had to make that difference Wagner used to talk about. It was why he'd begun looking into the corruption himself, had started quietly a while ago if the truth be known – Wagner's return had just given him the impetus he needed. Spurred him on to redouble his efforts.

Which was why, when the bar was crowded again, full of cheering cops, he was all the way over here at the back on his own. The people in his division didn't like narks, couldn't stand what they called the rat squad, but it might come down to that eventually. To get their precinct back on track once more.

"It's... It's not so bad."

"I know just how far it's slipped... On that note, how's work, how're things in the department? Any headway with weeding out the bad apples?"

"It's... an ongoing process."

"How many of the cops that frequent Brubaker's are owned now?"

Too many, thought Adlard, looking around.

"Perhaps you could do with a little help."

It was what Wagner had asked him for, way back, only he hadn't been up to the task. Didn't want to get involved. Now he had done, yes, he could probably use some help himself.

"Henry, there you are," said a voice and he looked up again. Davis, his former 'partner', who he'd successfully managed to evade on the way in. Not that he'd be offering to buy him a drink this time (thankfully, because that beer Davis drank was worse than piss). Not when he was one of the first people Adlard had started investigating, the results even more shocking than he'd imagined. "Been hearing some worrying things about you, my old friend. Hoping they're not true."

Adlard didn't answer him. They barely spoke anymore, even when they were at work.

"But just in case, here's something for you to think about." He took the newspaper he had jammed under his arm and placed it on the table in front of the detective.

"What's this?" Adlard picked up the paper, a recent copy of *The Post*; he could feel something inside it. A lump of some kind, like the print had a tumour. Opening it up, he saw an envelope inside.

"Your bet, on Fraction." Davis nodded back towards one of the screens that couldn't be seen from here. Where the boxing match was still going on, the competitors – Fraction and Johns – knocking different kinds of lumps out of each other. There were still a couple of rounds to go. "It came good, if you know what I mean?" Davis flapped a hand. "Now, I know you haven't dabbled in a while, but… Look, just accept the win, okay?"

"I didn't place a bet, *Lieutenant*." Adlard spat out the last word, this man's new rank, only earned because of his loyalty to a certain outside party.

"I placed it for you, Detective." He sighed. "I'm trying to look out for you, believe it or not buddy." Davis wasn't his buddy, not anymore, if he ever had been. Far from it. And when his partner skirted the table now and nudged his shoulder, Adlard grabbed his arm and slammed the envelope into his open hand.

Davis looked around him, then nodded and tucked the money back into his pocket. "I see. Disappointing, but not unexpected. I don't suppose there's any use in asking you to just leave things be?" Again, Adlard said nothing. "Okay then, so I'll leave you with a word of advice: watch how you go. It's a dangerous city."

"Let me ask you this, Henry, do you feel safe on the streets in Glaive City?"

Adlard watched him wander off, then took another sip of the whiskey and couldn't help noticing the headlines on the newspaper Davis had left behind him.

"Henry, I read the papers."

About what had been happening in the past couple of weeks, the foiled bullion robbery, stopping a human trafficking ring from Europe, the raid on the club and the fire… All businesses connected to The Maniac, unofficially of course.

"Hey, maybe Glaive City has its very own vigilante ridding the streets of scum!"

The words of the man who'd just tried to bribe him, who worked for that self-same scum – not that Adlard could prove it. Wasn't the kind of help they needed, though, was it? They needed to clean up their act, get rid of the rotten eggs on the force; Christ alone knew how.

Adlard pushed the newspaper aside, finished the rest of his drink – the only one of the evening – and put on his longcoat. Then he made his way out through the bar, past faces he knew wouldn't even give him the time of day now.

Only Ellis, the old beat cop who'd been involved in that whole shitstorm back at the waste plant nodded, and Adlard nodded back. He was a good bloke; if it hadn't been for him Wagner might well have ended up dead for good. Still on desk duty, still walked with a limp, but Ellis had done his duty.

Then Adlard was outside. He screwed his fedora onto his head, as was his habit, and looked up at the night sky. Blue-black clouds like bruises were passing over the moon, his breath was misting. Adlard jammed his hands into the pockets of that longcoat, walked slowly round to the back of Brubaker's, to the car park. Towards his Mustang, surrounded by squad cars.

He was almost at the vehicle, had his keys out and ready to open up, when he suddenly froze. Heard the noises behind him, off to the side of him. Figures, men: five, six of them, dressed in black, all wearing ski-masks. Enough of them… Enough to send a message.

"*It's a message.*"

Adlard took them in, left, right, in front of him as he turned. "Evening fellas. What can I do for you?"

One of them laughed. Another said: "You could try running. Give us some sport."

"You know what, boxing's more my sport," Adlard replied.

Then they came at him, and he got some good licks in – he could still hear the cheering as the match droned on inside Brubaker's, almost accompanying the fight out in the car park… if you could call it a fight. Never thought about drawing his firearm till another man whispered in his ear, "If you don't back off, Emily's next!"

That did it, and out came the revolver – but it was forced back and up, sending his bullet into those already wounded clouds. The echo rang out across the car park, then his gun was wrenched from his grasp and he was kicked to the ground. Adlard remembered thinking that if they carried on he might not even make it, might end up in a coma like that guy they'd found in the cage at the docks: punched so hard it had knocked his soul out of him, that's what the docs had said. If he'd even had one in the first place, that was.

"Enough," he heard one of them say.

Only it *hadn't* been one of them. There was something just a little… off about that voice. Something not quite human. Adlard raised his head, saw from the way they were all looking at each other in confusion that none of these men had uttered the word.

Then it began, another figure breaking into the middle of them. Adlard barely had time to blink a few times before it was done, the whole thing a blur of fighting moves he hadn't seen the likes of before. Fast, accurate. Designed to do one thing and one thing only, disable these attackers: possibly forever.

When he was done, the figure stepped back. Bodies were strewn all around the car park. Just like those reports from the heist, from the docks, from the club – and those poor fuckers had barely made it out of the fire alive, including that Badger guy who was one of Miller's generals.

The figure, a hooded figure Adlard now saw – again, same as in the eyewitness descriptions – stepped towards him and he flinched. But somehow he felt this person meant him no harm, indeed a hand was extended to help him up.

"Y-You're him, aren't you?" Adlard wheezed. Even as he said the words he could hear how stupid they were, how obvious it was. "The vigilante from the papers. The one they're calling—"

The whole hood nodded, but he kept his face well

out of sight. "I'm here to help," he told the detective, cutting him off.

"We… we don't need…" Repeating what he'd been thinking earlier, that this person had left a wake of victims behind him, people with broken or severed limbs, people in comas, people with third degree burns; not undeserved, it had to be said, but who'd appointed *him* judge and jury? Adlard stopped, however, feeling the pain from the kicking, looking at the prone men, remembering how they'd threatened Emily and how he couldn't possibly have protected her from this. Thinking about how hollow those words he'd been about to say were.

"Everything you need is on the passenger seat of your car," said the hooded figure in black. And Adlard peered through the window, saw a manila file. "To stop the rot."

"But—"

The sound of more men now, cops rushing from the bar. "His name's in there," the vigilante said, pointing back at one of the guys. A man approaching, walking with a limp.

"Detective, are you—" Ellis froze when he saw the figure Adlard was with, what he'd done.

"He trusted you," the vigilante continued after a pause. "Wagner. And you… you led him astray." Adlard saw the man wince at those words, saw him hang his head, and when he looked up again there were tears in his eyes. "But you were taken care of, right?"

"My… my family." Adlard raised an eyebrow at Ellis' reply. "They threatened—"

The vigilante held up a hand to silence him. "I don't care. I just need you to pass on a message for me. Tell him I'm coming. I'm coming to take out the trash." Ellis gaped at the figure, who was striding towards something. Swinging a leg over, climbing onto it. The thing looked like an extension of him even as he gunned the engine. "He'll know when. Tell him I'm coming to fuck him up!" shouted the vigilante, then put his head down and guided the bike out of the car park.

Davis had emerged by now, was barking orders at the uniformed men to get in their cars, to chase after this criminal.

But Adlard couldn't help smiling, just a little. Knowing that what this criminal had left behind might fuck all of them up, the people like Davis, like Ellis – now that one was a real surprise! – knowing that he was going to get that help.

Whether he liked it or not.

* * * * *

He sat in the dark.

In his home. Not the one Henry had visited – Blake doubted he would have brought him the housewarming gift for this place – but his real home. The one that suited him, the new him. The one an old friend of his father's had helped him construct, a guy whose life his dad had saved once down in those mines. All done under the table naturally, or under the ground in this case (for that kind of money, Wagner could have arranged anything on the quiet; and no, the irony wasn't lost on him that some of that payoff had undoubtedly been the original cash he'd refused). Who would question people digging in an old cemetery? Especially one hardly anybody visited anymore.

The dead deserved company, didn't mind being shifted around a little if they got it: stacked behind that toughened glass to make room for his underground lair. The one he sat in now, regarding not simply the coffins on either side, but the tank made of the same transparent material as the walls. The one he'd spent a lot of time in of late. Now he'd got the levels just right…

It had been trial and error for a long time, the tubes that injected the yellow serum into him – the results of any number of painful experimental drugs trials, theses by chemists barely out of university, but which had now been perfected – the needles that stimulated parts of his torso many doctors didn't even believe in. The result had given him the ability not just to walk again, but to move faster than any ordinary human. Gave him not only his strength back, but the strength of several men. Allowed him to train even harder than he'd done when he'd first got into martial arts, allowed him to learn some that hardly anyone was aware of. Even create a couple of his own.

He'd been telling Henry the truth when he said that he'd never found a real cure, though, especially for how he looked. But that was okay. It was the way he was *meant* to look, his real disguise a mask he wore in the daylight hours.

Blake's eyes flitted to the vehicle he'd been using to get around, a variation on the bike he used to ride. There were a number of bullet-holes on the sides, mainly from when the cops had been chasing him the previous evening, but he'd outrun them eventually thanks to the jets fitted on the back. And the cannons on the front had come in particularly handy during that bullion heist to clear the blockade.

Now he stared ahead of him, at the computers on the desk there. The most sophisticated system money could buy, which had helped him ferret out the names on that corrupt cops list. Which had helped him tie together all of Miller's operations, to link him to the illegal production of Trip. Just in front of these banks of monitors were his souvenirs so far, a small chunk of that gold he'd saved from the raiders, a cigar (not the cigar that had started the fire, that had burned white-stripe, but a reminder), and the remaining twin's gun. The very gun he'd used to shoot Miller in the face; he'd recognised it instantly. When he got round to it, he'd have to create some kind of museum.

And he'd saved the clippings from *The Post* too, scattered around the place chronicling his exploits so far. It was someone there who'd given him his name, the one Henry had almost spoken. The driver from the heist had described a hooded guy with a scythe who'd saved him. "Looked like Death I swear, but he was a man… A Death-Man?"

The European slave-women he'd freed had whispered "Morte" when asked to describe their liberator. So some bright spark journalist had put both of these together and come up with… Mortis-Man. Yeah, it was cheesy, Blake had to admit, but the more he'd rolled it around on his tongue the more it seemed to fit. Just like it seemed to fit his ride, which he'd jokingly named himself the 'Mortis-Cycle'. He was already drawing up plans for something bigger, something that would encase him in a bullet-proof cocoon and maybe even be able to fly!

Blake could almost picture himself driving that out at night, along the tunnel which had also been dug in from the other end of the lair – and opened out some distance from the cemetery. As opposed to the one that opened with a lever under the gravestone above that read, 'Here Lies J. Black: Death is Only A Horizon.' Part of a quote from Rossiter W. Raymond he'd rather liked. Seemed appropriate, as he'd been not only an author and scholar but also a mining engineer…

It was from here that he'd waged his war, picked his battles as Henry had once suggested, and picked them well. But he hadn't gone for the leader first. No, he'd got rid of the generals this time. Put them out of the picture, and left the last one to savour. The big one.

Soon he'd ride out and face his real destiny, with the darkness at his back.

Soon Blake Wagner, the Mortis-Man, would have his final revenge.

* * * * *

The waste disposal plant looked deserted, plunged into darkness like that: a hulking black shape against a black night.

But Mortis-Man knew different. There were people at home, *he* was at home. The Maniac as he liked to call himself these days, and it was just as fitting as the name Mortis-Man himself had inherited. As he rode towards the building, which appeared even more run-down than when he'd been here last, he pressed the button that would bring his cannons to bear. He wasn't going to sneak around on this occasion. Why bother? They knew he was coming, he'd warned them through Ellis. Sent the message he knew would get through.

That Miller had probably been waiting for since all this began, or at the very least since he'd begun to undermine the man's authority. To take back the city. Mortis-Man waited until the last second, then unleashed the firepower of those cannons. They ripped through the metal of the front wall, creating a door where there hadn't been one before. Big enough for him to power through, ducking and letting the front of the bike take the strain.

No sooner had he ridden in than it started. Mortis-Man noticed them only at the last minute: mounted rocket-launchers; clearly motion-activated, because now they spat their own load at him. Gritting his teeth, he pulled on the handlebars and tugged the bike left, then right. He managed to avoid one of the explosions, but another caught him off-guard and blasted the bike sideways, then a further one targeted the vehicle itself. He just about had time to leap off the thing before it struck, blowing his ride apart. The Mortis-Cycle was a tough cookie, but not *that* tough.

"How nice of you to join us!" came a voice over the intercom system. He couldn't tell whether it was scratchy because of the age of the machinery, or Miller just sounded like that now. But it *was* Miller. "I got your little message! Coming to take the trash out, I love that! I do enjoy a good pun!"

From his crouching position, Mortis-Man grunted and looked around him, but couldn't see any more missiles trained on his position. Maybe he was too small a target? What he could see were figures, lots of figures. Far from being deserted, this place was fuller than it had been in years, even when it was operational. Guards? He couldn't tell, but it would make sense for Miller to have a small army waiting here for him. That didn't matter, he'd fight a thousand armies to get to that man.

However, the closer they got, the more he could see of them: especially as weird coloured lights had kicked in, flashing red, green, yellow… These people didn't have weapons, weren't brandishing machine-guns or anything; they looked like ordinary members of the public, not even the kind of despicable folk who'd been in that club the night of the fire.

"In honour of your visiting us, and a certain very special date, we thought we'd throw a party! Only nobody wanted to come to it. Boo! So, we had to round up a few bods and get them in the mood!" Music struck up from somewhere, the kind of song you'd find playing at a children's disco or whatever. Mortis-Man looked from one face to another, some snarling and snapping like animals, others with their eyes rolling back up into their heads, still others clawing at something only they could see in the air above them. He knew exactly what this was from looking into the Trip situation, the batches Miller had demanded more of. He'd dosed the lot of them!

A woman, the closest to him, ran at Mortis-Man, grabbing him. He tried to pull her off safely, without hurting her; she didn't know what she was doing. Then there was a man there, and another woman, surrounding Mortis-Man, swamping him. He wasn't about to start fighting innocent members of the public, no matter what Miller had done to them – it wasn't their fault.

"What's the matter? They just want to dance!" shouted his arch-enemy. "Maybe a kiss or two. And that's just the men!" He guffawed, the sound thick and guttural; stomach-churning. Mortis-Man needed to finish this quickly, get these people medical help before it was too late. But that wasn't going to happen when they were currently piling on and on.

He picked a spot on the landing above, flung out his blade on the end of its wire, which wrapped around the railing up there. Then he depressed a button, which pulled him up and out of the crowd's clutches. A tool he'd designed himself, Mortis-Man had got one of the finest weapon-makers in the world – Master Miyazaki – to construct this unique 'three-in-one' instrument. It could be used for fighting, absolutely, but also for getting him out of tight spots like this one.

No sooner was he on the next level than he had to untangle the wire, and put it to its other use. These were definitely guards up here, men with guns running towards him. Aiming at him. Firing at him. Mortis-Man spun the scythe, the blades rotating like the top of a helicopter. Bullet after bullet was batted back at the guards, striking them in shoulders, thighs, kneecaps. Their own firepower working against them. He tossed the scythe between his hands, returning the volleys like a professional tennis player, putting all the guards out of commission by the time he was finished. One took a bullet to the side and spun, dropping over the railing. The crowd gravitated towards where he'd landed like zombies after fresh meat. With the final handful of bullets, he targeted the speaker system and killed that dreadful party music.

Making his way along the upper level, Mortis-Man retraced his steps from all those years ago, entering a room he was all too familiar with. The place where he had been 'born', on this very day so long ago. He stopped when he saw the throne made out of garbage… No, thrones, plural, because two more sat on either side of the main chair. And though the middle one was empty, there were people on the other two. Mortis-Man stepped closer, his eyes adjusting to the gloom once more. Making out the features, what there were of them. Making out the texture of the skin and bone.

Because sitting – or should that be lolling? – on those two thrones were a couple of corpses. Two people who looked like they'd been dead for some time. Looked like they might have been quite at home in the place where his underground lair resided.

"Seeing as it's a special occasion, my birthday in fact! I thought I'd dig up dear old Mommy and Daddy," said the voice, continuing its strange commentary – but he still couldn't tell where it was coming from. *Birthday…?* Of course, because this had been the place, and the date, that Miller had also been born again. As his aptly-named alter-ego. Mortis-Man took another step, then another. "Oh, and we have party games too!"

Guards appeared from behind the thrones, and he tensed, braced himself. But they weren't holding weapons at all; instead they had syringes in their hands. And the needles of those syringes were embedded in—

"No," breathed Mortis-Man, seeing the children held there, ranging from about six to ten years old, of both sexes, a couple crying and sniffling. "You maniac. You're insane!"

"Now you're getting it! That's kind of my schtick these days."

"Let them go!" Mortis-Man demanded. "Let them go, right now!"

Nobody moved, apart from a couple of kids shaking.

"Okay..." Mortis-Man narrowed his eyes, slowly reaching inside his cloak. Quicker than any of the guards could follow what was happening – and certainly quicker than any of them could inject that poisonous Trip into the kids' systems, which would undoubtedly kill anyone of their age – he released what he'd taken from his belt. Miniature versions of the hand-held scythe, also courtesy of Master Miyazaki, which spun and flew through the air, breaking off in several directions at once.

They lodged in the hands holding those syringes, forcing the guards to drop them almost as one. And suddenly Mortis-Man was moving forwards like one of those missiles that had blown up his bike. He struck out with kicks and punches to the face, whipped his main weapon across one guard's chest which sent him reeling into a wall.

Bending, he whispered to the children, "Run and hide!" and they didn't need telling twice, evacuating the room in seconds.

"Aww, spoilsport!" Miller moaned. "We'll have to play another game instead, then."

There was movement off to the left of him; swift, urgent. Mortis-Man just about had time to avoid the blow from the katana as it swept through the air and bit into the floor. He glanced about him, saw his attacker and was taken aback. He knew before coming here the damage those gunshots must have caused to Miller but hadn't been quite ready for seeing the real thing. That lopsided grin, caused by plastic surgery on his ruined cheek, his missing eye where another bullet had gone in; was still somewhere in the guy's brain if you believed the rumours.

Then there was the way he was dressed, in a kind of

giant romper-suit – a far cry from the more fashionable and expensive attire he used to wear. It was just a reflection of how far off the reservation he'd clearly travelled.

Mortis-Man's hesitation almost cost him dearly, because in his other hand The Maniac was holding an Uzi. Ordinarily that wouldn't have been a problem, because his suit should have protected him, but as his foe pulled the trigger and fired the first of a number of rounds, one of them caught him in the ribs and he realised they were armour-piercing bullets.

Stumbling sideways, Mortis-Man threw himself over the thrones, tipping one of the side chairs over and pitching the skeleton – mother, father? if that part was even real – from its seat. The Maniac didn't seem to care about shooting at them, because he fired now into those thrones, the only cover Mortis-Man had. And not very good cover at that, because the bullets tore right through them.

He'd been left very little choice, had to emerge at some point. But Mortis-Man spotted a way to kill two birds with one stone. Launching himself at the wall, he bounced off it like a pinball and slammed sideways into The Maniac – knocking him off his feet. His Uzi flew out of his grasp and slid along the floor, out of his reach. Full of what seemed like nervous energy – and perhaps another side-effect of that piece of metal in his brain – The Maniac was up again instantly, whipping his sword back and forth.

He didn't have the training, but his random slashing was unpredictable – and Mortis-Man was injured. One blow caught him on the right shoulder, between the gaps in his armour. Not a fatal strike, but enough again to put him on the backfoot. Looking up, he saw the blade whipping towards his hood, his head, and he just about had time to bring up the scythe to block it.

The Maniac laughed. "A game, a little dancing... See? Now give us a kiss!"

Grunting again, Mortis-Man depressed another button on his scythe, and the handles extended – one side stretching out into The Maniac. A few inches higher and it would have plunged into his chest, but as it was it ripped through his Babygro and into his stomach instead. It was The Maniac's turn to grunt, coughing up bloody redness. "Heh, heh..." he managed, dropping his katana and holding on to the staff part of the scythe with both hands, pulling himself forwards and looking under that dark hood. "Y-You going to kill me now?"

"Death's too good for you. It was too good for *all* of you."

Another feeble laugh. "I-I know who you are."

Mortis-Man hesitated, looked up so his own skull-like visage could be seen, then asked: "Who am I?"

"Y-You're my nemesis! You're Mortis-Man!" He spat the words out with more blood from his lips. "A-And... and I'm The Maniac."

Mortis-Man reached out and hauled the person who had once been Miller off the end of his blade, let him sag to the ground. It was then and only then that he heard the sound of sirens outside. "What did you do?" he asked.

"W-What anyone would..." Maniac hawked up more redness "...would do when they knew an intruder was coming. I-I called for help... called the cops," came the reply.

"I called in backup."

The threat inside had already been dealt with by the time they entered.

Gas had knocked out the people downstairs in the waste disposal plant, people who'd been acting crazy – a real laugh-riot as their new lieutenant would have called it – and now they were scattered all over the floor.

Uniforms with masks on were reporting that it was safe to venture in, that the gas was dispersing, especially as they'd opened the main front doors. Safe for Adlard and the troops to venture in first, followed closely by Davis and Mack. Yes, Chief Mack had wanted to oversee this one personally, so he'd said. "A delicate matter," was how he'd phrased it. To Adlard it all seemed pretty cut and dried.

He looked up to the next level, to the walkway, and saw them emerge. The figure in black first who'd saved him that night in the car park, and Adlard was still nursing the bruises from that one. The hooded figure who'd left him the files which he'd sat on for a while, trying to work out what he was going to do. The person who was dragging the man they called The Maniac along with him, holding what looked like a needle in his other hand.

"Those people need urgent medical attention," he called down to them.

"No shit," whispered Adlard to anyone who'd listen.

"And there are kids up here, they're in hiding and scared."

Kids? The detective said to himself. Had that lunatic been using them as hostages or something?

"Then there's this," said the figure, Mortis-Man as the media was now calling him. He dragged The Maniac to the top of the steps and threw him down them, letting him roll head over heels. Adlard watched the bundle come to a stop; the man was bloody, broken, but still alive it looked like. More fodder for the ambulances that were also outside with the squad cars.

"What are you waiting for!" This was Mack, pushing his way through. "Get up there, arrest him! Arrest the vigilante!"

Adlard felt something nudge his shoulder, turned and saw Davis there. "You heard the boss, get that fucker!" Adlard sneered at him, then he punched him squarely in the face. The man went down immediately, and stayed down.

"What... what are you—" Mack began, but Adlard already had his gun out and was pointing it at his head.

"You're under arrest, former Chief." He'd been waiting until the last moment, until he could be sure he had backup here, and now he saw a lot of faces in those uniforms that he didn't recognise. State police he'd called in, as well as IA – having handed over evidence of the corruption in Glaive's police department. Already, the uniforms on the take had started to be rounded up, Mack just hadn't known about it beforehand. Adlard had wanted to do this publicly, in front of the other cops from their precinct. To show them things were changing, about to change for good if he had his way.

And yes, technically he should be ordering the lads to go up there and arrest Mortis-Man, but for one thing he'd rather arrest The Maniac when he was conscious again. Arrest him and sling his ass in Lovecraft Asylum, for his links to the Trip network if nothing else. And for another, the next time Adlard looked up again, after he'd cuffed Mack – who'd been swearing like a trouper as he was handed off to a state policeman – there was no sign of that vigilante. Just a couple of those kids he'd talked about, wandering out now they thought it was safe to do so.

Safe… Safe to come inside here, the city safe from The Maniac – for now – him and Emily safe. Would feel a whole lot safer now walking those streets, knowing a certain someone would be patrolling them. At some point their paths would cross again, Adlard realised that, and they might not see eye-to-eye about things. He might even have to try and arrest the guy, for all of his good intentions.

But for now he was walking back outside again, looking up and seeing not a black and bruised sky, but light there. The darkness withdrawing, as the sun rose over the horizon. As morning came.

And a new dawn arrived for Glaive City.

* * * * *

The sun was so strong that day, the brightness reached well into the living room through the windows.

The day he knocked again, as Blake thought he would. Had been expecting him, maybe not on this late afternoon, but at some point after the events of the preceding week. The only shock was he hadn't come before now. Blake was alone this time, so he opened the door with the remote control to see Adlard standing there on his doorstep in his longcoat and fedora.

"Henry! Well, this is a pleasant surprise," he lied. Not about the pleasant part, but the surprise. Like he'd lied about a lot of things. "Come in, come in."

"Blake," said the detective, taking his hat off and holding it in front of him like a shield.

"What brings you here again so soon? Not that it isn't good to see you."

The man came in and started as the automatic door closed behind him. Catching his breath, he wandered into the room where Blake was sitting in his wheelchair. "I..." He shook his head. The man had questions, obviously, but wasn't quite sure where to start. How to articulate them. "How are you?"

"Since we last talked? I'm fine." Blake inched sideways a little and sucked on his oxygen. It wasn't just for effect this time, the bullet-wound on his side – now just a bad bruise he'd told the carers happened falling out of his chair – was hurting today and his special drugs had long-since worn off. Indeed, he looked exactly what he was – a cripple who needed help to breathe, who had good and bad days. "You, though..." Blake touched his mask and nodded at Henry, who was still sporting his own bruises from that beating in the car park.

"Oh, this? This is nothing," said Adlard, mirroring his actions. "I've had worse."

"You and your lot have been busy recently," Blake told him, like he didn't already know.

"How did you—"

"I read the papers, remember?" Adlard nodded. "Seems like you had some help, as well... Look, why don't you sit down, Henry?"

He seemed like he was thinking about it, then remained standing. "Blake, can I ask you something?"

"Sure, anything." Here it came, the reason why he'd driven out here again in the first place.

"Are you... I mean, you've read about what happened with The Maniac? How he was taken down?"

"Of course," replied Blake. "I'm delighted. Can't stand bullies. Like I said, though, you had some help. This… what was his name?"

"Mortis-Man," Henry said simply. "He took apart Maniac's operations, led us to those Trip production plants, his distribution network. There'll be no more of that crap coming into the city now."

"Good, that's good."

"He even sent an antidote to the hospital where those poor people were being treated for their bad Trips."

"Again, good. Right?" Blake recalled bringing the syringe back from the plant and running the substance inside it through his computers, working out how to properly treat those unfortunates The Maniac had dosed. "And the situation with the corrupt cops in your division. The papers said all that had got cleared up."

Henry nodded once again. "Might even be a promotion in it for me. There's an opening after all."

"Davis?" asked Blake.

"Davis," Henry confirmed.

"So why… You don't look very happy about it all? Seems to me like the guy did you a big favour. That he started to fix things."

"Blake, a lot of people were hurt."

"All of them deserved it, I guess," came the retort. "And no-one died, I read that somewhere."

"Wrong. Officer Ellis threw himself off the roof of his block last night."

There was a hesitation before Blake said, "Suicide?"

Henry nodded. "Confirmed this time, not like Moore."

"Why?" asked Blake, pretending he didn't know.

That part hadn't been reported by the papers, and his friend laid it out for him. "I see."

"Yeah. And I can't help wondering about... Well, the timing of you coming back and all."

"I told you, Henry. That was to face my fears. The anniversary and everything."

"Yeah, I know what you said."

"And what...?" Blake chuckled and started coughing, had to take an even bigger drag on his oxygen. "You think *I* might be Mortis-Man?" Another laugh, louder this time, so he reined it in. *Don't overegg the pudding.*

"I'd be lying if I said it hadn't crossed my mind."

"Get a doctor here right now, in fact get a team of them. Ask them if I'm capable of running around the city doing the kinds of things they describe in the news. Jesus, I *wish!* I'm even interviewing a personal nurse this week, her name's Simone I think."

"But the timing... I don't believe in coincidences." That detective's instinct of his.

"Have you ever thought that this... Mortis-Man, right? This guy just chose the anniversary of The Maniac's creation as well. The day I shot him."

"Yeah. The day you shot him and he... His men... I can't help wondering if maybe you found some of those cures you were talking about when I first visited."

Blake waved a hand at the chair he was in. "Like I said, they didn't work out – clearly."

"Or maybe you found someone who could get you the revenge you wanted for all that?" Henry mused. "A mercenary? Money like yours could buy someone really good, I'd imagine."

"You'd imagine? And what an imagination you

have, Henry! I mean, come on!" Blake laughed again.

Adlard looked at him sideways. "Yeah, maybe you're right. Who'd believe any of it."

"Not me, that's for sure. But I'll tell you one thing, this Mortis-Man fella whoever he is, I kinda like his style. Don't you?"

Adlard remained silent.

"Listen, Henry, I still haven't cracked open that whiskey. I think I could manage a couple of glasses today, if you'll join me? Celebrate your promotion?"

The detective rubbed his chin, thinking about it.

"And I have some cards around here too, if you fancy a hand or few?"

"I... I don't know." Henry looked at his watch. "I should really be getting back to Emily. She worries."

Blake shrugged. "Give her a ring, she'll understand. She's a good woman, I'm certain of that."

Adlard smiled. "She is. Right, okay, you've talked me into it."

"Bottle and glasses are back there in the kitchen. You know your way around, old friend," said Blake thumbing behind him. And then he watched as Henry's smile widened, as he tossed his hat onto the couch and went off in search of the booze.

He didn't enjoy deceiving the man, but Blake doubted he'd see his point of view on the whole vigilante thing. Perhaps one day. But for now, the identity of Mortis-Man must remain a secret. There was still much to do, criminals on the streets of the city who needed reminding.

That although it was bright today, the darkness could return. That they didn't own it, couldn't revel or hide in it. That it wasn't their protector or friend, because he was the one who'd been embraced, adopted by the absolute darkness.

That this city, Glaive City, was his home. *His* city, always would be. And soon they would find out, they would understand…

Why the darkness would be no safe place for them anymore.

Another Life

All those lives, different lives.

If she cared to, and especially at this time of the month, she could see – *smell*, more accurately – the content of their days, their years, so far on this planet. But even if she couldn't, with some you could tell their life-story just by looking at them, even if they hadn't been here on this particular night.

Take the man in the booth not far from the door, nursing his Sam Adams. Looking down into the beer, and up occasionally to scan the room – attempting to catch the eye of some female, but not confident enough to get up and ask any of them out. Probably for the best, dressed as he was. Mommy's boy, had lived with her – *looked after her* – until she'd died… fairly recently, a sniff confirmed. Father had passed away early, leaving them enough to live on, meaning the son had never had to go out to earn a living. Meaning he could devote all his time to the woman, who'd made sure his dedication to her was ingrained from an early age. It had left him with very few social skills, indeed she was surprised he was even out tonight – and at a bar like this. But then loneliness could be crippling, could be worse than physical pain sometimes.

Diana understood that better than most.

Her turn to look down into the drink that was in front of her, a vodka and tonic. The clear surface reflected her features back at her, the lines on her face more noticeable than they had been even five years ago when she was in her early forties, instead of approaching the big five-zero. The redness of her hair from a bottle now instead of the natural ginger it had been, growing up and into her twenties and thirties. Oh, she was still considered a looker for her age – nowhere near some of her contemporaries, and given the life she'd led any one of them might have appeared twenty years older than they should have done. A *hard* life, that's what some would have put it down to.

She looked away, looked back across the bar again. Searching the faces, sniffing once more – picking up the false bravado of one guy at the back who was chatting up a woman, giving it all the patter when in real life he couldn't even stand up to his boss at work. Would cry himself to sleep most nights, never having been able to keep up a relationship for very long; they'd always see right through him in no time at all. If he'd drop the bullshit and just let someone in, he'd get exactly what he wanted – a woman to spend the rest of his, admittedly pitiful, life with. Someone to share things with, to talk to. It was an itch he just couldn't scratch.

Then you had the flip side of the coin, the guys with *too much* confidence. Who targeted those of the opposite sex who had even less self-belief than the man with the chat. Who'd been through brutal, messy divorces, leaving them with no self-respect whatsoever. There was one now, homing in on a woman who was barely forty but had been through all of that and more. Been cheated on, lied to, told she was ugly – when in fact if she used half the make-up she did she'd actually be quite stunning. Make-up as a mask, a shield. Covering up who you were for a night like this. Everyone wore one, but some masks were more necessary than others.

And look, yes, already she was falling for his heavy-handed technique. He'd get what he wanted from the woman, then leave her in some hotel room feeling used and unloved, just like always.

It would serve that bastard right if Diana just—

No, not him. It would draw too much attention. Besides, he was busy with his conquest. Once he'd got another couple of drinks inside her, they'd be off; sometimes he needed drugs to help... weaken their resolve, but not this time. He had it all planned out. She might not even make it to the hotel, might just end up in the back of his pick-up with her legs in the air. Maybe next time, Diana said to herself. She was good with faces, even had his name now – Wayne – his scent, and was sure she'd see him again. If she felt so inclined, would even be able to track him to the trailer where he lived, lie in wait for him to emerge and then...

Diana's gaze swept across the room again. Singles' Night – it brought them all out. Was why she came. As much as Wayne believed himself to be a predator, he had nothing on her.

She paused, spotting the man with greying hair in the corner.

He had a different look to everyone else in here, seemed so out of place it was unreal. For a second they locked eyes, then he looked away again. Took a sip of the whiskey that was on the table in front of him. Diana sniffed. Nothing. She got nothing from him, and frowned. That never happened. So what—

"…sitting here?"

The voice wrenched her from her thoughts, and as she turned to take in the fella by the side of her, Diana's frown deepened. *Christl! It couldn't be…* She almost dropped off her stool. Then she blinked, shook her head, told herself that no, it absolutely couldn't – and indeed wasn't. But the similarity was amazing.

"Are you okay?" he asked her.

"Are you still pure?"

"I…" She turned back to look for the man in the corner, but he'd gone – and Diana faced front again, faced the man who was talking to her. "Sorry, what?"

He ran a hand through his boot-black hair, smiled with teeth that were unnaturally white. "I asked if anyone was sitting here." The man gestured to the empty seat beside her, and she shook her head again. He parked one buttock on the stool, left one leg dangling. The man was wearing a white shirt and dark trousers that might have been the bottom half of a suit. "Good. That's good."

"That's good. I'm glad you're still pure, sweetie. Still Pop's little girl."

It was even there in his voice. Practically the same… And now Diana found herself looking at another reflection, of a past that she herself had lived. The content of her own days and years on this planet. Though strangely she flashed back not to him, to his voice – but to *her*. The mother she'd lost so early, the opposite of the guy with the Sam Adams. A warmness, feeling safe in her embrace (one of the last times): the woman who'd named her after a goddess, told her she was special. Magical.

Then nothing but him. Her father, Roy. And that had been fine, he hadn't been a bad parent – a little on the strict side, but then what would you expect from such a deeply religious man as him? Only beat her when it was really 'necessary', or he wanted her to be quiet. He used to tell her that God had taken her mom because it was his will, and she was now up in Heaven at His side, enjoying the benefits eternal life could offer. Hadn't known her at all, though, had he? Not really.

Roy had worked at a local delivery place: good, honest grind, either behind the counter or driving parcels out to people; used to joke during the festive season that he was Father Christmas making his rounds. Or Poppa Christmas, as he called himself. It put food on the table and a roof over their heads, even if it was only a flat in their tiny hometown of Nowheresville USA.

It wasn't really until she started to grow up, until boys began taking an interest – and they were only friends from school, just buddies as they tended to be before you'd even hit ten. But that had been enough to set him off, to try and isolate her. And it had only got worse after that, moving up to High School. He'd set curfews for her, made sure she was back home straight away after lessons ended, that she was in her room doing her homework. Occasionally, out in the schoolyard, she thought she saw his delivery van go past. Just keeping an eye on her, spying, making sure the boys there weren't *too* friendly.

"You know all about right and wrong," he'd said to her on the way back from church one Sunday. "Listen to those lessons you've been taught and you won't wander far off the path, sweetie. You make sure you stay pure."

Not that he ever believed her as she grew into a teenager, thought stuff was going on even in school hours, his paranoia ramping up to dangerous levels. That's when he'd really started to show her who was boss, and why she shouldn't step out of line. His belt, his fists, it was all the same to him. All to keep her pure, keep her on the 'straight and narrow'. She wasn't a bad girl, but that didn't seem to matter to her Pop. He thought the worst, whatever she said. It was around then Diana began to dream of another life, of being someone – anyone – else.

Maybe of being a superhero, like the one she shared her name with, dressed in red, blue and gold. From the comics Abi Huston would lend her and she'd devour, hiding them away in her room, imagining what it would be like if she had powers herself. Pop had found a couple once and ripped them up, said they were putting subversive ideas in her head. His weapon of choice that evening: the wooden spoon, careful only to leave welts where nobody would see them – and back in those days folk didn't really care anyway. She had to wonder where God and Jesus fitted into all this, thought that surely *they* wouldn't approve of such behaviour.

Then that day had come, when all of a sudden in class she'd known what Jackie Bishop had been doing over the weekend with Howard Flanagan down in the woods; the kind of things her father was imagining she was getting up to, but wasn't. Nobody was taking the wooden spoon to Jackie, but Diana had also known what would happen in nine months' time. That Jackie would have twins, and have to drop out of school altogether. How she'd known all this – and it had all come to pass, *all* of it – was beyond her, though hadn't her Aunty Glenda who'd visited one time mentioned something about her mother having 'the sight': past and future, Glenda had insisted, her mother had been able to see it all. She hadn't stayed around for long after that, and had never been invited back.

Was that it? Had Diana inherited this ability from her mom? Maybe she did have powers after all, maybe that's what the woman had meant when she said Diana was special. Magical.

If only it had been that simple.

She'd begun noticing it all the time after that, could tell things about people if she concentrated – though it was always strongest at a certain time of the month. Not *that* time, a woman's time, when she'd often catch Pop rooting around in the bathroom bin for evidence that she wasn't like Jackie Bishop. He needn't have worried, Diana was terrified of going anywhere near boys by then: thanks to him.

Not even at the prom, when she'd been asked out by several but had said no to them all – preferring to just go alone, and get picked up by Pop afterwards for the debrief. Of course, he hadn't believed her then either that nothing had been going on – and it was during his thrashing with the belt that she blurted it out. What she knew about him and the women he saw on his route, the other deliveries he'd been making all these years – good, honest grind – including when her mom had still been alive.

That had made him pause for thought, stand back and gape at her. "You're just like her," he'd said then. "Cursed! You have the Devil inside you, child! Aren't pure, could *never* be pure!"

But it was as he'd come at her that final time she'd

realised. Realised how her mom had really met her end, that his attempts to drive out what he thought was a demon had resulted in that woman's premature death; God acting *through* him. Not suicide as the authorities concluded, a hanging, but murder. As Roy saw it, he was releasing his wife – genuinely believed that she was now in Heaven. That he'd sent her there.

Another reason to keep an eye on Diana, in case those tendencies ever surfaced in her, regardless of all his good work. Something else surfaced during that attack, though. Perhaps not all the way, but enough to make her Pop think twice this time – something in her eyes, and in his when he saw it – enough to make him go and fetch his gun instead. Something that definitely wasn't 'pure' as her father always called it.

Diana had escaped, crashed out through the front door – shouldn't have been able to do that, because it was solid wood, locked and bolted – and she just ran. Had no idea where she was going or how she'd even survive, just knowing that anything was better than this. Embarking on another life, away from her Pop.

She'd woken up that first morning, emerging from something of a daze, in someone's barn – her dress shredded in places. Diana had begun crying into her hands and thought she'd never stop. Didn't have a clue who to turn to. Maybe her Aunty Glenda? But she had no idea how to find her, let alone get there. Her father had kept her away from that side of the family, from *every* side of the family, come to that.

So, when she couldn't really stay in the barn any longer, Diana set out and started walking. She walked, and walked and walked, up the road as far as she could – was lucky enough to be picked up by a retired couple in their sixties on their way east, who asked questions about the state of her, but didn't push for the answers. Diana ended up staying with them at their place for a few weeks, just to get her head together, but moved on before she started to get too attached.

She figured that a life on the road was the only way to keep a low profile, the only way to avoid the authorities who might be looking for her. God alone knew what crap Pop had told them about her. Diana got by, after a fashion, working jobs that didn't really need references or even real names – waitressing, handing out flyers, cleaning. Like her namesake, she didn't need a man to look after her. She had to be strong, had to learn to survive on her own wits. Telling herself it was better to be alone.

But that hadn't lasted long, and when money dried up and winter would come around, she'd turn to other methods of making a buck. A self-fulfilling prophecy, becoming the very thing that her father always thought she was. Being used, but being paid for the privilege; sad sacks she'd tried to block out, tried not to 'read' because it upset her too much.

"Aren't pure, could never be pure!"

Retaining control, or so she told herself. Using some of that cash to get good and loaded, even high, at that certain point in the month when she feared she'd become the 'demon' her father had witnessed. Getting by, while all the time dreaming of another life. A better life.

It had gone on like that for years, until she'd met Rick. She'd noticed him at the launderette a few times before, with his basket of clothes which told her he was single. But on this one occasion he'd smiled, said hello, then after a certain amount of initial awkwardness asked her if she wanted to have a coffee with him. Diana had concentrated and attempted a reading, but all she'd got was that he was a nice man. Had the power not been at full strength that day, or had the way she'd felt about him even in those first few moments clouded her judgement? Had the love she'd felt for him later done the same, just like it did with so many other women who didn't even have her abilities? Too blind to see what's right in front of their eyes, or smell it either.

That coffee had turned into a drink, a dinner, a series of dates… Then before too long a night back at his place where he'd shown her what it really meant to make love, as opposed to having sex. The closeness two people could feel when they became one. A different kind of magic. Yet not even then did she—

"…like a drink?"

The voice cut in again, and Diana was back in the present. Back with the guy who'd sat on the stool beside her, as he eyed her up and down: taking in the low-cut satin top, the leather skirt and stocking-clad legs. As he asked her if she wanted another vodka. She necked back the drink she had and nodded.

He smiled at her, asked the barman for two and held his glass up for her to clink, which she did. A drink, a dinner, a series of dates and then… No, not this time. And was it her imagination, or did this rube look like Rick as well? The dark hair, the smile.

She was good with faces.

Only because, looking back now, Rick looked like Pop – and how screwed up was that? Should have rung a warning bell right there and then, only it didn't. Was that why she'd done everything in her power to please Rick, to get back that feeling of being wanted which had vanished when her father looked at her a certain way? To try and get back to being safe again…

Once more, the memories intruded. Diana on her wedding day, having used those fake papers to arrange it all – it was surprising the kind of people you got to know in her line of work, the contacts you made. She'd only ever lied about that one thing to Rick, her past, and he hadn't pressed her. Said that he didn't need to know all the ins and outs, that whatever she'd gone through it was another life. Not this one, with him.

Funny how the past and the present blur into one, though, isn't it?

They'd only been married a couple of weeks, only just back from the honeymoon actually, when he hit her for the first time. It had been a surprise, definitely, came out of the blue. Some minor disagreement about something, she couldn't even remember what – the shock of it had wiped away all traces – and there it had been, the punch to the stomach that winded her, doubled her over. He'd left her on the floor of their new apartment, while he went out to have a few drinks with the boys from the firm. Had that been what the argument had been about, Diana not wanting him to go? Wanting Rick to stay with her that Friday night instead? Was that unreasonable? Apparently so.

When he'd returned, smelling of booze, all apologies and horny as anything, she'd told herself that it had been a misunderstanding. How could she have gotten it so wrong? She couldn't have, her senses told her he was a nice guy.

But, of course, it had happened again. Again and again. The violence, the possessiveness – her not being able to leave the house, while he could do what he liked. Except… except she needed to, at that special time of the month. Needed to get away so that he wouldn't see what she was, especially now she'd cleaned up her act – gone to AA and everything, couldn't use drink or drugs to subdue it. Needed to get away so that Rick didn't realise that she was—

"—*not pure, could* never *be pure!*"

Cursed!

Luckily, it tended to coincide with when he went on his benders – often staying out all night, and telling her he'd been at a pal's house when she knew the truth of it. That he'd been with one of his sluts, cheating; making his deliveries, like Poppa Christmas. The stupid thing was, Diana had put up with it, for *so* long! Her namesake – *both* her namesakes – would have been ashamed of her, but she couldn't see any way out. Only to dream, to hope for another, better life.

That was when fate forced her hand. He'd been waiting for her when she returned one night, sitting in the dark, smoking. She saw the red tip of his cigarette even before she put the light on.

"Where have you been? It's nearly four in the morning!" Where had *she* been, like he had a right to know. Just a husband's right, Diana told herself, but she couldn't even answer him; didn't even know herself, just that she'd had to get away. Not let him, let *anyone* see what her father had seen.

He was rising and striding towards her then, but she was holding up her hands. "Rick no, please… I'm pregnant." She'd been waiting to tell him, for the right moment – if there ever was such a thing.

Her words stopped him in his tracks, just as those revelations had done with her Pop so long ago. But if her words had shocked him, then his next ones were just as much of a surprise to her. "Is it even mine?" he asked.

She was about to yell, about to scream at him: "*Of course* it's yours!" She hadn't been with another man since she'd met Rick, hadn't wanted – let alone needed – to. Then it was too late, because he was already ploughing ahead, intent on finishing what he'd started, probably believing it *was* someone else's – if it even existed. The punch was harder than ever, right in the stomach again.

And then the baby really didn't exist, would never be carried to term let alone be born. Diana felt the exact moment it happened, because she'd started to develop a bond that surpassed the usual mother and daughter connection. Clutched at her stomach and breathed in heavily, felt all the waste, everything that child could have been.

Everything Rick had taken away from her.

Felt that, and felt something else besides. She felt angry. No, *furious*! Diana couldn't hold it back any longer, didn't want to. This was something beyond the usual urges that she escaped to fulfil, so that she didn't hurt anyone unintentionally. Some livestock, woodland creatures – then she was able to rein it back in. Not tonight. Not after this.

She could see it on Rick's face, see it in his eyes. Saw the same fear Pop had experienced, only Rick didn't have a gun in the house to fetch. Couldn't stand the things. It wouldn't have stopped her anyway.

Not unless it had been filled with silver bullets.

Then she was on *him* for a change, raking him with her claws, tearing out his throat with her teeth, killing him not for food, but for revenge. Something she should have done long ago. By the time she was finished with Rick, there was very little left. What wasn't splattered all over the walls, the floor and ceiling, she'd chewed and swallowed, savouring the final moments of him. It was why, she often thought to herself later, she'd never been able to get a sense of Rick's future when she sniffed him. Because he didn't have one. She'd seen to that.

A brutal, messy divorce.

Diana hadn't been able to stay after that, not even long enough to gather her things or get any money together – because she could hear the sirens even as she changed back. A concerned neighbour most likely, complaining about the noise. "Sounds like someone's being murdered in that apartment!" Sort of. Thank Christ she hadn't married Rick under her real name…

So she was on the road again, only this time she had relished it. Freedom, an escape. Yet another life. Alone. She'd found more deadbeat jobs, but never turned to the oldest profession ever again. And she'd learned to embrace this… 'curse', what she was. Embrace and control it, make it work for her. Do what her mother had never been given the opportunity to.

Only problem was, livestock would no longer satisfy. Not now she'd tasted Rick, tasted human flesh. Not even AA would be able to help her with that one. Which was why she hunted, usually only those who deserved it – or she thought she was doing a favour. She was too old for clubbing, and hadn't really been into that when she was younger anyway – too busy making ends meet. Dating sites were fertile ground, out of the way bars, Singles Nights…

"…get so lonely sometimes, don't you find that?"

She'd been drifting again, not really taking any notice of what the man was saying to her, so Diana just nodded. It *was* a lonely life, this one she led. Couldn't let anyone else in, not just because of what she was, but because of what they might do to her. She'd had enough of that. No more.

"Yeah, me too. You… you don't look like the kind of woman who needs to hang out at evenings like this one, if you don't mind me saying." He smiled again with those oh-so-white teeth. Diane sniffed him up now, knowing he couldn't be Pop (that man had taken his own life a few years after she left, she'd heard, blew his brains out… just couldn't handle what he'd married, what he'd spawned). Knowing also it couldn't be Rick, that was impossible. No, this guy – the doppelgänger – his name was Tatum, and he worked at Lucky Marv's Used Cars.

Treated women as abysmally as her father and husband had, though. There was a string of them behind him, all of whom had fallen foul of his abuse. Maybe not physical, this time, but mental. A game-player. It was just a bonus surely that he looked like Pop, that he looked like Rick.

Well, she had a few games in mind for him.

"That's very kind of you."

"Not at all. You're, well, you're beautiful…' He waited for a name, but when it wasn't forthcoming he told her his instead – the one she knew already.

"Look, do you want to just blow this place?" Diana said to him. "It's pretty dead anyway." *Though not as dead as you'll be soon*, she thought to herself.

"Er, yeah. I mean, if you're sure?" Wasn't used to it

being so easy, it had thrown him.

"I'm sure," Diana told him, a confidence that hadn't been in her voice when she was growing up, nor when she'd been Rick's bitch. "Let's go." She noticed him watching as she shuffled forwards on the stool, allowed him a glimpse of the tops of those stockings. *Make the most of it*, she thought, *because I'll have a few more sights to show you before the evening is over.*

They grabbed their coats, his a blazer-style jacket as she'd thought, hers a fur – fake, naturally. Then they made their way outside, Tatum holding the door for her like the gentleman he wasn't. Diana cast a look up at the sky, clouds rolling across the full moon.

"You know, this kind of thing doesn't usually happen to me."

"No?"

"I mean, a woman like you… You're so—"

"Direct?" Diana offered, to help him out.

"Yeah, that's it. Direct. You know your own mind."

And yours, as well.

"Life's too short to be anything else," said Diana. "Don't you think?"

He smiled again, nodded. "So, where do you want to go? My place? Your place?"

"What's wrong with right here?" she said.

Tatum swallowed dryly. "What, here? In the car park?"

Diana looked around, spotted the cameras trained on the space ahead of them. Shook her head.

"My car, you mean?"

She shook her head again. "Round the back, there's an alleyway." Diana knew it all too well, had already scoped it out. Knew it, and others like it. Had used them before.

"You're keen, aren't you?" There was a hitch in his voice, and surprise – like he thought it would have taken much more than buying a drink to get her this far. Never in a billion years thought he'd be screwing her behind the back of that very bar twenty minutes later.

"Why wait?" she said to him. "Life's—"

"Too short, yeah. You said." He grinned now, nodded. "Okay, after you then." Tatum held out his hand, once more pretending to be the gent. But when they got to the alley in question, he started to reveal his true colours. He grabbed Diana and pushed her back against the wall, breath coming in short bursts. Then he was up against her, grinding against her—

Good, honest grind…

She could feel his hardness jabbing into her thigh. His mouth was on hers, hands all over her as if he couldn't decide which bit to explore first.

Diana pushed him off easily.

"What?" he said, genuinely surprised. "I thought this was what you wanted."

"Not quite," Diana said to him.

"So what… Don't tell me you've fucking changed your mind now, because…" He let the sentence tail off, but the inference was clear. Now they were here and in the heat of the moment, he was getting what he wanted whether she liked it or not. None of this was helping his cause.

"Because what?" she pushed. "What are you going to do about it, if I have?"

Tatum smirked. "I've already done it," he told her.

Diana was aware of someone else in the alley with them. Two people in fact, no, three… a couple of them wearing caps. How had she not picked up on that before? Tatum wasn't alone. Wasn't the only one intent on getting what he wanted tonight. How had she not— She took a step, almost lost her balance and had to reach for the wall.

He… the bastard had drugged her. But how? In the drink? She'd been watching it the whole time, hadn't gone to the head or anything. Besides, stuff like Wayne used wouldn't work on her. So…

"Not feeling great, Diana?" asked Tatum. How the fuck did he know her name? Her *real* name. "Aww, a pity. That'll be this." He tapped his lips, then produced a chapstick from his pocket. "I make it myself, infused with tiny particles of silver. Oh, don't worry, it won't kill you – just slow you down for a little while, long enough to do what we need to."

Silver? Diana was aware she was frowning again. Not only did he seem to know who she was, *what* she was, but he knew what weakened her.

Weakening her resolve…

This whole thing had been planned, more so than anything Wayne could have come up with. But how? She'd 'read' this guy, smelled Tatum and—

"Now, I know what you're thinking. How could you have got it so wrong? Of course, I'm not Tatum. I don't work on a car lot. But the guy I took this from does." He produced something else now from his other pocket. "Just another product in our beauty line. Sweat from one Tatum Jones, sprayed on." The man who wasn't Tatum demonstrated by pressing the top and Diana got another whiff of the person who was: his past, his future. A mask, a shield. "It works a treat, totally confuses the target."

Target? Shit!

The other men were getting closer now and with one sniff she knew who *they* were, just as they knew everything about her. Hunters, professionals belonging to a… a league. People who left nothing to chance. They'd even gone through their ranks to find someone who looked a bit like her father, like Rick – exploiting another one of her vulnerabilities.

They had weapons now, she saw. One held a lethal-looking silver machete, another a large Bowie knife, the final one a small hand-held axe. Quiet weapons that wouldn't draw too much attention. Diana tried to will the change, to bring it on, but it was frustratingly out of reach, like an itch she just couldn't scratch.

'Tatum' stepped forward again. "You were right about one thing, life *is* short – for you!" Then he punched her in the stomach, doubling her over. The recognisable pain came back to her as she slid down the wall. The pain, the memories again. The hurt, the anger. The loss. "All right," said the man, nodding to his companions, "let's finish this."

Diana's eyes narrowed, willing the change – even looking up again at the moon for help. And it was as she did so that she saw it, a silhouette actually moving across that silvery circle, like a much hairier E.T. Moving, falling, dropping behind the hunters with a growl.

They turned, but were way too slow for this creature – which towered above them, clawing machete-man out of the way in seconds. He landed against the opposite wall, bones crunching, his weapon clanking to the ground.

There was very little room to manoeuvre in that tight

space, and though the hunter with the knife made a lunge, it was easily dodged by this new player in the game. Then suddenly the hand that had been holding the knife was separated from the arm. The man clutched this stump to his chest, blood pumping blackly from it as he screamed.

"Look… look out!" Diana cried, pointing to the creature's right – where the hunter with the axe was bringing the weapon downwards. Would have embedded it in his opponent's head had it not been for the warning. Now, instead, a large paw sank into the man's chest, pulling him in so that huge teeth could do their worst, biting into his face and tearing most of it away with a wrench of the head.

Fake Tatum backed away, mouth hanging open. He wasn't sure how the tables had turned so quickly, but that wasn't really important right now. He needed to get away, run. Live to fight another day, because life was—

The huge wolf turned its attentions toward him, dropping the axe-man at its feet. It was only now, close-up, that Diana could see the streaks of grey in its fur. The look in its red and yellow eyes. These men weren't the only ones who could disguise their scent.

It was about to lunge, to attack, when Diana shouted: "No!" The wolf turned towards her, and they locked eyes for the second time that evening. It cocked its head. "He's mine!"

And now, mustering all her strength, channelling all that hate and fury – Diana changed. She easily matched the other wolf in size, snarling and howling as she rose to her full height.

The man in front of her, the one who looked like her father, her ex, and probably now wished that he didn't, pissed his pants. He tried to get away, but that just made it all the more satisfying for her. The attack was even more ferocious than the one all those years ago that had ended Rick's life.

When she was done, when she finally looked up again – chewing on bits of the final hunter – the other wolf was gone. Vanished, just like he had from the bar earlier. Diana sniffed the air, but of course she couldn't smell him, didn't have a hope of tracking him.

Then she realised why he'd fled. There was no sign of the hunter with the missing hand, he'd got away; the only one who had. She wondered who the stranger was, whether this would now cause trouble for him? It would definitely alert *her* to the fact hunters were on her tail.

She wondered also, if she'd met the stranger when she was younger, whether things might have been different. Whether they would have got on, even had a chance at making it. Making something… Both the same, shared experiences. Not alone.

Diana shook her head. A fantasy of a better life, a different—

No. Enough. She wouldn't do that anymore. No more dreaming. It was time to go, before the sirens came again. Time to hit the road once more.

Thanks to the stranger, the only man who'd ever been there for her when she needed him, there would be more content, more to fill up her days and years – hopefully.

And for that she would always be grateful.

* * * * *

From the rooftop, Neil watched the van drive away.

He would track it, follow the guy with one hand (a familiar move he'd used before, another parallel) and take care of him – but by now he'd almost certainly alerted more of his kind. Neil would be on their radar now, just like she was: the she-wolf back there he'd helped. He didn't like to interfere, and their reputations went before them; if he hadn't believed it then, he did after witnessing the savageness she'd displayed below. The female of the species was most definitely more deadly than the male. Briefly, he wondered what had made her quite so brutal.

She could've taken care of the whole lot of them easily, if that hunter hadn't drugged her. Trap or no trap, she would have polished them off in no time. And he began to think himself, that maybe a companion on this journey, this trip he'd begun after leaving his hometown, might not be such a bad thing after all.

Might not have been a bad thing from the start, if he'd hooked up with one of them instead of hanging around with his mates. Maybe none of the awful things that had occurred would have happened if he'd had someone like her to share life with. To talk to. His friends, his wife, his child… all those different lives, gone. But with her, with the woman back there—

Neil shook his head. It was too late for all that, it had already happened. That had been his fate and his story wasn't over yet. This shit would come back to bite him, he knew that as well; it always did. You reap what you sow. But he'd deal, the same as he always did. Anyway, that was for another time. Another place.

Another life to come.

Story Notes

White Shadows

I wear a few different hats as a writer, and this one was written with my P.B. Kane YA one on for a collection of those stories with the same name. Now, I like to think that my YA stuff can also be read and enjoyed quite easily by adults, which is what the tale is doing in this collection as well, but you be the judge. It's inspired by the kinds of winters I remember from my youth, proper white-outs we never really get these days – or at least not where I live. The last one I can remember was about ten years or more ago when the snow was halfway up the front door.

My memory of the really bad ones – depending on how you look at it, because if you were a kid it was great as the schools would all close – is full of things like power-cuts and putting food from the freezer outside in the garden so it didn't go off. But if you went out playing, parents would also warn you that if you weren't careful you could get lost out there or even 'eaten up' by the snow… probably one of those things adults told kids back then to scare them shitless and keep them safe. That idea, or image, has always stuck with me though and was the germ of what 'White Shadows' eventually became. Living snow that could actually eat you up.

Amazing the stuff from your childhood that can cause nightmares later on, isn't it?

The Cursed

This is one of a handful of stories I wrote as a bit of a palette cleanser after finishing my third HQ/Harper thriller – when I was doing about 5k words a day for weeks. And all this while lockdown was going on, which must have added a depressing spin to them. I think the older we get the more we look back on our lives and how things could have gone differently, rightly or wrongly, and very often the things that didn't go the way we wanted are our own fault. Sometimes they aren't, but for the character in this one that's definitely the case.

I should also probably explain that an anthology called *Cursed* that my better half Marie and I edited had just come out the previous March. In fact it was a signing event for this at Forbidden Planet's Megastore in London that was the last thing we went to before everything started to go sideways with the pandemic. What an appropriate year to bring that one out, eh? Anyway, I have this tendency to get a bit jealous when editing themed anthologies – not simply because of the talent on display in them (and trust me when I say we've had some cracking names and stories in our anthos over the years), but because they got to write tales based on whatever the book was about.

For example, our *Hellbound Hearts* anthology for Pocket Books/Simon & Schuster, which were tales inspired by the novella that spawned *Hellraiser*, directly led to my writing one of the books I'm still known for today: *Sherlock Holmes and the Servants of Hell* published by Solaris. I have a few Alice tales bubbling away as a result of co-editing *Wonderland*, too. But yeah, this time round it was reading lots and lots of stories with curses in them, and it got me thinking about how you might inadvertently mess your entire life up by cursing someone but not being specific about it, or not even believing you have the ability to do it in the first place. How it might backfire on you actually, because it's based on hatred and curses always, always teach the person using them a lesson too.

Maddy the Monster

When I was putting together a sequel to my British Fantasy Award-nominated *Monsters* collection (Alchemy, 2015), I needed to write some new material. And as I was using a particular favourite story of mine called 'Michael the Monster' – inspired by Ray Bradbury's *The Homecoming* (we have a wonderful edition, hardback and illustrated by my old friend Dave McKean) – I thought it might be a nice idea to pen a sequel, so they could bookend the collection.

'Michael…' also has a bit of a *Fly II* / *Splice* vibe to it, in so much as it's about a genetically modified creature who is making money for his masters but only able to go out at Halloween when nobody will give him a second glance. At the end of that one, Michael escapes and evades capture. 'Maddy the Monster' moves things along a bit, and we catch up with the story mid-revolution, complete with rumours about what he's been up to since. You don't necessarily have to have read the first story to enjoy this one, as I purposefully made it self-contained, but I'm sure Steve Shaw at Black Shuck won't complain if you bought a copy of the gorgeous hardback that is *More Monsters*.

The Queue

I've always wanted to do a kind of film noir *Double Indemnity* kind of story, but from a different angle – and regardless of what Donnie thinks, this *is* my version of *The Postman Always Rings Twice*. Only I've put my kind of spin on it, the kind where you get punished forever for doing the kind of things Donnie and Grace (if it really is Grace) do in their lives. The kinds of things love makes you do, because love can drive you crazy, making you impatient, especially if you're not the most patient of people to start with.

But the idea for the punishment came from standing in so many lines in hotels, waiting to get checked in. The kind of queues we British folk are always moaning about, but find ourselves in time and again. That are, frankly, already like a level of Hell. Queues where you can't see any movement, can't see to the front or the back – especially at conventions as you're waiting to get checked in or registered. Now just imagine being in one of them actually for ever, with no hope of escape – and even if you do, you really don't want to get checked into that particular hotel/prison. Pretty scary stuff, I reckon.

Crumbs

This was the first modern horror fairy tale I wrote after compiling all of them so far in the first volume of *Kane's Scary Tales*. It took over a decade to get enough together for that one, including stories like 'Sin', 'Snow' and 'Giants'. Put together with the books in the *RED* trilogy, which again took ten years to write and were a modern horror version of *Little Red Riding Hood*, I was just a bit fairy-taled out for a while.

But when I was asked for a novelette for an anthology a year or so ago – which didn't happen for some reason, probably COVID-related – I started to think about them again and the ones I hadn't covered. Like *Hansel and Gretel*... Again, putting together *Cursed* was a big influence in that department because Lilith Saintcrow did us a wonderful version of that story, in a unique way only she can, and it sort of kick-started my desire to do more. I'm already thinking about a few others, but yes, 'Crumbs' will definitely be in a second volume of *Scary Tales* at some point down the line.

Pure Evil

An old story now, but one I still have a fondness for and which hasn't been seen in quite a while. Being a horror fan, I obviously love all the tropes, including asylums and mad scientists, and this one definitely reflects that. It might seem a bit hokey by today's standards – might even have seemed that back when I wrote it – but this is my homage to things like *Creep Show*, which has just returned in the safe hands of Greg Nicotero for the streaming channel Shudder. So, y'know, it's not meant to be taken too seriously.

Having said that, I still think that the idea of having something inside us that makes us do some of the horrible things we do is quite a potent one. Yes, it does take free will out of the equation completely and lays the fault at something else's door, but then again I do that with the Controllers stories too (see the collection, published by Luna Press). Having no free will can be just as frightening as *choosing* to do such things, I think.

Mortis-Man: Origins

The original Mortis-Man tale, which the Sinister Horror Company published in my *Death* collection, was definitely a fun romp. My homage to the superheroes and comic books I grew up with, and I had a blast writing it. Similarly, readers have told me they had fun reading it too. In 'The Return of Mortis-Man' we catch up with our protagonist at the end of his career, and indeed his life, so it made sense if I was ever going to do another one it had to be a prequel (although now I am having ideas for a third one, which is most definitely a sequel) and in a sense I gave myself the blueprint for 'Origins' in the original. We hear how Mortis-Man came to be, so this was just filling in the blanks I told myself.

Not only did it turn out to be a more serious affair than its predecessor, much darker and harder to write, it ended up being about 10k wds longer! Just goes to show that when you set out to write something, that isn't always what you'll end up with. Nevertheless, I am quite happy with the results – whether you guys think it works or not is another matter entirely! Oh, and yes I continued my trend from the first story of giving the characters the names of comic book creatives, just to add another dimension to my tribute.

Another Life

Returning to Black Shuck Books now, and I'm proud to say that my mini-collection *The Spirits of Christmas* (which is still available should you need a winter chill around the festive period) was the first in their Shadows line of handy pocket-sized paperbacks. Steve Shaw and I were chatting over a drink about this, how maybe to follow it up somehow – and the thought occurred to me that I could gather together all the tales in what I was starting to think about as *The Life Cycle*; essentially catching up with a guy's life at three points – young, middle-aged and old man – but someone who just happens to be a werewolf.

We were coming up just a little short wordcount-wise, so I was wracking my brains as to what I could put in there that might be halfway related. And it was then that I started thinking about all the time between stories in the originals, and how it was conceivable that my main character Neil might have come across another wolf but at right angles. I mention that he's travelled a lot, so I could set I anywhere conceivably, and I didn't want to do another male wolf story so I figured it would be fun to do something from a female point of view, as I do enjoy writing from that perspective. And so 'Another Life' was born… It's since spawned a sequel itself, 'Lifeline', which you can find in Horrific Tales' anthology *Leaders of the Pack*, and I'm having ideas now for a third one which would tie up this particular strand and turn the whole thing into a trilogy, just like the first *Life Cycle*. More on that as and when…

So, there you have it. I do hope you've enjoyed reading these stories, and the ramblings about them here. As always, thank you for joining me and keeping me company on yet another bookish adventure. Without you, the readers, there really would be no point.

Acknowledgements

My thanks to Mark Miller at Encyclopocalypse for being willing to take this one on, and to Cavan Scott for his amazing introduction, not to mention Christian Francis for the stunning cover. As always, hugs and massive thank yous to all my friends in the writing and film/TV world, for their continual help and support in the past. A very special thank you, though, to people like Mike Carey, Jason Arnopp, Neil Gaiman, Joe Hill, AK Benedict, Michael Marshall Smith, Kelley Armstrong, Rio Youers, Christopher Fowler, Stephen Volk, Peter James, Simon Clark and so many more. Finally, a humongous thank you to my family, in particular my 'words are not enough' wife Marie.

About the Author

Paul Kane is an award-winning, bestselling writer and editor based in Derbyshire, UK. His short story collections include *Alone (In the Dark)*, *Touching the Flame*, *FunnyBones*, *Peripheral Visions*, *Shadow Writer*, *The Adventures of Dalton Quayle*, *The Butterfly Man and Other Stories*, *The Spaces Between*, *Ghosts*, the British Fantasy Award-nominated *Monsters*, *Shadow Casting*, *Nailbiters*, *Death*, *Disexistence*, *Scary Tales*, *More Monsters*, *Lost Souls*, *The Controllers*, *The Colour of Madness* and *Darkness & Shadows*. His novellas include *The Lazarus Condition*, *RED* and *Pain Cages* (a #1 Amazon bestseller). He is the author of such novels as *Of Darkness and Light*, *The Gemini Factor* and the bestselling *Arrowhead* trilogy (*Arrowhead*, *Broken Arrow* and *Arrowland*, gathered together in the sell-out omnibus edition *Hooded Man*), a post-apocalyptic reworking of the Robin Hood mythology. His latest novels include *Lunar* (which is set to be turned into a feature film), the short Y.A. novel *The Rainbow Man* (as P.B. Kane), the critically-acclaimed and award-winning *Sherlock Holmes and the Servants of Hell* from Solaris, the sequels to *RED – Blood RED* and *Deep RED – Before* from Grey Matter Press, *Arcana* from WordFire Press, plus *Her Last Secret* and *Her Husband's Grave* (another recent sellout at Amazon and Waterstones) from HQ/HarperCollins (as P.L. Kane)

He has also written for comics, most notably for the *Dead Roots* zombie anthology alongside writers such as James Moran (*Torchwood, Cockneys vs. Zombies*) and Jason Arnopp (*Doctor Who, Friday the 13th, The Last Days of Jack Sparks*) and as part of the team turning *Clive Barker's Books of Blood* into motion comics for Seraphim/MadeFire. His stand-alone comic *The Disease*, published by Hellbound Media, was also a 2016 Ghastly Award-nominated title in the 'One Shot' category. Paul is co-editor of the anthology *Hellbound Hearts* (Simon & Schuster) – stories based around the mythology that spawned *Hellraiser – The Mammoth Book of Body Horror* (Constable & Robinson/Running Press), featuring the likes of Stephen King and James Herbert, *A Carnivàle of Horror* (PS) featuring Ray Bradbury and Joe Hill, *Beyond Rue Morgue* from Titan (stories based around Poe's detective, Dupin), *Exit Wounds* – a crime anthology featuring the likes of Lee Child, Val McDermid, Dennis Lehane and Jeffery Deaver – *Wonderland* (a finalist in the Shirley Jackson Awards) and *Cursed*, the last three also from Titan.

His non-fiction books include *The Hellraiser Films and Their Legacy, Voices in the Dark* and *Shadow Writer – The Non-Fiction. Vol. 1: Reviews* and *Vol. 2: Articles and Essays*, plus his genre journalism has appeared in the likes of *SFX, Fangoria, Dreamwatch, Gorezone* and *Rue Morgue*. He also co-wrote the afterword to the latest edition of Stephen King's *Night Shift* collection. He has been a Guest at Alt.Fiction five times, was a Guest at the first SFX Weekender, at Thought Bubble in 2011, Derbyshire Literary Festival and Off the Shelf in 2012, Monster Mash and Event Horizon in 2013, Edge-Lit in 2014, HorrorCon, HorrorFest and Grimm Up North in 2015, The Dublin Ghost Story Festival and Sledge-Lit in 2016, IMATS Olympia and Celluloid Screams in 2017, plus Black Library Live (Warhammer 40k) and The UK Ghost Story Festival in 2019, as well as being a panellist at FantasyCon and the World Fantasy Convention, and a fiction judge at the Sci-Fi London Film Festival. He is a former Special Publications Editor of the British Fantasy Society and is currently serving as co-chair for the UK arm of the Horror Writers Association.

His work has been optioned for film and television, and his zombie story 'Dead Time' was turned into an episode of the Lionsgate/NBC TV series *Fear Itself*, adapted by Steve Niles (*30 Days of Night*) and directed by Darren Lynn Bousman (*SAW II-IV*). He also scripted *The Opportunity*, which premiered at the Cannes Film Festival, *Wind Chimes* (directed by Brad '*Hallows Eve*' Watson and which sold to TV), *The Weeping Woman* – filmed by award-winning director Mark Steensland, starring Tony-nominated actor Stephen Geoffreys (*Fright Night*) – *Confidence*, directed by award-winning Mike Clarke (*A Hand to Play*, *Paper and Plastic*) which stars Simon Bamford (*Hellraiser*, *Nightbreed*, *Starfish*), and *The Torturer* directed by Joe Manco of Little Spark Films. Loose Canon/Hydra Films have just turned Paul's novelette *Men of the Cloth* into a feature called *Sacrifice* (aka *The Colour of Madness*), starring *Re-Animator* and *You're Next*'s Barbara Crampton. His work for audio includes the full cast drama adaptation of *The Hellbound Heart* for Bafflegab, starring Tom Meeten (*The Ghoul*), Neve

McIntosh (*Doctor Who*) and Alice Lowe (*Prevenge*), and the *Robin of Sherwood* adventure *The Red Lord* for Spiteful Puppet/ITV, narrated by Ian Ogilvy (*Return of the Saint*). You can find out more at his website <u>www.shadow-writer.co.uk</u> which has featured Guest Writers such as Dean Koontz, Robert Kirkman, Charlaine Harris and Guillermo del Toro.

Other Books by Paul Kane

Novels

Arrowhead

Broken Arrow

Arrowland

Hooded Man (Omnibus)

The Gemini Factor

Lunar

Sleeper(s)

The Rainbow Man (as P.B. Kane)

Blood RED

Sherlock Holmes and the Servants of Hell

Before

Deep RED

Arcana

The Red Lord

Her Last Secret (as P.L. Kane)

The Storm

Her Husband's Grave (as P.L. Kane)

Novellas & Novelettes
Signs of Life
The Lazarus Condition
Dalton Quayle Rides Out
RED
Pain Cages
Creakers (chapbook)
Flaming Arrow
The Bric-a-Brac Man
The P.I.'s Tale
Snow
The Rot
Beneath the Surface (with Simon Clark)
Blood Red Sky

Collections
Alone (In the Dark)
Touching the Flame
FunnyBones
Peripheral Visions
The Adventures of Dalton Quayle
Shadow Writer
The Butterfly Man and Other Stories
The Spaces Between
Ghosts
Monsters
The Dead Trilogy
Shadow Casting
Nailbiters
Death

The Life Cycle
Disexistence
Kane's Scary Tales Vol. 1
More Monsters
Lost Souls
The Controllers
White Shadows (as P.B. Kane)
The Colour of Madness: Official Movie Tie-In
Traumas
Darkness & Shadows

Editor & Co-Editor
Shadow Writers Vol. 1 & 2
Terror Tales #1-4
Top International Horror
Albions Alptraume: Zombies
The British Fantasy Society: A Celebration
Hellbound Hearts
The Mammoth Book of Body Horror
A Carnivàle of Horror: Dark Tales from the Fairground
Beyond Rue Morgue
Dark Mirages
Exit Wounds
Wonderland
Cursed

Non-Fiction
Contemporary North American Film Directors: A
Wallflower Critical Guide (Major Contributor)
Cinema Macabre (Contributor)
The Hellraiser Films And Their Legacy
Voices in the Dark

Shadow Writer – The Non-Fiction. Vol. 1: Reviews
Shadow Writer – The Non-Fiction. Vol. 2: Articles & Essays
Leviathan – The Story of Hellraiser and Hellbound: Hellraiser II (contributor)
Hellraisers

9 781959 205982